Intuition

Intuition

C. J. OMOLOLU

WALKER BOOKS
AN IMPRINT OF BLOOMSBURY
NEW YORK   LONDON   NEW DELHI   SYDNEY

First published in the United States of America in June 2013
by Walker Books for Young Readers, an imprint of Bloomsbury Publishing, Inc.
www.bloomsbury.com

For information about permission to reproduce selections from this book, write to
Permissions, Walker BFYR, 1385 Broadway, New York, New York 10018
Bloomsbury books may be purchased for business or promotional use. For information on
bulk purchases please contact Macmillan Corporate and Premium Sales Department at
specialmarkets@macmillan.com

Library of Congress Cataloging-in-Publication Data
Omololu, Cynthia Jaynes.
Intuition / C.J. Omololu.
        pages   cm
Sequel to: Transcendence.
Summary: Events from Cole's past life in sixteenth-century England begin
to intrude on her blossoming romance with Griffon.
ISBN 978-0-8027-2371-0 (hardcover) • ISBN 978-0-8027-3464-8 (e-book)
[1. Reincarnation—Fiction.   2. Supernatural—Fiction.   3. Secret societies—
        Fiction.   4. Love—Fiction.]   I. Title.
PZ7.O54858In 2013   [Fic]—dc23   2013014753

Book design by Nicole Gastonguay
Typeset by Westchester Book Composition
Printed and bound in the U.S.A. by Thomson-Shore Inc., Dexter, Michigan

2   4   6   8   10   9   7   5   3   1

All papers used by Bloomsbury Publishing, Inc., are natural, recyclable products
made from wood grown in well-managed forests. The manufacturing processes
conform to the environmental regulations of the country of origin.

To my parents,
who taught me how to listen

Intuition

One

The best part about being Akhet is that you remember everything. The worst part is that you forget nothing.

Every day I remember more about the other lives I've lived—as a lady in England in the sixteenth century and as an Italian cellist in the nineteenth—but there's nowhere I'd rather be than right here, sitting on the back of Griffon's motorcycle, my arms around his waist, holding him so close I can feel his muscles shift as he kicks the bike into gear. I press myself into the back of his worn leather jacket as we cut through the wind over the blur of asphalt on the Great Highway, the sun glinting off the waves to our right, the dunes leading into Golden Gate Park on our left.

Peering around his shoulder, I catch a glimpse of Griffon's eyes in the rearview mirror, and I can tell he's smiling even though the rest of his face is hidden by the helmet. As he turns his head, I can see the very edge of the scar on his cheek, and it sends a shiver of regret through me. The mark is finally fading, but even if it disappears completely, I'll always know what happened and how close I came to losing all of this.

We stop for a light and Griffon puts both feet solidly on the ground to steady us, reaching down with his hand to give mine a squeeze, the Akhet vibrations between us whenever we're close now just a normal part of our relationship. It's these little moments of connection that I love the most—a casual touch on my arm or the way he grabs my hand when we're crossing the street. The almost unnoticeable gestures that tell the world we're together. As the light changes, Griffon puts the bike in gear and I tighten my grip on his waist as we surge forward, enjoying the comfort of knowing Griffon would do anything to keep me safe.

As we approach the turnoff to the zoo, bright triangles of color pop against the blue sky up ahead. Dad used to bring me out here to watch the hang gliders when I was little, and every time one of them leaped off the edge of the beach cliff, a scream would catch in my throat in that split second before the wind tossed them high into the sky. Now for the first time I get what that thrill must feel like. As the bike glides along the asphalt, I understand how it feels to let everything go, to trust in something greater than yourself and allow the rhythm and the motion to carry you away.

We pull into the zoo parking lot and Griffon holds the bike steady so I can slide off. I put my hand up to check my ankh necklace, more out of habit than anything else; it was almost four centuries before it was given back to me, and I'm terrified of losing it again. Mine is bright silver with a dark red ruby, while the ankh Griffon keeps tucked into his shirt is plain bronze on a thick black cord. Despite the differences, the meanings of both are the same—eternal life.

As Griffon secures the bike, I glance up at an ancient pink building on the other side of a chain-link fence. As soon as I see the intricate plasterwork over the three doors that face us, a tremor of recognition sends a jolt through me. Despite the fact that I don't remember it, I know I've been in there before.

I loop my fingers through the wire diamonds of the fencing and try to get a better look. The building's old and obviously abandoned, with different colored paint patches where someone has tried to cover years of graffiti. I close my eyes, trying to prepare myself for the worst, but I'm not pulled into a memory this time—it's just images and feelings floating through my mind. The anxiety in my chest eases as I realize that I'm not going to be thrown out of my present into another time and place. Not knowing when the blackouts are going to happen has been the hardest part of becoming Akhet.

Looking around, I can sense that at one point there was water here, lots of water—not the ocean, but something that feels almost as big. In my mind I can hear happy squeals and the sounds of splashing. I picture people in bathing suits that go down to their knees, still wearing stockings and tall, lace-up boots.

Griffon's fingers wrap around mine. "What is it?" he asks, standing behind me at the fence and glancing up at the decrepit building. He bends down and kisses me lightly on the back of my neck, and I shiver. I'll never get tired of the sensation of his lips on my skin.

I blink a few times to shake the rest of the memory out of my mind. "I'm not sure. I remember water here . . . a lake or something."

Without any explanation, Griffon understands that what I'm talking about wasn't just years ago, but decades. Centuries even. "Maybe you came here when you were visiting with the orchestra that time. That would have been the late eighteen hundreds, right?"

"Eighteen-ninety-five," I say. "That was the date on the news-paper articles about Alessandra's death."

A golf cart approaches and we turn to see an old guy in a khaki zoo uniform watching us. "Can I help you with anything?"

"Maybe," Griffon says. "What was this building?"

The guy squints up at the crumbling carvings and peeling paint. "The old pool house," he says, frowning. "It's a crying shame what's happened to it over the years. Back in the day it was beautiful."

"So there was a pool here?" I ask, a little confused. What I felt seemed like more than just a pool.

He gestures toward the cars. "Only the biggest one in North America. Ran the whole length of the parking lot—a thousand feet and then some. They say you could even see it from space."

That makes much more sense. The biggest pool in North America would just about fit.

Griffon glances at me, but neither of us is surprised. When it comes to places we've been to in the past, Akhet are never wrong. "When was that?" he asks.

The old guy scratches his head. "Let's see. I think the pool opened sometime in the late eighteen hundreds. Filled with water from the ocean, but heated too—amazing technology for the time. I swam here as a really little kid, so they must have closed it in '70, maybe '71. They paved it over to make the parking lot a few years back."

The late 1800s. I look back at the faded pink facade, the sounds of laughter and splashing water still echoing in my ears as the man drives away. "It is a shame."

Griffon smiles sadly at me as we turn and walk toward the zoo entrance. He takes my hand, but doesn't say anything. He must go through this all the time—seeing something from his past that's now old and decayed, the echoes of the lives that experienced it still faint in his ears. I wonder if you ever get used to it. Griffon squeezes my left hand gently, careful to avoid the fingers that are still numb from the accident. I love seeing our hands together, his dark skin against mine more of a complement than a contrast. "I've got this," he says, reaching for his wallet as we approach the ticket window.

"No way," I insist. "Rayne and I come here the first weekend of summer every year. This is our tradition, not yours, so I pay this time."

Griffon hesitates, but I stare him down. "Okay," he says. "This time." He looks around the entrance. "Where are we supposed to meet them?"

I pull my phone out of my pocket. "I got a text from Rayne while we were riding. She and Peter are heading for the bears; they'll meet us there."

I lean into Griffon as we walk through the front gates, still amazed at the way everything turned out. "I'm so glad you introduced them. Rayne deserves someone good." I feel almost possessive as I look up at him—his beautiful lips with the inviting curve at the top and amber eyes that give just a hint of the abilities that lie behind them. It's impossible to imagine my life without him in it. "And this way I get to hang out with both of you, and everyone's happy."

"I'm definitely happy," Griffon says, leaning down to nuzzle my neck. "Never been happier."

I laugh and pull back slightly. "We'd better stop or we'll never make it to the bears."

"Okay by me," Griffon mumbles. "We could just go back to my house and lock ourselves in for the rest of the day. For the rest of the week."

I force myself to take a step back, the thrill at the thought of being alone with him coursing through my body. Part of me wants to spend every minute with Griffon, waking or not. "I can't bail on Rayne." I push him toward the path that goes past the lion house. "This way."

As we turn the corner, an Asian couple blocks the path, gesturing wildly and shouting things I don't understand. The man looks frantic and the woman is on the verge of tears, her eyes shining and her face red.

"Hang on a second." Griffon drops my hand as he walks over and says something in their language. The couple looks both surprised and relieved, and fire off some rapid sentences, pointing up the pathway.

"Hey, Cole," Griffon calls back to me. His voice is steady, but I can hear the urgency in it. "See if you can find someone who works here."

I don't know what's going on, but I can tell it's something bad. I feel panic rising as I turn the corner and see a woman in a khaki uniform. "We need help!" I say, pointing up the path. "This way."

Griffon and the couple rush over as soon as they see us. "They think someone took their son," Griffon explains, while the parents look on with fear in their eyes. "About two years old. They were with him over by the lemurs a few minutes ago and when they turned around, he was gone."

The employee gets on the radio to relay the information, and in seconds there's a crackly response. "What was he wearing?" she asks.

Griffon quickly translates the question and then their answer. "A red striped shirt and a brown hat."

I hear the description being relayed to radios throughout the zoo, then there's nothing but static for a few long moments. The man reaches over to grab the woman's hand, and I see him squeeze it hard. Griffon smiles and says something that I don't understand, but it seems to reassure them in some way and they both nod in reply.

We all jump as the radio crackles, and the park attendant answers. She grins, and I feel my whole body release the tension that's been building for the past few minutes. "Someone's bringing him over—they found him watching the chimps."

His parents can't wait; as soon as they spot the employee carrying the little boy, they race over to him, their happy cries not needing any translation. After scooping him up and covering him with kisses, the mother comes back to Griffon and takes his hand in hers, nodding rapidly as she talks.

Griffon flashes his smile and bows his head as she says something to him that I can tell is a thank-you.

"That was scary," I say as we watch the family go into the lion house together, each of the parents holding tight to the boy's hand. "What language were they speaking?"

"Mandarin." He shrugs. "I told you I was Chinese . . . before."

"Handy," I say, teasing him to cover up the awe I feel whenever he does something unexpected like this. Putting an overturned chess set back together, each piece in the same place it was before, switching languages without even thinking about it, reading pages of text faster than he can turn them; it's going to take a lot of lifetimes for my abilities to catch up to his.

"Hey, it was the least I could do. I remember the panic of losing your kid in a crowd."

I know he doesn't mean anything by it, but that comment hits me full force. Griffon once had a kid to lose in a crowd. And probably a wife to go with it. Reminders of his past lives always sting a little, even though I know it's just a fact of being Akhet. Our past is always woven in with our present. We walk a little way in silence, each of us wrapped up in our own thoughts. As we pass the hippos, there's a rustling in the bushes and a bright blue peacock steps out onto the asphalt, dragging its tail feathers on the ground.

Peacocks roam all around the zoo, but I've never seen one this close before. He stands a few feet away, his blue head shimmering almost green in the sun as he tilts it toward us. The bird shakes his body and puffs his tail feathers out for just a second before they settle back on the dirt. Slowly he moves toward us just as some screaming kids run by, sending the huge bird diving for the bushes and out of sight.

Griffon walks to where the peacock disappeared and comes back with a long, shimmering feather in his hand. "Looks like he left something for you."

I reach out to touch the delicate colors that seem to shift and change in the light. Pulling the strands through my fingers, I feel a moment of panic as I'm drawn into a memory, one that's centuries older than anything here at the zoo.

"My darling Allison, have you never heard a peacock's call before?" Connor asks, green eyes shining with amusement as he watches my surprise.

The peacock's cries are startling as he lifts his head again and opens his mouth to the sky, the repeated caws echoing over the grounds of the manor house and disappearing into the English countryside.

"I've heard them from inside the sitting room," I answer. "But never in such close proximity. There aren't many wild peacocks in Cornwall, I'm afraid."

Connor looks at the bright blue birds that peck at the land, looking for their next meal. "These descendants of the original pair have lived on the property almost longer than my family has. It's always striking that a bird with such astoundingly beautiful plumage would have such a grating and ugly cry."

"'Tis unfair that the males are allowed to dress in brilliant colors and inventive patterns, while the females are simply dull, gray birds," I tease.

The peacock closest to us takes a few steps in our direction, the blue of his head and neck shimmering like something other-worldly in the sun. As he turns toward me, he raises his tail in a display that takes my breath away—a fan of hundreds of feathers, dotted with blue and green, waving just slightly as he proudly turns so that the colors catch the light.

"It appears you have an admirer," Connor says. He turns to me, his face all seriousness. "More than one, I'm afraid."

My heart surges as the distance between us closes and I can't help but look at him directly. His kind eyes are set in a face that is as handsome as any I have ever seen. I can feel the heat from his body on my skin as he reaches to cup my chin in his hand. "You are more beautiful than any peacock."

I long to have the sensation of his lips on mine and hope that Mam is right, 'tis only a matter of time before we have leave to be together. Until then, I shall bide my time and play my position to the best advantage. "You make me blush, sir," I reply quietly, trying to suppress the excitement that I feel.

"I hope I have the opportunity in the future to do more than simply make you blush," he replies, tracing my cheek with his thumb.

I turn from him so he won't see the desire on my face. Connor is so capable in every aspect, I'm not entirely convinced that he is unable to read my thoughts. The peacock turns and flicks his tail feathers in my direction, lowering them to the ground as he starts to walk away. He is so close that the feathers brush the bottom of my brocade gown and I bend down to feel the silken strands as they pull through my fingers.

Something tickles my cheek and I reach up to brush it off, feeling the soft strands of the peacock feather that Griffon's holding. The image from the memory flashes through my mind and I shiver as I realize that something behind Connor's eyes, something undefined, is familiar in a way I don't want it to be.

Griffon's face shows concern as he studies me. "Everything okay?"

I push the memory of Connor down as far as I can and try to erase the heaviness that's sitting on my chest. Whatever our relationship was in the past, Connor doesn't have anything to do with my life now. Griffon and I have been through so much in such a short time, I'm sure we're meant to be together. We're destined for each other.

I stand on my tiptoes to give Griffon a quick kiss. "Better than okay," I answer. "It's fate that we're here, in this lifetime, together again." A chill runs up my spine as I feel traces of the passion and desire that Connor's green eyes stirred in me. In the sixteenth-century English me. "And you can't mess with fate, right?"

Two

Maybe you can't change your fate. But you can change your mind.

"I can't do this. We need to go back," I say through gritted teeth, my hands in a tight grip on the bridge's metal railing—the only thing separating me from certain death.

"I thought you were finally getting over your fear of heights," Janine says. "After pulling Griffon back onto the roof of a three-story building, I figured walking across the Golden Gate Bridge would be a snap."

"You'd think that," I say. My stomach is churning as I stare straight out at the horizon, past the skyscrapers of San Francisco on one side and the hills of Marin on the other, to the point where the dark green ocean meets the edge of the world. "But then I had adrenaline going for me, what with Veronique pointing a gun at the two of us."

"Come on, Cole. Just look down," Janine says, bending over the railing toward the water hundreds of feet below like it's no big deal.

"That's what I'm trying to avoid. You know how much I hate this." Watching my best friend fall from a rooftop a century ago makes me uncomfortable standing on a ladder; forget about being a few hundred feet above the waves of the bay.

"Which is exactly why I thought the bridge would be the perfect spot for our empath lesson." The beads on the ends of her long braids make a clacking sound as she pulls away from the railing and looks at all the other pedestrians on the sidewalk. "Name a place in the city that contains more emotion." She leans in toward me. "Think about it: you have the giddy tourists snapping photos on their phones to send to the folks back home, and the commuters driving their cars over the bridge, worrying about the errors in the latest spreadsheet." Janine pauses. "And then you have the people who are so afraid they're going to fall that they can barely move."

I allow myself one quick look down, and it just confirms my worst fears. My hands start to sweat and I panic, sure that I'm going to lose my grip on the railing. "It's not so much that I think I'll fall," I confess to her as a bike rider whizzes past us on the sidewalk. "It's that I'm afraid that for one split second I'll allow the crazy part of me to take over and I'll jump. Because I know I'll regret it in the first millisecond after my feet leave the concrete."

"Most people do," she says, watching the whitecaps on the water below us. "I know an Akhet who died this way in his last lifetime. Said the same thing—regretted it all the way down

until he hit the water. Splat." She takes one last look over the
edge and I know we're both counting the seconds it would take
for a body to fly through the air and land with the smallest
splash down below. "Come on, let's walk."

"I don't think I can," I say. We had only made it a few hundred feet away from where the water hits the rocks on shore—
not even to the middle of the bridge—before I had to stop.

"You can," she says. "Just put one foot in front of the other."

I let go of the railing with one hand. "On one condition. I get
to walk closest to the road."

"Okay," she says, starting off without me. "But you know
you have a much greater chance of being hit by a car crossing
the bridge than you do of accidentally flinging yourself off the
side."

"I'll risk it," I say, already feeling a little better now that I'm
a few feet away from the edge.

Janine gives me a smile that looks just like Griffon's. Although
her skin is darker than his, certain gestures or expressions
remind me that, despite the fact they're both Akhet, Janine is
definitely his mother in this lifetime. I wonder if it's weird for
her that I'm with him.

I look around at the people on the bridge. Even though it's
unusually bright and sunny for a San Francisco summer day,
the wind up here is fierce, and most everyone pulls their jackets
tightly around them. "So are we really going to do a lesson outside? In front of all these people?"

"It'll be fine," she says. "Maybe things will go even better
in the fresh air." Which is a nice way of saying they haven't
been going so well the last few weeks cooped up in her office

at the university. If the past few training sessions are any indication, my empath skills may be as developed as they're ever going to get.

"If you say so."

"I say so," she says. "Haven't you heard it takes ten thousand hours of practice to master anything? I'm sure you put at least that into the cello over your lifetimes."

Janine glances at the scar that runs down my left arm. The shattered window has been fixed for months, but the physical damage to my hand seems to be permanent. In a split second and with a single shard of glass, Veronique managed to change the course of my life forever. Instead of touring the world playing cello, I can barely hold a bow, much less manage the complicated fingerings that an orchestra demands. "Look," she says. "The cello brought you a long way in this lifetime. And from what you're remembering, it sounds like it took you a long way in the past too. But maybe that phase is over now."

As much as I know she's right, I wince at hearing the words out loud. They seem so final. "Mom and Dad don't want to admit it's over," I say. It's so much easier to push my anxieties off onto them. "They think this is all just a temporary setback, that I'll be back to playing in no time despite what all the doctors say."

"And what do you think?"

I take a deep breath and risk a glance back down at the water through the slats in the railing. "I don't believe in miracles."

Janine looks at me. "Sometimes a miracle is just a lot of luck and sweat in disguise."

I nod, not trusting my voice. I don't know what I think anymore. One minute I know my cello career is over even before it
began, and I'm okay with that. The next minute, the thought of
never playing in front of an audience again feels like a punch in
the stomach.

"Maybe you won't be able to play at the same level anymore," Janine says. "But maybe there are ways you can utilize
your other skills to make the greatest difference."

"But my empath skills suck so far."

"They don't *suck*," Janine says, and I can't help smiling. She
never swears, and even that word sounds funny coming out of
her mouth. "You've done it before; you were able to harness
those skills when you needed them most. You just need more
practice to be able to do it on command." We walk a little way in
silence and I look up at the tall orange metal towers that hold up
the cables on the bridge.

"Even though you were gifted with the cello as a child," she
continues, "your parents still got you lessons, didn't they? This
is the same thing. Taking an innate skill and honing it until
you're a master. And since a true empath is rare, these skills
are more important than ever."

"What for? Even if I do figure out how to do this and become
an empath, how is that going to help anyone?"

"Mankind's greatest failing is not understanding one
another—a lack of communication between individuals and cul-
tures. Someone like you, who can bridge the gap, so to speak"—
Janine grins at her own joke—"who can make one person truly
understand how another feels and be able to probe the depths of
a person's psyche to find a hidden meaning? That would be

invaluable." She pauses. "Not to mention being able to tell when a person is lying. The Sekhem are already asking how your training is coming along. Trust me, they're interested."

Even though she's said variations of all this before, it still sounds so unreal. Me, being a valuable part of such an important organization. Crazy. "Then I guess we'd better start practicing."

Janine stops on the edge of the sidewalk and puts her hands about two inches in front of mine. "At some point, you might be able to read people without even touching them, by sensing the magnetic field that surrounds them. For now, we're going to concentrate on using physical contact. I just think it's easier that way."

"Except for the usual Akhet vibrations, I don't feel anything."

She shrugs. "It's a theory I'm working on. This level of empathy is totally new to all of us, but I think with your innate abilities, you can become so sensitive that physical contact won't be necessary." She turns and starts walking again. "Let's go this way around the tower," she says, pointing to the left. "It's less crowded on this side, and we can decide if we want to go all the way across or turn back."

"I already vote for turning back." There are a few people at the railing, mostly taking pictures or craning their necks to see the top of the tallest tower. But there's one older guy in a blue jacket who stands out as if he has a spotlight on him. Everyone else fades into the shadows as I study him. He's not doing anything at all, just standing motionless at the railing, but even from here I can feel that something's not right.

"What is it?" Janine asks.

"That guy right there. Don't you see him?"

"Which guy?"

"The one in the blue. Something's going on with him," I say. His eyes aren't looking down, but are fixed in the distance. Both hands are gripping the railing so hard his knuckles are white, and one foot is poised on the bottom rung. "I think he's going to jump," I whisper.

"Then you need to go make contact with him," she says quietly, her eyes focused on his back.

I can feel panic rising in my chest. "How? Do I just go ask him if he's about to kill himself?"

Janine nudges me forward. "You'll think of something." She glances at me. "Anything's better than the alternative."

I take a few steps closer, with no idea how I'm going to do this. In order to read him, I need to touch him, to make contact with him in a way that won't startle him. I'm within a couple of feet when I pretend to trip, going down on one knee, grabbing at the man's arm as I fall.

I'm hyperalert as my hand makes contact, and in a flash I feel overwhelming despair and sadness wash over me. It's as if death is already too close. "I'm so sorry!" I say, putting both hands on the sidewalk to steady myself both from the fall and from the strength of his emotions.

"Are you okay?" he asks, looking startled. He reaches down to help me up.

"I think so," I say. I look into his eyes behind thick black glasses, wondering what happened in his life that brought him to this place. "Are you?"

He tilts his head and releases my arm. Instantly, the emotions vanish. "Sure," he says, a puzzled expression on his face. "Why wouldn't I be?"

"I just saw you standing here. And you looked a little sad."

He shakes his head and gives me a slight smile. "I was just admiring the view," he says with a shrug, his voice betraying no emotion at all. "Not every day you get to stand on a bridge and look at such a beautiful city."

I begin to feel unsure of myself. Either he's a really good liar or he really wasn't planning to jump. "Right. Of course. It's just that I—"

"What's going on, honey?" A thin woman with a camera around her neck walks up and slips her arm through his. She has on a purple knit hat that doesn't look out of place up here, even though it's June. I'm startled to see that he's not alone. Why would he bring her here if he was going to jump?

"Nothing," he says, giving her a kiss on the cheek. "This young lady tripped, and I was just helping her up."

I look back at the sidewalk at the imaginary crack that caused my fall. "He was." I nod to the man. "Thanks. They should really fix that. Someone could get hurt."

"That's terrible," the woman says with a frown, squinting down at the sidewalk. She smiles up at the man. It's obvious she adores him. "I'm glad he could help."

"Are you sure you're going to be okay now, miss?" the man asks.

I have no idea what just happened here. He seems so stable now. Did I read him wrong? "I'm sure," I say, giving him a wide smile that I don't feel. "I'll be fine."

"Great," he says. He pounds his fist twice on the railing and then turns to walk back toward the San Francisco side, arm in arm with the woman.

Janine squeezes my shoulder as they walk away. "Great job," she whispers. "How did it feel?"

"It wasn't *great*," I say, frustration clouding any satisfaction I might have. "I don't think I read him right at all. At first all I could feel was an overwhelming sadness, but then he just acted so normal."

"Maybe you were right," Janine said. "And maybe by talking to him at the crucial moment, it passed. Sometimes people don't want their problems solved. They just want to be seen."

I glance back at the couple. "Or maybe he's just a tourist admiring the view."

"You have a nice day," the woman shouts over her shoulder, giving a little wave. As the sleeve of her jacket falls back, I see a clear plastic bracelet around her too-thin wrist. I look at the hat covering her head and see that there's no hair peeking out from the bottom of it. It's then that I understand—she's the one who's dying, not him.

"You too," I shout back. Sometimes it sucks to be right.

Three

"What time is Griffon picking Owen up at the airport?" Rayne asks as we dodge the crowds on Haight Street.

"About an hour ago," I say, digging around in my bag for my bus pass. We've spent the day hanging around my house, but now I have to go teach cello at the studio. I complain about having a job, but I'm secretly glad to have somewhere to go during the week. A whole summer with nothing to do would make me antsy. "Kat wanted to go with him, but I talked her out of it. Griffon is his best friend, and the ride from the airport is probably the only time she won't be hanging off Owen this whole trip."

Rayne wrinkles her nose. "Is it going to be weird hanging out with your sister so much?"

I stare at her. "Um, yeah. Which is why you have to promise not to leave us alone with them. Kat is already talking about all the parties we're going to while he's here; you and Peter need to come along to break up the ick factor."

She laughs. "We'll try."

The sidewalk is thick with tourists, but the strange hand on my arm is still startling, and my blood runs cold when I turn to see who grabbed me. For a second I can barely breathe. I knew this moment was going to come sooner or later; she's been sanctioned by the Sekhem for what she did to us, but there was not much more they could do. I've rehearsed this over and over in my head, all of the things I want to say to her, how I need to stand up to her once and for all, but I'm caught so off guard that I take two steps backward.

"Cole!" Veronique says, as if our meeting on the street is some kind of happy coincidence.

"What do you want?" I'm glad that my tone is as flat and lifeless as I mean it to be.

Veronique smiles and shakes her head. "Nothing. I just saw you and your friend across the street and wanted to say hello. Because it's been so long." She looks physically like the Veronique I first met last year—her dark hair shiny and not a strand out of place, but there's something in her eyes that reminds me of the frantic woman up on the roof with a gun aimed at Griffon's head. It's been almost two months since that horrible day, but I can see right away that not much has changed.

"Not long enough," I say. I glance at Rayne, who's standing to the side. After all that happened between us, I forget she's never actually met Veronique, never come face-to-face with the one who almost took it all away. Not like I'm going to introduce them now.

"Oh, come on," Veronique says, as if we just had some small argument that can be washed away with a few words. "All's well that ends well, right? Everything turned out okay."

"*Okay?*" I repeat, my voice louder than I intend it to be. I look around to make sure nobody is close enough to overhear. "The last time I saw you, you were trying to kill Griffon." The scar on his cheek and the one on my arm are evidence that she did in fact mean to hurt us both; nothing that happened was an accident.

Veronique glances at Rayne, obviously not knowing how much to say in front of her.

"Rayne knows all about us," I say. "All about what you did."

"Right," Veronique says, smoothing back her hair. "That's why I wanted to talk to you." There's a pause as Veronique hesitates, staring at her hands. "Look, I was wrong, and I wanted to say that I'm sorry." She looks straight into my eyes. "For everything."

I wait, but Veronique doesn't offer any more explanation. "Sorry?" I repeat, my voice again too loud. I concentrate on lowering it. "For which part? Sorry for stalking me? For permanently destroying my left hand as well as my career? For almost killing Griffon? Which part are you *most* sorry for?"

Rayne puts one hand on my trembling arm, as I vent the anger I wasn't aware I'd hidden inside. I can't look at Veronique right now. Every time I remember the sharp blast of the gun followed by the image of Griffon going over the edge of the building, I feel sick inside.

"It's okay," Rayne says, in an attempt to be reassuring.

"It is definitely *not* okay." I've gone over and over it for the past couple of months, but Veronique hasn't been here to answer for any of it. Now is my chance. "You don't even understand what you've done." I lean forward, my breath coming hard and fast as my heart pounds. "The scar Griffon's going to carry for the rest of his life." I pull up my sleeve and hold my arm out for her inspection. "My scar that hides the real damage inside. I can't play anymore; I'll probably never play in front of an audience again. And for what? I had nothing to do with Alessandra's death in that lifetime." At this point, I don't care who hears me.

Veronique waits quietly until I'm done. "You're right. I deserve all of that and more. I take full responsibility for everything I've done. I was stupid and stubborn. All I could see was an opportunity for revenge, to silence the anguish that's followed me from one lifetime to the next." Her eyes tear up. "I was blinded by my love for Alessandra, and it's prevented me from moving on in this life. From being able to form relationships, to pursue my passions. And it was love that made me do things I can't take back. I just thank God that everything ended up as well as it did."

"Not all of us are so thrilled," I say quietly, not wanting to let her wrap everything up in a neat little package.

"I'm seeing a therapist." Veronique nods at Rayne. "She's Khem, but someone who understands what it means to be Akhet."

Rayne's looking at me for clarification. "Khem is someone who's not Akhet," I explain, just as Janine did for me. I stare down Veronique. "But most Akhet don't use it. It's like slang, a derogatory term for someone who doesn't know, who's ignorant."

Veronique holds her hands up in front of her. "I didn't mean anything by it. In fact, she's been really helpful in sorting some things out." She looks at me. "Giacomo has gone back to Italy. Alone." She laughs. "Or maybe not so alone by now, who knows?"

I have to admit I'm surprised that her boyfriend left her. Giacomo stood by her even though she loved a ghost. He was ready to kill for her. "I'm *so* sorry to hear that." I make sure that she hears my tone.

She shrugs, either not getting my sarcasm or choosing to ignore it. "It's better this way. Even he couldn't compete with my memories. That's what I'm trying to learn to deal with. I may never find the essence of Alessandra again, and I have to come to terms with that. All I ask is your forgiveness."

"Why in hell should I forgive you?" I say. "I trusted you, and you completely betrayed me. Why should I waste any more time listening to you?"

"You don't have to," Veronique says quietly, her eyes fixed on the sidewalk.

The expression of resignation on her face is pathetic and only makes me more angry. "Good to hear," I say.

I turn to go, but Veronique grabs my hand. "Come on." Her voice is almost desperate. "Don't leave like this."

I push her back as hard as I can, knowing that people are starting to look at us, but not caring at all. "Get your hands off me!"

Rayne jumps between us, one hand on each of our shoulders. "Stop!" If I wasn't watching carefully, I would have missed it. As soon as Rayne touches her, Veronique flinches slightly and something unreadable crosses her face.

"Oh my God," she whispers, putting a hand to her mouth.

Two red spots appear on her cheeks, and I can see her hands trembling. Rayne isn't Akhet, I know that, so I have no idea what's causing this reaction.

"You're insane." I turn my back on Veronique, hopefully for the last time. I have nothing else I want to say to her. Ever. "Come on, Rayne, I've heard enough. Let's get out of here."

I pull the cello out of its case and lean it against my shoulder, the familiar weight letting me exhale for the first time in what seems like days. Music is something I don't have to think about; it's something I absorb without trying, and I'm grateful for every opportunity to lose myself in it.

At least that's how it used to be. With a sigh, I pull the cello away from my left shoulder and set it against my right. Holding and playing the cello with my left hand is totally second nature, and to turn that around, to play the notes with the other side of my body, is something I'm still not used to. People compare it to trying to write with your other hand, but relearning how to play the cello this way is more like learning how to breathe underwater—impossible. Not that I don't appreciate it. Griffon went to so much trouble and expense to get this right-hand cello built for me; it's the most amazing gift I've ever gotten. And I suppose I am getting better—every day it's getting a little easier, and even though I'm a long way from playing concerts again, at least I can still teach.

Reaching for the bow with my left hand, I catch a glimpse of the raised, red scar that runs down the inside of my forearm, and immediately my anger at Veronique bubbles up in my chest all over again. Like I'd accept some halfhearted apology for everything she did. As I waited for the bus, I tried several times to text Griffon to tell him, but eventually I put the phone away. No sense getting him all worked up just as Owen arrives, and this way I can choose my words more carefully.

I close my eyes as my fingers stumble through a piece I wrote a couple of years ago, mostly finding the right notes on the right string, but without the confidence I'm used to. There's no life to the music; it feels flat and empty, and the longer the bow pulls at the strings, the worse I feel. I stop trying for the right notes and start sawing at the cello, the bow making a mind-numbing screeching sound as it scrapes the bridge. Ever since the accident, I've had to put on a brave face, had to become the poor injured musician who will use all of her talent and ambition to overcome the setbacks. But it's not going to happen. I know that now. I probably knew it the moment I woke up in the hospital with my arm wrapped in white bandages. Impatience and anger well up in my body, the frustration that's been building for weeks finally exploding in my hands. As the notes fade into the air, I throw the bow across the room and watch it clatter against the wall. For a split second I feel better, but immediately the guilt sets in. It isn't the cello's fault it can't sing. It's mine.

Crossing the room to pick up the bow, I catch a glimpse of Herr Steinberg's face in the window of the practice-room door. He's looking at me with a measure of understanding, not the pity I'm used to from other people. I can feel my cheeks flame up, knowing that he's witnessed my ridiculous temper tantrum. He catches my eye and glances down at the doorknob, the studio signal for "Can I come in?" I nod and pretend to adjust the strings of the cello, knowing that I can't look him in the eye right now without losing it. Even though I realize that knowing how to play the cello effortlessly isn't really a gift, only a memory of a skill I learned in another lifetime, not having an outlet for my emotions leaves me frustrated and angry.

I can feel the pressure in the practice room change as he opens the door, closing it quickly behind him. "Do I get to hear?"

I shrug, fiddling with the tension on the bow. "Not much to hear."

Herr Steinberg's eyes crinkle up at the corners as he smiles. In all the time I had away from the studio after the accident, I missed his steady presence the most. He's been my teacher in one way or another for almost ten years, and even though I know that letting me teach at the studio was sort of a pity gesture because I can't perform anymore, I appreciate it. "I find that hard to believe," he says. "But you don't have to if you don't want to."

"I'm not ready." Tears spring into my eyes despite biting my lip to try to prevent them. I sniff and give him what I know is a sad smile, but it's the best I've got. "I played better when I was seven."

"As you were the most talented seven-year-old I've ever met, that's not so bad." He glances at my custom right-handed cello. "It'll come back, not to worry." He pauses. "Do you have a minute? There's something in the lounge I want to show you."

I glance at the clock. "I have a few minutes before my next lesson. What is it?"

"You'll see," he says mysteriously, leading the way down the hall. Herr Steinberg has a lounge set up for families to wait in while students are at their lessons—there are toys and games and even a mini fridge full of juice boxes for kids who behave, and I can hear kids laughing and parents talking softly as we approach. When we reach the doorway, I see Griffon sitting on the couch in the middle of the crowd, concentrating intently on something on the low table in front of him. He glances up and his face breaks into an embarrassed smile.

"It's for you," he says, turning back to the table. "But it's not done yet."

I peek over his shoulder to see him working furiously on an Etch A Sketch. I blink hard and have to catch my breath when I see what he's doing. On the gray screen is a perfect picture of me in a long black gown playing the cello. The right-handed cello. "That's amazing," I say, constantly surprised at what he can do.

"It is," Herr Steinberg agrees, and a bunch of the parents nod. One girl scoots closer to Griffon to get a better look.

"I had a little time on my hands." Griffon shrugs like it's nothing. Like anyone can just walk in here, grab an Etch A Sketch, and make it look like fine art. "I dropped Owen off at your house to see Kat and thought I'd come by."

"I'll be done in about half an hour," I say.

"Great," Griffon says, his hands twisting the little white knobs on the front of the toy. "That should be just enough time to finish this."

"Is that your job?" one of the boys asks.

Griffon laughs. "No. It's just fun."

"You should totally do that for your job," the boy says, a hint of awe in his voice.

I see my next student sitting right next to Griffon on the

couch, with an unusually blank look on his face. "Zander," I say. "Let's go."

"Right," he says, nodding. He looks at Griffon. "That's cool."

That's about the highest compliment anyone's going to get from this kid, but I can't say that out loud because his mom's standing right next to me. We walk back toward the practice room, Zander kicking the cello case in front of him every step of the way. I try not to sigh because it's not really fair to dislike an eight-year-old, but every half hour spent with him feels like an eternity. His mother has gone out of her way to tell me how smart he is, how he's a genius with the computer, already skipping grades at a rapid pace, but that doesn't hide the fact that basically, he's kind of a frat boy in training.

"Hey, Nicole," Zander says, plopping down in the chair opposite mine.

"*Miss* Nicole," I correct for the hundredth time. Herr Steinberg insists on the proper respect in the studio.

"Whatever," he says, looking around. I hate to say it because he's just a kid, but whenever his lesson rolls around, I make sure my bag and any other valuables are locked away in the teachers' lounge. He always looks like he'll pocket anything he can get his hands on. "Is that guy your *boyfriend?*" He draws out the last word like we're on a playground somewhere.

"Maybe," I say, although I know I'm smiling.

"Do you guys have sex?"

"Zander!" I say, looking up to make sure the door is shut behind us. "That's not the kind of question you ask somebody."

He stares me down. "I'm guessing the answer is no, then."

I sit down in my chair. "I am not talking about this with

you." I lift up the cello and put new music on the stand, mainly to avoid his eyes. "Did you practice?"

Zander looks at me like I'm an idiot. "No."

I sigh. His lack of improvement is going to mean another lecture from his mother on my teaching techniques. That her darling boy sucks at cello has to be my fault, rather than the fact that he hates it and never practices. I set the music on the stand between us. "I'm not even asking you to spend ages on this." I'm not sure why I'm bothering with explanations. "Just a couple of hours a week."

"A couple of hours that I could be doing something more useful," he says, reluctantly dragging his cello out of its case. If it's possible to feel sorry for an inanimate object, I wish that his poor cello could find a more deserving home. I know his parents bought it new last year when we started working together, but it's already covered with the dings and scratches of a much older instrument.

I set my bow on the stand and turn to face him. "Why don't you quit? Let's just stop this huge waste of time and go out there and tell your mother you really don't want to do this."

I can see the conflict on his face as he thinks about what I just said. For all his snarky comments and bored attitude, he's afraid of his parents. More than anyone, I know how heavy parental disappointment can be. "I can't." He sighs and picks up his bow. "Let's just get this over with."

"Amen to that," I say, picking up my own bow and fingering the first note.

Four

I can't believe I let you talk me into taking the bus," Kat complains as we walk down Fillmore toward the bay, her stiletto heels on the sidewalk sharply echoing her agitation.

"What else are we supposed to do?" I ask. "All six of us can't fit into a cab, and getting two would have taken forever. Not like it's going to kill you to take a bus every once in a while."

Kat glances back at me from where she's marching slightly ahead of the rest of us. "You don't know that. From the looks of some of the people on there, a person might actually end up dead." She stops, bracing herself against a building, and lifts up her foot. "Besides, I think I got gum on my shoe."

Owen grabs her around the waist and sweeps her down the street until she squeals with pleasure. "If I had it my way, I'd get you your own personal limo for transport."

They stop, and Kat kisses him on the lips quickly, then

so deeply I have to look away. Owen's thick Scottish accent makes everything he says sound sexy to her, so every time he speaks they end up in a lip-lock. I've never hung out much with my sister before, and now I know why—the display has left me slightly sick to my stomach.

Griffon grabs my hand and grins at me, and I wonder if this is weird for him too. I'd hate that his best friend is dating my sister, except for the fact that if I'm being honest, Owen chasing after Kat is the only reason I'm with Griffon now. I turn to see what's keeping Rayne and Peter only to see them leaning up against a building, locked in an embrace. "Seriously?" I shout back at them. "You too?"

"It's not a bad idea," Griffon says, bending down for a quick kiss. I laugh and try not to give in to the sensation or we'll never get there. Which would actually be pretty okay with me.

"All right, guys, let's go," Kat commands, in the lead once again. She straightens her dress and takes Owen's hand. "It's just down here on Beach Street."

"Fancy," I say as we approach a modern loft building, looking slightly out of place among the old Victorians on the street. The windows flicker with candlelight, and I can see the shadows of people moving behind the sheer curtains and hear the hum of synthesizer music that seems to vibrate through the walls. "Does this whole place belong to Francesca?" I know Kat's boss has to have some money lying around—not every twenty-one-year-old gets to run her own clothing store—but even I know that buildings down here aren't cheap.

Kat turns to face me. "Yes. Promise you won't embarrass me. This isn't some little-kid party. Francesca and Drew have a lot of influential friends, big people here in the city. Don't blow it."

The mention of Drew's name makes my smart-ass comeback catch in my throat. The only reason I agreed to come was because I wouldn't have to see him. "I thought you said Drew was still out of town."

"He is," she answers. "He had to do some business thing in LA. Why?"

I glance at Griffon talking to Owen on the sidewalk. I haven't told him about meeting Drew at the shop or the fact that he recognized my ankh. I don't know how to explain my feelings about Drew when everything is so new with Griffon and me. "No reason. Just curious."

Griffon joins me on the stairs as Kat pushes the door open. The house is lit with a combination of candles and little twinkling white lights. Every surface seems to shimmer, and the effect makes me a little bit light-headed, like I'm trapped in a fun house mirror.

The front room with all the windows is crowded with people who look like they've just come from a gallery opening— well dressed, but with something a little artsy about each one of them: oversized rings here, fuchsia hair there. I look around, but it doesn't take long to figure out that everyone here is older than we are, and I'd take bets that we're the only high-school students to ever attend one of her parties.

"I'm going to find Francesca." Kat takes Owen by the hand and leads him through a doorway, leaving the rest of us alone while she shows off her prize. At least she isn't going to hang around and babysit.

Rayne puts her hand on my shoulder and whispers in my ear. "Good thing we brought our own cute boys, because there's nothing but old men in this place."

"You're not kidding," I say. All of the guys in this place are in their twenties at least, looking like they just got off from their nice, responsible jobs. Nobody is paying any attention to us; they're just standing in small clumps, drinks and tiny plates of even tinier food in their hands.

Griffon slips his arm around my waist. "Want me to get you a drink?" He glances at a long table filled with bottles and glasses.

Rayne looks at me and shrugs, answering the unspoken question about whether we should drink real drinks or not. I look around. No keg in sight. Since we were at a fancy party, maybe it was time to be a little fancy. "Um, a glass of wine. White."

"Sauvignon blanc or chardonnay?" Griffon's grin gives him away.

I shove him in the arm. "You pick."

"I'll help," Peter says, and the two of them walk off into the crowd.

Rayne drags me over to the window. "Wow, check out this view. You can see the Golden Gate and the boats in the marina from here." I stand next to her, watching the lights on the boats bob up and down on the water. "What exactly does Kat's boss do again?"

"She owns a clothing store on Union Street," I say.

"Must be some expensive stuff to afford a place this nice."

I wrinkle my nose, remembering the nearly empty store

with its artsy, highlighted displays. "I suppose," I say, absently picking at the paint stain on my jeans. At least I'd traded my Vans for some black flats.

Rayne nudges me with her shoulder. "Places like this always make me uncomfortable. I don't think I'm meant to hang around rich people." She glances around the room as if she's looking at the exhibits at an aquarium.

"Me neither," I agree. I see Peter and Griffon across the room, laughing at something the guy next to them said. I watch how easy Griffon is in this place, with these people; he seems to melt into any environment and look like he belongs wherever he is, like some sort of social chameleon. I wonder if that's a skill you can learn.

Rayne follows my gaze. "I wish Peter was as into me as Griffon is you." Her voice is tinged with sadness.

"He is! What are you talking about? I've seen the way he looks at you."

Rayne's cheeks blaze with pleasure and she turns back to the window to try to hide it. "You think so? It's just that you can tell that Griffon would do anything for you. I mean *anything*."

I think back to that day on the roof, where Griffon said that he'd die for me if that's what it took. "He is pretty amazing." I swallow hard to keep the image of him clinging to the side of the building out of my head. "But so is Peter. We're both lucky."

Rayne stands up straight and pokes me in the side, nodding toward the drinks table. "Who's the old lady? She totally looks like she's hitting on Griffon."

I turn to see a woman standing close to him, almost pushing Peter out of the way. She's gesturing as she talks, the massive diamond on her right hand catching the light every time she moves. The woman puts her hand on Griffon's arm every chance she gets, in a way that seems more than friendly, and makes me more than curious. Most Akhet have a habit of touching people in order to get information, but she's taking it a little far. Griffon backs up a tiny step, but she follows him, closing in on what anyone can see is his personal space. He's smiling, but shaking his head at everything she says—his face is a mask of embarrassment. Griffon hasn't glanced over here, but he must know that I'm watching. Drinks in both hands, he turns to walk away, but she folds something into his back pocket at the last second.

As much as I want to, I can't pretend I didn't notice. "Who was that?" I ask as the two of them hand us our drinks. I take a sip of the golden liquid to try to push down the annoyance that's rising inside of me. Rayne stands next to me with her arms folded across her chest, always ready to be on my side, which is one of the things I love about her.

Griffon laughs, his dark eyes looking endless in this dim light. "It's no big deal."

I'm not sure what to say, because I know what I saw.

Peter grins and shrugs his shoulders. "You might as well tell her."

"What?" I look at Griffon in confusion, wondering if the woman is Akhet and he can't say anything. Peter doesn't know about us. I told Rayne everything when Veronique tried to kill Griffon, but Peter doesn't have a clue about past lives or Sekhem—any of it.

"She just gave me this." Griffon digs around in his pocket and holds out a crumpled business card.

It's thick and has letters embossed in silver. "'Mary Belle'?" I read, and look back up at him.

Griffon rolls his eyes. "She's an agent."

"Apparently she owns the biggest modeling agency on the West Coast," Peter says. He grins. "At least that's what she said. And she set her sights on your boyfriend here. Practically begged him to come in and see her. Apparently he's got 'the look.'"

I smile, feeling like an idiot. She's not Akhet. Just a cougar. "I could have told her that."

"Did you think she was hitting on me?" Griffon grabs my hand and squeezes.

"No," I say. Rayne shoots me a look. "Yes. Maybe."

Griffon leans in and kisses me. "As far as I'm concerned, there's no one but you in this place."

"Smooth talker," I tease, relief making me relax at last.

Rayne takes a drink and looks around. "Wonder where the people with the teeny tiny food are. I'm starving."

"I saw some trays near the kitchen," Peter says, reaching for her hand. "You guys want anything?"

I hold up my wine. "I'm okay," I answer, watching the two of them disappear into the crowd.

Griffon and I stand quietly for a few minutes, and I can't help noticing some of the women in the room glancing our way. Or, rather, Griffon's way. All the eyes on him make me a little jealous, but I get it. With his dark skin and golden eyes, Griffon draws attention everywhere he goes.

Just as I'm starting to get uncomfortable, I feel his hand on my arm. "The guy by the bar told me this place has a great view. Let's go find it."

"You can see the boats from this window."

"Yeah, but he says there's a better one. Grab your jacket." Griffon leads me out of the room toward a doorway at the end of the hall. The cold, wet air hits me as soon as we push it open, and I pull my jacket tighter. The fog hasn't completely rolled in yet and you can still see some stars in the black sky overhead. There's a set of stairs that snake along the outside of the building, and Griffon heads for those.

"You first?" he asks, looking up.

I turn to him. "Why? So you can watch my butt from below?"

He holds up his hands in surrender. "You caught me. I was going to say that I was just trying to be polite, but look who I'm talking to. The human lie detector."

I follow his glance up the stairs. They go up three stories and disappear at the roof. "Can't we just enjoy the view from down here?"

Griffon kisses the palm of my hand. "You know this is a different rooftop. Nothing's going to happen, I promise." He makes a big show of looking around. "No Veronique in sight."

I smile, but it just pokes at the guilt I've been carrying around with me, because I haven't told him about running into Veronique. At first I could never find the right time, and now that it's been almost a week, I don't know how to bring it up. It seems like she listened to me, though, because I haven't seen her since.

"Let's go check it out," Griffon says. "And if you don't like it, we can come right back down."

I totally agree when people say you should face your fears. I just don't want to face mine. I hear loud laughter from the hallway on the other side of the door and suddenly, desperately want to be alone with him. "Okay. But just for a minute."

As soon as we reach the top, I suck in my breath. The view from up here is really amazing. I can see over the Marina Green to the dark water under the Golden Gate Bridge. The cars on the bridge look like a river of light as they flow to Marin, where the edge of the fog licks at the hills.

"There's Alcatraz," Griffon says, pointing to some tiny dots of light in the middle of the water.

"Would you believe I've never been there?"

"I haven't been there this time," he says. "But I visited last time, in the seventies, when they'd just opened it up to the public. It was pretty creepy back then—they did this one demo where they'd lock you in one of the solitary confinement cells for two minutes. It was pitch black and silent, and two minutes seemed like forever. I heard they don't do that anymore, though."

I watch Griffon as he speaks, loving that this conversation about a trip he took in a past lifetime seems normal. Our normal. "We should go and check it out."

Griffon takes a step away from the stairs, and I notice the rooftop deck for the first time. The surface is covered with wood like a regular deck, but it runs the whole length of the roof, the fact that we're the only people up here making it look even bigger than it already is. Over in one corner are a nice outdoor table and a set of chairs, and closer to us are a thickly cushioned couch and some chaise longues that look like they'd be more at home in a living room than on a roof in the middle of the city. "Hey, a fire pit." Griffon walks to the big copper bowl by the couch. "And there's wood."

I slowly walk over to him, feeling safer as I move away from the edge of the roof. Griffon reaches into his jacket and pulls out a silver Zippo lighter. "And now we have fire."

"Do you always carry a lighter with you?"

"Habit. I got used to having one." He gestures with his fingers like he's smoking.

I make a face, trying to imagine him with a cigarette hanging out of his mouth.

"Come on," he protests. "That was, like, forty years ago. Everyone smoked then. It's not like it is now." He bends down, flips the lighter around with one flick of his wrist, and holds the flame to the small sticks of wood in the bottom of the pit. "Even in this lifetime, a nice, solid lighter seems like a good thing to have." He blows on the flame and I can hear the wood crackle as it catches fire, a few sparks shooting up into the sky before they burn out completely.

Griffon flops onto one of the lounge chairs, patting the small space beside him. "Let's pretend we're camping. Somewhere high up in the Sierras next to a little lake in front of our roaring campfire."

We sit quietly for a minute, staring at the flames. "Two truths and a lie," I say, bringing up the game that made me like him in the first place. "My turn."

"Make it good this time."

"I'll make it easy. I know you stink at this. Okay; I once got attacked by a bear while camping, I've been snorkeling with dolphins, and I can make chocolate chip cookies without looking at a recipe."

Griffon makes his thinking face, scrunching up his mouth

until I have to laugh out loud. "Um, for some reason I believe that anyone who inhales chocolate like you do can whip up a batch of cookies blindfolded in the middle of the night, so I'm guessing that one's true."

"You're one for one."

"Last month you told me that you'd been to Hawaii twice, so I'm going to say that you've been snorkeling with dolphins."

I frown. "I never told you about Hawaii."

He looks at me like I should know better. "It was May fifth. A Sunday. And we were sitting in my living room watching TV. A commercial for an airline came on, and you said that you'd been to Hawaii twice, once when you were three and then again two years ago." Griffon smiles. "Is that good enough?"

"Show off." I laugh. It's hard to argue with someone who has an eidetic memory. "It'll do. So the lie?"

"Is obviously that you were attacked by a bear." He grabs my hand. "In fact, these hands are sissy soft. I'll bet you've never even been camping in your life."

"Not true! I've camped plenty. And for your information, I *was* attacked once. It was by a baby deer on the way from our tent to the bathroom, but still."

"Car camping doesn't count," Griffon says, pulling me down to him. "We should go backpacking sometime. Just the two of us in a tiny tent in the big mountains."

"Ooh. Sign me up." I settle in next to him, pushing myself against the length of his body until he rolls onto his side and puts his arms around me from behind. I watch the fire dance in front of us, feeling the warmth from its heat on my face and the warmth from Griffon's breath on the back of my neck.

"Did you bring the marshmallows?" I ask, turning my head toward him.

Griffon laughs. "I knew there was something I forgot. You should never go to a posh party in the Marina without a bag of marshmallows."

I roll over so that I'm facing him, wrapping one leg around his. Reaching up, I ease my fingers through his curls and then trace the side of his face. "If I was Kat, I'd make you go get some."

Griffon pulls back and smiles. "If you were Kat, I'd make Owen do it." A serious look passes across his face. "But I'd do it for you. I'd go and get you anything you want. Even marshmallows." He pushes a strand of hair away from my face and leans down to kiss me, his lips soft but urgent, and I can feel the desire in his touch. The vibrations that always exist whenever we're together become insistent and almost visible in the small space between us. I run my hands up the inside of his shirt, feeling the muscles of his back contract and goose bumps form as I touch his skin. He keeps his hands outside of my clothes like he usually does, feeling the contours of my body through my jeans as he runs his fingers down my thigh. I inch toward him, closing off any remaining space between our bodies.

My fingers slide down where his jeans meet his skin and he moans softly, pressing against me with even more urgency, his hand firmly on the back of my neck. I can feel his hesitation and silently urge him to keep going, to not stop at that invisible line we've respected all of these weeks.

I sense the moment it changes, and reach up to pull him to me even harder, but Griffon's breathing heavily and pushing himself away from me on the lounger.

"We need to stop," he says, and I can hear the effort it costs him to force the words out.

I reach for him again, wanting the connection I felt just a few seconds ago. With everything we've been through together, I'm not a kid anymore. "No we don't. There's nobody else here. Just us. I want to show you how I feel."

Griffon hesitates, and I can see the emotions playing on his face. He squeezes his eyes closed and shakes his head. "I know how you feel. You don't have to prove it to me."

"I know I don't *have* to," I say softly. "I want to."

He bites his lip as his eyes search mine, looking for the truth in my words.

With centuries of experience behind him, sometimes he seems like an adult—but sometimes he's every inch a seventeen-year-old boy. I run my hands up his shirt, smiling when I see him flinch. "Why are you hesitating? It's not *your* first time."

Griffon looks at me seriously. "It's my first time with you."

I watch his face in the flickering orange light, wanting to lock this one moment in time so that I can go back to it over and over again. I wonder if it will be different when I remember my other first times. If it will make it any less special. "It doesn't matter whether we're in some fancy hotel room or right here under the stars. I want to be with you."

Without saying anything, he bends down and buries his face in my neck, tenderly kissing the curve behind my ear. The air around us seems to have changed, taken on a weight of expectation, and I feel a thrill of anticipation and fear run through me.

I'm so focused on his touch that I don't hear the voices on the stairs until they're almost to the rooftop. Griffon must hear them at the same time because he jumps back from me, and the two of us frantically adjust our clothes as Kat and Owen appear at the top of the stairs.

"I knew it!" Owen shouts, and I can hear the pride in his voice.

"Oh. My. God." It doesn't take a genius to recognize Kat's angry voice. "I told you not to embarrass me!"

I struggle to sit up, my heart still pounding at what almost happened. "Which is why we're up here *alone* and not making out in the middle of the living room."

"Right," she snaps. "Like everyone in the place couldn't look at the two of you and know what you've been up to."

Griffon glances at me with a smile, and I can't help laughing. "So what are *you* doing up here, then?" I ask. "Just coming up to check out the view?"

Kat looks at Owen, and even in this light I can see her face get red. "As a matter of fact, we were."

"Which is exactly what we were doing." Griffon points to the other lounge chair. "Have a seat. It's not so cold with the fire going. I'm going to go get us a couple more drinks."

I watch Kat and Owen settle into the chair, thinking about how much I don't want to spend the whole evening watching them make out. I want to go back to the place Griffon and I were just now. "I'll go," I say. "Besides, I want to check on Rayne. I didn't tell her we were up here." I slide off the chair before Griffon can object and grab the glasses. Bending over to give him a quick kiss, I whisper, "Be right back."

I know I'm grinning as I open the door at the bottom of the

stairs, but I can't help it. As frustrated as I am at getting interrupted, it felt so right. I lift my sleeve up to my nose just to get
the faint traces of his scent, to nudge the last ribbons of memory
of what we almost did. Of what we're still going to do. Soon.

I'm not paying attention to anyone as I walk down the hall
toward the living room, just thinking about Griffon up on the
roof and how much I want to get back there with him. Which is
why I'm caught totally off guard when I hear a shout coming
from the crowd in the kitchen.

"Cole! Wait!"

I stop and glance through the doorway, but the person who
emerges from the crush of bodies is the last one I expect to see
at this party. I'm so stunned to see him again that I can barely
get his name past my lips.

"Drew."

Five

"I heard you were here," Drew says in his thick Australian accent, glancing behind him as he follows me into the hallway. "I've been looking all over for you."

"I thought you were gone," I say, taking a step back from him. Even though I know I can't avoid him forever, I didn't think I'd be face-to-face with him so soon. My hand goes automatically to the ankh around my neck, and Drew's eyes follow. He reaches out to touch its silver curves, but I shrink back from his hand, which seems to snap him back to reality—the reality where we barely know each other.

"You didn't call," he says. He takes a step toward me, and I can feel the faint but insistent vibrations between us. "I was hoping you would."

"I don't know what you're talking about," I say, staring at the hardwood floors to avoid the intensity of his blue eyes as he looks at me. With his short blond hair, he's not my type at all, but I can't deny that he's very good-looking, and it's a little intimidating. As far as I'm concerned, Drew's just a jewelry designer who is practically engaged to Kat's boss. And also happens to be Akhet.

Drew takes a step back, and I can feel the intensity of his energy ease, as if he's consciously forcing himself to slow down. "Is that how we're going to play this?" He nods slowly, but I know it's not with approval. "I thought you'd be glad to see me after so long. All things considered."

I glance behind him, half expecting Francesca to step into the hallway any minute, but only one fairly drunk guy weaves past us, not paying any attention. I look Drew straight in the eyes, hoping that I can stop this conversation before it goes too far. If we don't acknowledge it, then I can keep it from being true. "I barely know you. I met you twice in the shop, and you like my necklace. I don't know what else you think is going on here, but that's all we are to each other." I hear the words and close my eyes, willing myself to believe them. *That's all we are to each other.* I can't let myself think about any other possibility.

Drew stands so close I can feel the warmth of his breath on my skin. "You and I both know that isn't true. You know exactly who I am to you. Who I've been to you. I can tell that you remember."

"You're wrong," I say, looking past him. Not daring to look right at him for fear of what I might see there. "I don't remember." I inhale, trying to make myself believe those words. "I don't remember anything."

"Why would you say that?" Drew asks, and something in his voice makes me meet his eyes. I'm surprised to find a glimmer of hurt behind them. His voice trembles as he continues. "It's taken centuries to find you again, and I thought you'd be as thrilled as I am to finally be together in the same place, in the same lifetime."

I think of Griffon upstairs on the roof and want nothing more than to be back there. No answer I can give will satisfy Drew, so I turn to run back to the stairs, back to Griffon so that I can make this all disappear.

But Drew's reflexes are quicker than mine. He reaches out and grabs my arm as I turn, and it feels as if a strong current of electricity is connecting the two of us. Drew is a more powerful Akhet than I'd imagined. I can feel his hands catching me as my knees buckle from the impact of the jolt and the memory that starts crashing all around me.

The ground beneath us trembles from the pounding of the horses' hooves. I look up at Connor, fear crawling over my skin even as I try to deny what is coming.

"We must run," I say, throwing myself into his arms. Panic rises through my body. "We have to go." I turn to pull him down the long stone hallway, but he stands fast. "They'll find us here!"

"My dear Allison, there is nowhere left to hide," he says quietly, with more comportment than I thought possible at such a moment. His calm control of any situation is one of the things that drew me to him, but right now I want to beat on his chest and spur him into action. What little time we have left is fleeting, certainly he must see that? "They have the grounds surrounded,

I'm sure of it," he continues, lifting my face with his strong hand. "We have no options left. To fight them now will only put us both in danger. I will not risk your life as well."

There is a distant pounding at the main door, although I know the servants have long since gone to the country. "We can't just surrender into their hands!" I cry, frustration at the situation spilling over until I can no longer stop the hot tears from flowing.

Connor reaches around and frees the pendant from my neck, then slips the ruby earrings from my ears. Folding them into my palm, he whispers, "With these jewels and the others in your chambers you shall have means to get away. Keep them hidden, whatever you do."

He bends to kiss me, and for one brief moment it is as if we are the only two people left on Earth. I cling to him desperately, wanting to remember what may well be our last moments together. His lips press against mine, the intensity of his emotions matching the beat of my heart and the heat from our bodies causing the silver in my hand to warm. I feel our connection growing stronger even as our time together grows shorter.

I barely register the noise in the hallway as the soldiers gain entry. It is only when Connor is ripped from my arms that the reality of the moment catches hold and I start to scream. "Connor! No! Make them stop! You can't leave me!" I fall to my knees before the tallest soldier as his compatriots hold my husband roughly by the arms. "I beg of you, sir. You are making a grave mistake!"

I smell the leather of his spotless black boots as the man towers above me, a thick piece of parchment in his hands.

"Connor Wyatt," he proclaims. "You are to be remanded to the custody of His Majesty's representatives to be tried for treason against the crown."

The soldiers shout as they wrestle Connor down the hallway, although he is putting up very little protest. The tall one brushes me aside as if I am nothing but a speck of manure on his boot as he turns to follow the others toward the door.

"Connor!" I scream, disbelief rising at the scene that is unfolding before my eyes. "Don't leave me! Connor!"

With one last burst of energy, he manages to turn back so that I can meet his eyes. "I will always love you, Allison. Never forget. No matter what happens, I will love you. Ad vitam aeternam."

For eternity. At those last words, the soldiers reach the door and wrestle him out to the waiting horses, which snort and paw at the ground. The dust has barely settled on the drive when I collapse on the cold stones of the doorway, fully and completely alone as silence descends upon the house.

I feel a solid wall at my back as I shake off the memory from so many centuries ago. Drew is holding me up by both arms, watching my face intently. He knows what's just happened. He may not know the details, but he knows I remember something. His blue eyes search mine as I feel a pounding of denial in my ears. Drew can't be right. He can't be Connor.

"Are you still going to deny it?" he whispers.

My hands are shaking and the feelings of abandonment and loss have settled into my chest as if that all just happened seconds ago. Tears jump into my eyes as I picture Connor's face again as he's led through our door for what I know is the last time. I look around, taking in the murmur of conversation from the other rooms, the faint smell of candle wax, the clinking of glasses from the bar. I'm here in San Francisco at a party with my boyfriend, not in England in the sixteenth century. "I can't deny what happened then," I say in a whisper. I force my eyes to meet his, the essence of Connor still lingering in my memory. I have to stay strong, keep my emotions in this lifetime. "But that has nothing to do with now."

Drew grips my arms even tighter, his desperation almost visible. "It has everything to do with now, and you know it. After all we've been through." He moves in closer and I can see the light golden stubble on his cheeks. "We're destined to be together, Allison. We've always been destined for each other." I see his eyes shining as he speaks and know that he's fighting back tears of his own.

I can't let myself get pulled into these emotions. There's too much at stake now. Drew could have been anyone back then. Somehow he knew about the ankh and what happened. I remember loving Connor then, but I don't know anything about Drew now. "My name isn't Allison," I say, with as much conviction as I can manage. "Not this time."

Drew's stare is intense. "Allison, Cole; Connor, Drew. The essences are the same, no matter what the labels are."

I take a deep breath and pull up as much conviction as I can. "I don't know why you're doing this, but you're not Connor. I would know." I feel someone watching and glance over Drew's shoulder to see Rayne standing at the end of the hallway staring at us. "I have to go," I say, quickly twisting out of his grip before he can react. Without looking back, I walk toward Rayne, picking up the empty glasses where I must have dropped them.

I force my voice to remain steady as I reach her. "I was just getting some more drinks."

Rayne turns and follows me, glancing back to where Drew is still standing at the end of the hallway. "Are you okay? What the hell was that all about?"

Ducking into the living room, I force myself to keep moving. "That? That was nothing."

Rayne puts out a hand to stop me. "I've seen nothing before," she says. "And that definitely wasn't it. Seriously, Cole. What's going on? Who is that guy?"

"He's crazy," I say. I glance toward the doorway, but Drew is nowhere in sight. "He thinks we knew each other a long time ago. From before."

Rayne grabs the glasses out of my hands and sets them down on a bookcase. Opening the front door, she says, "I think we should probably have this conversation outside."

As soon as the door closes behind us, I take a deep breath. "I'm not cheating on Griffon," I say quickly. "I'd never cheat on him. He's the best thing that's ever happened to me, and I'd never do anything to screw that up."

Rayne looks at me, confused. "I never said you were. I know how you feel about him."

I catch myself. My emotions are stirring up guilt where it doesn't belong. "Remember the whole Lady Allison thing?" I ask.

"Yeah. The lifetime in England."

"Right. And Lord Wyatt? Connor Wyatt? The one we looked

up on the Internet?" I continue. "Well, Drew says he's . . ." I let the sentence trail off and stare at her, hoping that my gestures will save me from having to say it out loud.

For the first time, the concern in her eyes wavers. "Are you trying to tell me that the guy back there was really Lord Wyatt from England all that time ago?"

"I don't know." I shake my head. "He says he is, but I just don't know. He recognized this at Kat's shop a few weeks ago," I say, tracing the ankh with my finger. The memory of losing Connor is still tugging at the edges of my emotions, and I have to force myself to focus on the present. "I've been avoiding him ever since."

Rayne slumps down and sits on the low wall of the porch. "Wow. So you're saying he's one of you? I thought you said there weren't that many Akhet in the world. Seems like every time I turn around you're telling me about another one."

"I know. Griffon and Janine said that the same essences are often drawn to each other, like planets orbiting each other over many lifetimes. The fact that I'm remembering now seems to be bringing around every Akhet in Northern California." I look at Rayne. Even though she's my best friend, I wonder how she can possibly help me with this. "Promise me you won't tell Griffon. Or Peter."

"You said that Peter doesn't know about you guys."

"He doesn't. But don't even bring up Drew's name. I'll figure this out, but I don't want Griffon hurt." I remember the unrelenting pain and emptiness I felt during those days without Griffon, after I'd found out the truth about him. About who he'd been to me. "After all we went through before, I can't stand even the possibility of losing him again." I grab her hand. "Promise?"

"Promise," she agrees. "But I saw the way he was looking at you. I don't think this Drew guy is just going to go away. What are you going to do?"

"I'm not sure," I say. "But for right now, avoiding him is a good place to start. I'm not going back in there."

"You want me to go get Griffon? Tell him you have a headache and need to go home all of a sudden?"

I sit down beside her. "Would you? He's up on the roof with Kat and Owen. The stairs are at the end of the hallway."

Rayne leans over to give me a hug. "Look at you and all this drama. What happened to the boring, cello-playing geek from a few months ago?"

The craziness of the night boils up inside and I feel a tear escape down my cheek before I can brush it away. "I wish I knew."

Six

Come in," Janine calls from behind her door.

I poke my head into her office, surprised to see that she's not alone. An older woman is sitting in the upholstered chair next to her desk, and she gives me a welcoming smile as I glance at the two of them.

"Sorry! I'm early. I'll come back in a half hour." I've been so anxious to talk to someone about the Drew situation that I couldn't wait until our normal time to see her. I have no idea how I'm even going to bring it up, but I figure if anyone will understand, it's Janine.

"No, it's okay. Come, sit." Janine motions to one of the empty chairs at the small round table that takes up most of the room in her small office. "We were just wrapping up. This is Sue Takami. She's going to be a guest lecturer here in the fall, so I was just giving her some tips on the ins and outs of the university." Janine nods to me. "This is Cole. We've been working together for the past few months."

Sue smiles in my direction, her black eyes looking at me with a friendly curiosity, although she doesn't seem to want any more explanation about what kind of work a sixteen-year-old girl would be doing with a renowned university professor. "Nice to meet you." The name is familiar, but it isn't until she speaks that I recognize her—Natsuko Takami. The latest book she wrote won all kinds of prizes and is being made into a major movie; she's been on all the talk shows Mom likes to TiVo.

"You too," I say, trying not to get flustered and say something stupid. I reach out to shake her hand, and just before our fingers touch, I feel Akhet vibrations filling the space between us. I glance at Janine in surprise.

Janine's eyes open wide, but I can't tell if she's teasing me or not.

I look at Sue. "So you're . . ."

Sue looks quickly at Janine, and I feel a conspiracy in the room. "I'm a writer, if that's what you mean. I'm also a teacher. And a wife and mother." Her eyes almost disappear as she laughs and shakes her head. "I'm sorry, Janine. I can't stand to see the confused look on her face a minute longer." Her laughter turns into a grin. "I'm also Ahket. Like you. You're not wrong."

I exhale and try not to be annoyed. Janine likes to pull these little tests on me, and I always hope she's laughing with me and not at me. I smile at her. "I'm never sure if I'm imagining things, because it seems like Akhet are everywhere lately."

Janine's dark eyes blaze with interest. "Really? Who else have you met?"

Instantly I regret my words. "Nobody. Just, like, Veronique. And you guys."

"I think it's like learning a new language," Sue says kindly. "Suddenly, it seems like you hear it on every street corner."

I smile gratefully. "Yeah," I agree. "It is like that. Are you really coming to teach here?"

She nods. "I really am. Spirit Stories in Modern Literature."

"Sue is an old friend," Janine says. "I've been telling her all about you."

Sue tilts her head to look at me. "Janine says that you have budding abilities as an empath. That's fascinating, and a skill the Sekhem will be champing at the bit to use."

I shrug, slightly embarrassed. "I'm not very useful right now," I say.

"No room for false modesty here. Soon Cole's going to outgrow me as a teacher," Janine says. "She's picking things up so quickly that I've almost reached the limit of what I can show her. Pretty soon I'm going to have to pass her along up the ladder."

"Really?" Working with Janine has been so comfortable that the thought of trying to stretch my abilities with another teacher is a little scary. "I thought we'd just keep doing what we've been doing."

Janine laughs. "I'm like kindergarten as far as empathic abilities go. Within a few months, you'll be coming back to teach me what you've learned."

"Are you enrolled at the university?" Sue asks. "My seminar is usually for upperclassmen, but I can try to pull some strings if you're interested."

"That would be great," I answer. "But I'm still in high school. I'm going to be a senior."

"How exciting! Do you know what you're going to do after? Will you apply here?"

I glance at Janine. My future has changed so much in the past few months that I have no idea what I'm going to do. "I'd always planned on going to Juilliard. But . . . things have changed." Not only is Juilliard completely off my radar, but no music school is likely to accept an extraordinarily talented cellist who can barely play a note. "I had an accident and can't play anymore."

"A lot of Akhet don't even go to college these days," Janine says. "It's not like the Sekhem are going to turn you away if you don't have a degree. If you decide to go that route."

I stare at her. "Nice. A university professor telling an almost-senior that she doesn't have to go to college. My parents would love that."

"I'm just saying you have a lot of options now."

I consider that. I've never really thought about anything other than college. "Anyway, I have a few months before I have to really start worrying about it."

"Well, I'll be glad to help in any way I can," Sue says. "It's been so long since I've met an Akhet who wasn't Iawi—rather exciting to have someone new in the ranks."

I can tell from the way she's talking that Sue must have transitioned more than a couple of centuries ago. "Thanks," I say. In a rush, I remember what I wanted to talk to Janine about. "Listen, if you guys are in the middle of something, I don't want to interrupt."

Janine looks at me full on for the first time, and I force

myself to look at the floor. Even though she says she doesn't have many empath abilities, I can never lie to her. "Is that all you came for? Our usual session? Because I'm getting the feeling that there's more."

I glance at Sue. I'm going to try to keep Griffon out of this whole conversation, but I don't want it to be awkward for Janine. "It's . . . kind of hard to talk about."

"Sue was my mentor when I first transitioned. If anyone can help you with a problem, she can."

Griffon said that Janine isn't as Iawi as he is, but I know that this isn't the first lifetime she's remembered. "You guys were together before? That's part of what I wanted to ask about."

They exchange looks, and even though I know that telepathy isn't part of the abilities of even the oldest Akhet, sometimes I wonder. It seems as though the two of them are saying volumes with just their eyes. "It was many years ago," Janine says. "Centuries, actually. We've managed to maintain contact for the past four lifetimes."

"How?" I ask, amazed. "I mean, how do you manage to find each other again? Griffon said that it isn't like all the movies make it out to be."

"It's not," Sue answers. "Many times there is an extreme age difference, or geographical separation. The past fifty years or so, things have gotten much easier."

"What do you mean, easier?"

"Technology, for one," Sue says. "Computers, the Internet."

"Like some kind of Akhet database?" I ask. "You just put in your information and find people you've been connected to in the past?"

"That's not too far off," Janine says. "These days, we take advantage of the tools we have. In the past, the Sekhem kept the records. Traveling on foot and by boat to get around sometimes made reaching the Sekhem center impossible, particularly if you were part of a social class that couldn't easily travel."

"But if you were lucky, you could reconnect with people you'd already had a relationship with?"

Sue smiles at Janine. "The first time I met her, Janine was my grandson."

"And Sue was my grandfather," Janine adds, laughing at the look on my face. "Oh, come on. You must realize that Akhet reality means crossing gender, race, and class boundaries. Sue and I have been connected, just not in the way you might think; it's not like you can seek out your lost love through every lifetime. I already told you how things worked out between Griffon's father and me. No matter how strong your memories are of the other person, if both people don't share them, it won't work emotionally, even if it is physically possible."

My mind is racing as the two of them talk about finding other Akhet as if it's as ordinary as sending a text. "But what if two people had a relationship in the past, and it ended . . ." I search for the right word, remembering my feelings at the memory of Connor being dragged out the front door by the soldiers. "Tragically. Does that mean they're fated to be together if they find each other in the next lifetime? And, you know, if one of them isn't a grandparent or something."

"I've known some that have made it work in more than one lifetime," Janine says. "But it's not all that common; the odds are against you."

The fact that it's not common makes me even more convinced that Drew is wrong. He's not Connor. He can't be. "So if they're together again, and sort of the same age in the same place, does that mean that they should have the same relationship they had before?"

Sue watches me closely as I speak. "Are we talking specifics here, or just hypothetically?"

I can't look at Janine, because I know if I do, I'll tell her about Drew. I don't know if there's some sort of Akhet code, or just that mother-son bond, but I'm afraid that if I tell her the truth, she'll tell Griffon I was asking. "Hypothetically," I say, and force a short laugh. "I'm just trying to figure out how it all works."

"There's not a lot of data on it." Janine turns to Sue. "But it would be a fascinating study. I'm not sure that there's some outside force called 'fate' or 'destiny' that makes people act a certain way. I think you have to work out each individual case on its own." She turns the full intensity of her eyes on me. "What's his name?"

I look back at her, determined not to give it away, but I can see from her expression I've already lost. "Drew." I say it so softly that I can barely hear myself speak, but I can tell by the look on Janine's face that the name reached her just fine.

Sue sits up straighter in her chair. "And he's someone you met recently?"

"Yes. He knows my sister. And I saw him at a party the other night. He keeps trying to tell me that we were together in England in the sixteenth century." I look at Janine. "The same lifetime where I met Griffon."

I'm almost rewarded by the fact that Janine looks surprised. "So what does Drew want from you?"

"He said it was fate that we're together now. I could tell he was hurt that I didn't believe him. I was married to someone named Connor . . . before . . . and I remember parts of it. I have a strong memory of him being taken away by the king's soldiers. Something about treason. I think it was just after that that he was killed."

"And you're sure of these memories?" Sue asks. "This Drew person isn't imposing his memories on you?"

"I'm sure." I pull the ankh out of my shirt, the dark red ruby in the center almost glowing, despite the fact that we're inside under fluorescent lights. "I remember Connor giving me this back then. Griffon returned it to me after all this time."

Sue gets up and takes a step toward me. "May I see that up close?"

I nod, and she lifts the ankh up, examining the front and the back. "This is definitely from that time period."

"He had it made for me. I remember him saying that in a memory I had early on."

Sue looks at Janine and then back to me. "If he had an ankh made for you in the sixteenth century, then that means Connor was probably Akhet back then. It's not a common symbol for that time, at least not in England. He must be Iawi." She sits back in her chair and looks at the two of us. "How did the ankh end up with Griffon?"

I hesitate, but don't see any reason not to tell her the truth. "He'd gotten it as payment. For executing me."

She looks confused. "An Akhet executioner? I can't imagine."

"He wasn't Akhet then," I say quickly. "He was forced into it. And when he became Akhet in the seventeenth century, he spent most of a lifetime tracking down the family heirlooms that had been given to him so that he could hopefully return them one day."

Sue nods. "Interesting form of penance," she says thoughtfully.

"So you said this boy's name was Drew?" Janine continues. "How old is he in this lifetime? What does he look like?"

I close my eyes, trying to focus on the details and not the whole package. Because I'm not attracted to him, no matter how he thinks our past lives connected. No matter what I felt for Connor back then. "Twentysomething, I think. Tall, blond hair and blue eyes. With an accent. He's from Australia originally and does jewelry design for the shop where Kat works."

Janine looks thoughtful. "Hmm. He may be Iawi, but he's not Sekhem. I didn't even know anyone like that was nearby."

"Khered?" Sue asks Janine.

"Must be," Janine nods.

"What's Khered?" It seems like every day there's some new mysterious word they're throwing around.

"Khered are like children," Sue explains, a hint of disdain in her voice. "They're Akhet, usually newer Akhet, who don't want the responsibility of the knowledge and abilities that come to us over our lifetimes. They spend their time looking for personal gratification—fame, money, parties, drinking. Mostly frivolous activities. They generally shun the Sekhem and all we stand for, using up resources and enjoying themselves, and that's about it.

Improving the world for current and future generations isn't on their radar."

"Are there a lot of them?"

"More than enough," Janine sneers. "But I'm surprised that an Iawi is mixed up with Khered. Usually by the time someone's been around for a while they mature enough to leave that lifestyle behind."

Sue leans forward on her elbows. "So, what are you going to do about this Drew person?"

"Nothing, if I can help it." I look at Janine. "I know this is probably weird to hear because you're his mom and all, but I love Griffon, and I want to spend as much time as I can with him in whatever lifetimes we're lucky enough to be in together. We were drawn to each other after what happened between us last time. Griffon was the one who recognized that I'm Akhet, and he's been there through all the craziness that's happened since. If there's any fate involved, mine is to be with Griffon. Not Drew."

"Forgive me for saying this," Janine says quietly, "but you don't sound like you're trying to convince me. Sounds like you're trying to convince yourself."

Seven

"Watch that car!" Mom shouts, grabbing for the dashboard and pumping an imaginary brake on the passenger side. "He's pulling out!"

"I see him," I say irritably, turning the wheel to the left to avoid the Prius' bumper. Driving with her is always a lesson in patience, as well as three-point turns and parallel parking. She freaks out about every little thing. I can't wait until I take my driving test next month and can kick her out of the car.

"Get in the right lane. You're going to turn right up here."

"In, like, a mile," I say, putting on the blinker just to shut her up. "I know where I'm going." I wonder if I've had a driver's license in a previous lifetime, because driving doesn't seem all that hard.

"You should always anticipate your next move," she says,

craning her head back to make sure there's no car in my blind spot.

"And the next move of everyone around me," I finish for her. "I know. Maybe I should get my behind-the-wheel hours with Dad."

She turns to me, a pained look on her face. "Why would you say something like that? It's hurtful."

"I'm just saying that Dad doesn't get as . . . nervous as you do when we're driving."

"Well, forgive me for caring," she says, folding her arms and slumping in the passenger seat.

"I know you care. I just need you to care a little more calmly."

"Right!" she says, pointing. "Take a right here. The restaurant is just down this block. Look for a place to pull over."

I slow down, looking for the restaurant. "Can I stay out past curfew? Just for tonight? I'll be with Kat the whole time."

"We agreed on midnight," she says. "Nothing good ever happens after midnight."

I double-park next to the row of cars that line the street. "I'm sixteen," I say, my frustration mounting about my inability to change any of my parents' stifling rules. "Almost seventeen. Soon I'm going to have a driver's license, and with all of the money I've saved from giving cello lessons, Dad said he'd help me buy a car—"

"Look," she interrupts. "I know how hard it is to be young. To have your first crush. I'm just trying to help you make the right choices."

I get out of the car and slam the door. "I don't need that kind of help. I'm not a baby." I wish I could tell her how much I've been remembering lately. About being in England. About being an adult. That I really am not a little kid anymore.

A car pulls up behind ours and starts honking. I think for a second that Mom is going to give him the finger, but she just glares at the driver. "I know you're not. And soon enough you'll be away at school and can make your own decisions. But for now, the answer is midnight." She glances into the restaurant. I can see Kat and Owen standing just inside the door. "Call me if you need a ride home."

"I'll be fine."

Mom looks like she wants to say something else, but the car honks again, so she just gets in the driver's seat and pulls out into traffic, swerving to dodge a car that's pulling out in front of her.

Peter and Rayne walk up just as I'm reaching for the door, and Rayne lets go of his hand to give me a hug. "Are we late?"

"I don't think so. I just got here. Had a driving lesson with Mom."

"Ugh. How's that going?" Rayne asks.

"Fabulous."

The smells of garlic and lemongrass hit us as soon as we open the door, and I'm glad Kat picked Thai food for Owen's going-away party. Griffon's over in the corner talking on his phone, but as soon as he sees me, he hangs up and walks over to give me a kiss. "I missed you," he says, squeezing my hand.

"Me too," I say. I feel a pang of guilt about Drew. *I'll tell him,* I promise myself. When the time is right. I've got nothing to hide.

He pulls me over to the side so no one can hear. "Listen, I can't stay long. I've got some business things to deal with that just came up."

"Business?" I lean toward him. "Sekhem?"

"Yes," he says, glancing around. "Remember the break-in at our fuel cell lab in Switzerland?"

I nod. "Back when we first met."

"Right. Well, they've decided to abandon that lab and merge the operation with one in Silicon Valley. A couple of the people I work with are coming in tonight to start setting it up."

"So that means you don't have to go away this summer?" I know it's selfish, but that's the one thing that's been hanging over our heads—the fact that he could get called away to help at the laboratory in Europe at any second.

"Nope," he says, his face brightening. "Just to San Jose. I'll be a little busier here, but it's so much better for everyone."

"Much better," I agree. I look over his shoulder and notice that everyone's already gone from the lobby and disappeared into the dining room. As we get settled in our chairs, Kat sits so close to Owen that she's practically in his lap, but that bothers me less than it usually would. They really have spent almost every minute together that he's been here, and I know how she must feel now that he's leaving. I sip the sweet orange creaminess of my Thai iced tea, feeling the caffeine surge through my body, and try not to worry about everything else in my life.

Rayne splits her spring roll in half to let the steam escape as we pass the appetizers around. "Hey, I saw Veronique again today," she says. Her tone is casual, but I can tell by her face that she's testing me.

I stop mid-sip and watch the orange tea crawl back down the straw. "What? Where?"

"At the café. She came in right after me. We talked a little bit while we were waiting for our drinks." She takes a bite of the still-steaming roll. "She's pretty cool. Is there any way you could give her another chance?"

Griffon leans forward, his eyes full of concern. "What did you say about Veronique?"

Rayne looks back at me. "You didn't tell him?"

I'm trapped. I put one hand on Griffon's arm, but he doesn't move. "We ran into Veronique last week on the street. It was no big deal—she just wanted to apologize, but I told her I never wanted to see her again."

He shakes his head slowly, but I don't know if he's angry at Veronique or me. "Excuse us for a second," he says, getting up and throwing his napkin on the table. I follow him out to the empty hallway by the kitchen, anger trailing behind him like a plume of smoke.

"Why didn't you tell me?" he demands when we're alone. "You know how dangerous Veronique is." Griffon's eyes are flashing, and I instantly wish I could take it all back.

"I didn't want you to worry," I say as calmly as I can. "You told me yourself that there wasn't anything the"—I'm about to say Sekhem, but I swallow the word; there are still too many people around to talk freely—"they could really do about it. She's free to go wherever she wants."

Griffon's eyes seem to get darker. "Sometimes not all of us agree with their rules."

"I'm sorry," I say. I grab his hand and he doesn't pull away, which I take as a good sign. "I just knew you'd try to deal with it, and I didn't want any trouble. I guess I was hoping she'd go away."

He seems to soften a little bit. "How can I make you under-stand how dangerous rogues are?" he says. "They have no laws, no morals—they do exactly what they want, when they want, without any thought for anyone else, Akhet or Khem."

I squeeze his hand. "I don't think Veronique is at that level just yet."

Griffon squeezes my hand back and I know I'm forgiven. "Not yet. But she still can't be trusted. You have to promise me—no more hiding. If anything like this happens again, you have to tell me, okay?"

I look into his face and see the sincerity in his eyes. I swal-low hard. I have to tell him about Drew. "There is one—"

"Kat wants to know if you guys are coming back," Rayne interrupts. "She says she has an announcement." She looks from me to Griffon and I know she's trying to gauge the severity of this particular argument.

"Kat loves to make everything dramatic," I say.

Griffon looks back at me. "What were you going to say?"

I shake my head. "It was nothing." After all, Drew doesn't exactly count as a dangerous rogue Akhet. "Let's go back."

Griffon turns to Rayne. "Listen, Veronique is dangerous. If you see her again, call one of us. Right away."

She holds up her hands. "Okay, okay. I will."

Kat taps the edge of her knife on her water glass as we slide back into our seats. "Right, whatever you two are pissing about, shut up. I have some news." She giggles at Owen as he kisses her playfully on the neck. Whatever her big announcement is going to be, they take a break for a quick make-out session.

Tired of watching the two of them paw at each other, I glance outside. Despite the fact that it's dinner time, the sidewalk is packed with people dodging each other as they rush to their destinations. Most people are carrying shopping bags or takeout as they hurry by, but then I notice one person in the crowd who's not moving at all. Across the street, Drew is leaning against a telephone pole, motionless, looking like he's in the middle of a photo shoot. Our eyes meet and I feel instantly, inexplicably guilty. His expression is calm but expectant, as if he's biding his time, just waiting for something to happen.

"Are you kidding? No way! That's awesome!" The table erupts in loud exclamations and I know I've missed something big.

"What?" I ask, confused. Kat's eyes are shining like she just scored a big discount at her favorite shoe store.

"Isn't that romantic?" Rayne says excitedly. "Oh my God, can you imagine the stories they can tell to their kids?"

"What? You're pregnant?" I stare at Kat, wondering how she managed to keep all this from me.

Kat reaches over and smacks me on the head while everyone else laughs. "I'm not pregnant! Do you listen to anything? I'm going to go live with Owen. In London." As she talks, Owen sits there with a grin so wide it looks like his face is going to break open.

"When?" My mind feels like it's full of confusing information. I look over at Griffon, but his shrug tells me he didn't know anything about it.

"Next week," she says. "I couldn't get a flight back with him, so I'm meeting Owen there. Plus, that'll give me a chance to wrap up things with Francesca."

"But what about the Fashion Institute? Mom and Dad already paid for the first semester and everything. They're going to kill you."

"It's just a deposit. I'll pay them back once I get a job. And I'm looking into the London College of Fashion and the Royal College of Art. Anything I can do here, I can do there."

"Except me," Owen says. "You can only do me there."

Kat nudges him, but there's a smile on her face. I'm guessing Owen, with his accent, is the only person alive who could get away with a comment like that. "Stop."

"What about Mom and Dad?" I repeat.

"What about them? I'm eighteen, I can do what I want. I was set to move out in September anyway. I'm just pushing things forward a little bit."

"You're not going to tell them, are you?"

"I am," she says, glancing at Owen. "But not right away. And you better not either."

I sit at the table, my appetite suddenly gone, not wanting to make any more promises I'm not sure I can keep. Kat's right— she's eighteen and can do whatever she wants. She can meet a guy, go out with him for a couple of weeks, and fly halfway across the world to live with him, while I have to fight to stay out past midnight.

"I won't tell," I say, taking another sip of my drink. "But you can't just leave me here to deal with it all. You have to tell them before you go."

"Don't worry. I'll tell them before I go." She looks at Owen again and giggles. "Right before. Maybe I'll call them on the way to the airport. I can't believe I'm actually going to live in London!"

London. The Tower of London was where everything changed just a few short months ago. I glance out the window, my heart thumping, but at the telephone pole across the street there's nothing but a bunch of flyers flapping in the wind.

Eight

Griffon's house is dark as we walk up to the porch. Besides his bike, the driveway is empty, no sign of the red truck anywhere. "What's going on? Is Janine out?"

"All night." A sly grin spreads across Griffon's face. "She's at a conference in LA. We have the whole place to ourselves."

My insides flutter at the thought of being with him all night. Of waking up next to him tomorrow morning with his body curled around mine. Of everything that can happen in between. "I might have to unexpectedly be spending the night at Rayne's."

He smiles wide. "That would be great. Will your parents buy it?"

I shrug. Ever since Kat's big announcement at the restaurant last night, I seem to care a little less if they're mad at me. "It happens enough so that they won't get suspicious. I think they're having dinner together again tonight, so they'll probably be happy to have me out of the house."

"You think they're getting back together? That's so cute."

I wrinkle my nose. "I'm not sure about cute. I'm not sure they're getting back together either, just that they're hanging out a lot more than they used to." As much as I'd like for them to live together again, the thought that they might be doing more than just having dinner or going to the theater makes me a little nauseous.

Griffon unlocks the front door. "Wait here just a second," he says as he ducks inside. Something smells good, filling the house like it's been cooking all day. I hear him flip a switch, and in an instant the hallway and living room are rimmed with tiny clear lights that are hung everywhere. The effect is like soft candlelight.

"Oh wow!" He's got them strung through the banister all the way up to the second floor. "Is that a hint?"

He looks confused. "Is what a hint?"

"The lights on the stairs. They look like runway markers pointing the way to your bedroom."

Griffon laughs. "You have a dirty mind. I didn't really think of it that way, but now that you mention it . . ." He kicks the door shut behind us and swoops down to pick me up as he heads for the stairs. At the bottom step, he sets me down. "I'm just kidding."

I suppress a smile and fix him with my best stare. "I'm not." I grab his hand and pull him up the stairs to the landing.

Griffon laces his fingers through mine and bends down to kiss me. Just the slightest touch sends shivers through my body as if everything is on high alert tonight.

"I really did make you dinner," he says. "I'm an excellent cook."

"I bet you are," I answer, my words coming slowly as my body's reactions take over. "But right now, I want something else." There's a question in Griffon's eyes as I lead him up the rest of the stairs, and I know he's worried about pushing me too fast.

Griffon turns on the small desk lamp and his room is bathed in soft light. His bed is actually made this time, with a comforter and pillows propped up against the headboard. I have a suspicion that he might have even changed the sheets. The idea that he thought we'd end up here turns some of my excitement into nerves.

He walks over to where I'm standing next to the bed, and I feel suddenly awkward and unsure of myself. I've pictured this in my head a million times, but in the last few moments it's like my body has no idea what to do. Griffon inhales deeply as he kisses me, as if he's trying to imprint this on all of his senses. I close my eyes and kiss him back, relaxing a little as instinct starts to take over. My hands move under his shirt to feel his warm skin—we came up here so fast we're both still wearing our jackets. Griffon shrugs his off with one quick movement, but kisses my neck slowly as he pulls my leather jacket off one arm at a time and drops it onto the floor.

We separate, but the vibrations between us are so insistent that I can sense them even when we're not touching. Griffon sits on the bed and kicks his shoes off, reaching up with one hand to pull me down with him. A giggle escapes as I sit down next to him and I'm instantly embarrassed. "Sorry. I guess I'm just nervous."

"It's okay," he says. "We don't have to do anything you don't want to do." I'm sure lots of guys have said this in a similar situation, but I can tell from his face that he actually means it.

I want to take control of things, to show him how much I want him with me. To show him that Drew means nothing to me. With everything I've been remembering about my past, I feel older in a lot of ways, like tiny pieces of those experiences are making an impression on who I am today. I'm not feeling all that much like the sixteen-year-old I see in the mirror anymore. "I do want to. All I want is to be with you."

Griffon leans back against the pillows and I straddle his body, undoing each button on my shirt as he watches, not saying a word. Despite his silence, I can see him fighting for control, and I feel powerful with every gesture. When my shirt's undone, he reaches up with two fingers and eases it off my shoulders until there's nothing left but my ankh and the black lacy bra I stole from Kat ages ago, hoping for an occasion when someone besides me would see it.

Griffon's hand trembles slightly as he reaches up and strokes my neck, working his way down to my stomach and the top of my jeans. "You are so beautiful. The best part of every day is when I catch a glimpse of you, even if it's just for a few moments."

In response, I ease his T-shirt up over his head and toss it onto the floor, biting my lip at the sight of the smooth brown skin that seems to shine in the dim light. I reach out to touch the muscles on his stomach, feeling his desire as if it's a caress washing over me in waves, and the intensity of it scares me. All of a sudden I want this part to be over, to be on the other side of the big event so that we can move forward together. It's not that

I don't want Griffon to be my first time, because I do; it's just that there's so much expectation put on one moment in time that my heart starts to beat hard with anxiety.

Griffon pulls me to him, oblivious of the conflict going on inside my head. I try to quiet my fears and focus on the sensations, knowing I won't ever forget any of it, so I don't want to ruin it by thinking too much. I close my eyes and try to surrender myself to his touch, to the vibrations between us that are increasing by the second.

In the middle of a kiss, Griffon tilts his head back and looks me in the eyes, his thumb stroking the back of my neck. "Everything okay?"

"Yes," I say with as much enthusiasm as I can without sounding forced. "Of course."

I lean in to kiss him again, but Griffon pushes himself into a sitting position on the pillows. "I'm no empath, but I can tell you're lying."

I can't meet his eyes, knowing that I'm blowing what is supposed to be one of the most special moments in our lives. "I'm not lying. Everything's fine. I want to do this, I already told you."

"I hear you saying it, but I don't believe you. Cole, if you're not ready for this, we can wait. It's no big deal. I want to *be* with you. Not just have sex with you."

"I'm totally screwing this up," I say, sitting on the edge of the bed and turning my back to him. "You went to all this trouble, and I'm sitting here second-guessing everything. I want to be with you. All the way. It's just . . ."

"It's just that you're not totally ready," he finishes for me.

"And I didn't go to all this trouble only to get you into bed." He reaches out and tilts my head toward him. "Although, don't get me wrong, it's pretty much all I think about these days." His grin eases the guilt, but I know that he's telling the truth. "I did this so that we could spend an evening alone, have some good food, and let the rest of it happen when it happens." Griffon pulls me back down onto the bed and I ease myself into the natural curve of his body, my back pressing into his chest as he puts one leg around mine in a comforting knot. For the first time tonight, I relax and enjoy the feeling of his skin next to mine, not worrying about the expectations that might come with it.

We must have dozed off, because when I open my eyes again, the bedside clock says 10:34. It takes a quick second to remember where I am, but Griffon's easy breathing and his strong arm around my waist brings everything back. I shift carefully in the bed so that I can watch him while he sleeps, the long dark lashes brushing his cheeks and his fingers twitching slightly as he dreams. I reach up and touch one of the tight curls that cover his head. He's the most beautiful creature I've ever seen, and I make a quick wish that I can spend many more nights exactly like this. I ease myself into the crook of his arm so that I can feel his heart beating until he stretches and I can tell he's awake too.

"Hey there," Griffon says, his voice soft from sleep and a wide grin on his face. He kisses my neck and echoes my thoughts. "I want to wake up like this every day."

"I was just thinking the very same thing." I put my head onto his bare chest, amazed at how well we fit together. We stay like that, each of us wrapped up in our own thoughts, until I glance at his clock again and realize another half hour has gone by.

"I should go," I say, sitting up and rubbing my eyes.

"Why?" Griffon pushes himself up against the headboard. He lifts my hand and kisses the palm, an old-fashioned gesture that somehow works for him. "I'd love it if you'd stay. Plus I'm starving, and we haven't eaten yet."

The thought of spending the entire night in his arms is tempting. And I am pretty hungry. "Are you sure? Even without . . . you know."

Griffon laughs. "Yes. Even without 'you know.' I'm going to run downstairs and get the food. You just stay there and look beautiful in my bed for a few more minutes." He glances back at me. "Is it wrong that I love how that sounds?"

I stretch my arms over my head and arch my back, feeling his eyes on my body, knowing the effect it's having on him. "I love it too."

Griffon shakes his head. "You are making it so difficult to leave this room. Don't move. I'll be right back."

After a few quick texts to Mom, my plans for the night are set with surprisingly little effort. I realize I'm still wearing just my jeans and bra, so I reach onto the floor and grab one of Griffon's T-shirts, the spicy scent of him surrounding me as I pull it over my head and settle back onto the pillows.

Nine

Olivia runs down the hallway of the studio and smacks right into Herr Steinberg. The top of her blond head barely comes to his shoulder, and I can imagine what's going through her mind as she tilts back to look up at him, her green eyes wide with fear. As much as I love him, Steinberg scared the crap out of me when I was her age.

"Are you in a race, Ms. Miller?" Herr Steinberg asks, looking straight down at her, his face serious.

Olivia's voice is brave as she answers, "No, sir. Just thirsty. Miss Nicole said I could go get some juice. Sir."

"You may continue," Steinberg says, his eyes stern. "But you will walk in my studio from now on." I have no idea how he's keeping a straight face. I have to hide my smile behind the sheet music in my hand.

"Yes, sir," Olivia says. She looks back down the hallway at

me and I nod toward the lounge. She doesn't need to be told twice and takes off with a walk so fast it makes her whole body wiggle.

I take a deep breath before calling Zander into the practice room. "Ready?" I say to him with a smile plastered on my face. I have no idea whether my plan is going to work or blow up in my face.

He grunts and drags his cello into the room as I shut the soundproof door behind us.

"Wait a second," I say, as he starts to unlatch his case. "For the first part of the lesson, we're going to listen, not play."

Zander pauses and looks at me suspiciously. "What do you mean?"

I pull out my phone. "Well, I know that the cello isn't exactly your favorite thing."

Zander gives a snorting laugh in response. "You think?"

I glance up at the window in the practice-room door. "And I also know that your mom is going to keep dragging you here no matter how much either of us complains about it." I tap the screen on the phone. "So I thought I'd make you a deal. I'll only teach you to play cool new music instead of the classical stuff you hate if you try not to be such a jerk about it."

That gets him to break into a tiny smile, and I feel almost rewarded. "Like, what kind of music?"

"Well, lots of musicians are doing amazing things with the cello these days." I hit Play on the video I've loaded. "Like this woman. Her name's Rebecca Roudman. This is my favorite song she does—it's a cover called 'Sweet Child of Mine.'"

Zander scoots his chair over so that he can see the small

screen better. As he tilts his head down near mine, I get that particular little-boy smell of sweat, dirt, and something almost innocent coming off of him. He doesn't say anything as we watch her destroy the song on her cello, and when it's done he looks up at me. "What kind of cello was that?"

"An electric cello. Pretty cool, huh?"

He nods quickly. "It was almost like it was singing the words."

"Exactly. When you can't sing, the instrument can do it for you."

"Can you teach me to play stuff like that?"

"Yep. We'll start out easy and then get to the hard stuff as you get better. Rebecca's even from San Francisco, so maybe we can all go to one of her shows sometime."

"That would be cool," he agrees.

The look on his face almost makes me want to reach out and hug him, but something about Zander tells me he's not the hugging type. We spend the rest of the lesson watching videos of contemporary cellists, and I teach him a few new notes so we don't get in trouble for just watching videos the whole time. It's by far the nicest lesson I've ever had with him, and I'm almost sad to see him go when it's over.

I'm putting my music away when Steinberg's assistant sticks her head in the doorway. "There's a guy here for you." She looks at me with curiosity. "And he's totally gorgeous."

I blush and look down. Griffon's early. "Thanks. I'll be right out." I can't carry my cello on his bike, so I pack it up to bring to Herr Steinberg's office. It'll be safe there until tomorrow.

I know I'm smiling as I walk down the hallway, but I can't help it. Every time I think about seeing Griffon, I feel like I'm about to burst. The Etch A Sketch picture he made last time he was here is on a shelf in the lounge, and whenever I pass it, I feel a little jolt of pleasure.

"I hope you don't mind me coming here." The Australian accent startles me, and I look up to see Drew standing at the end of the hallway. "But I couldn't wait any longer to see you again."

"What are you doing here? How did you find me?" Panic takes over as I glance around. This is my territory, my safe place, and he has no business anywhere near it.

Drew ignores my question. "I need you to give me a chance. To explain things."

"I don't want you to explain anything else," I say, trying to keep my voice down. The truth is that I don't want to be convinced. Admitting he's right will change everything. Some people are staring at us with curiosity, so I push him into an open practice room and close the door. "I have a different life now. This has nothing to do with Allison."

Drew's face looks desperate as he speaks. "You don't remember," he says. "Or you would never say that."

I fold my arms and try to block out the few memories I have of the time Connor and I were together. I don't want to remember how I felt when he gave me the pendant. Or how I felt when he was led out the door for the last time. I think of Griffon's easy smile and it grounds me, so that I can face Drew again. "There's nothing you can say that will change anything. I'm with the person who's destined for me."

"You throw that word around pretty easily," he says.

"It's true. Griffon isn't just Akhet. He's Sekhem. And we're meant to be together."

Something dark passes over his features with this news. "Sekhem? So were the two of you happy together in a past lifetime? Did you sacrifice everything just to be with each other? Have you spent the past few centuries hoping against hope that you'd find the essence of the person you once loved so completely?"

"That's not fair," I say, trying not to absorb the meaning behind his words. "I've only just become Akhet. I have no idea what I've been doing the past few centuries—those are your memories, not mine." The image of Griffon on the executioner's stand passes through my head. How we knew each other then isn't important. "I'm with Griffon now. That's what matters."

Drew seems to shrink back at my words. He can't look at me as he reaches into his pocket and pulls out a small, black velvet jewelry box. "I made these for you."

I take a step back. "I don't want anything from you."

"I made them to complete the set," he says, holding it out toward me. He glances at the pendant. "They're meant to go together. Always were." He puts the box in my hand and folds my fingers around it in a familiar gesture. I'm too stunned to object when he whispers, "With these jewels you shall have means to get away. Keep them hidden, whatever you do."

I gasp as I recognize the words Connor said to me just before he was led away. We were alone in the room that day— there's no way anyone else could have known. I can't look at

Drew because I'm afraid of what I might see in his face. Of what I might see behind his eyes.

I hesitate, then turn the small box and lift the lid. Inside, nestled in a velvet liner, are delicate silver earrings, each with a bright red ruby in the center. I put one hand reflexively on my pendant as the room seems to recede around me.

"This!" the old man roars, yanking the pendant from around my neck. As much as I try to stand my ground, I flinch, and my skin burns as the chain is pulled free. "This is what you had made with the Raimondi Ruby?"

Connor steps forward to form a shield between me and his father. "It is mine to do with as I please. And I chose to give it to the woman I love. Return her property at once." His words are civil, but his tone is strong. The only hint of his anger is a slight trembling in his arm.

As an answer, his father spits in Connor's outstretched hand. "The woman you love," he says in mocking tones. "The whore. She is not fit to be anything but a concubine. Her low birth, her questionable parentage, her social graces—none of these things serve to recommend her to my society." The sensation is physical as he scans me with his greedy eyes. "Although I can see how you might succumb to some of her most obvious charms." The leer on his face is sickening as he runs one wrinkled finger across my cheek, flicking one of the ruby earrings that Connor has just given me.

In seconds the old man is flying through the air as Connor rushes at him. "Never lay a hand on my beloved again!" he screams, standing over the crumpled form. Despite my revulsion,

I'm grateful that Connor has no weapon, because I have no doubt that he would use it at this moment. Instead, he pulls my pendant free from his father's grasp. "Never touch her!"

Connor calmly walks back to me, folding the pendant into my palm and putting a protective hand on my arm as we turn to face his father. "I should go," I whisper, the first words I've spoken since we were discovered alone in the garden house.

"You should listen to her, for she is finally speaking some sense," his father says, pulling himself up to a standing position and straightening his tunic. I know that he won't easily forgive the physical display, but I can see that Connor's strength has made him wary. "She should go, and stop playing the lady." He stands at his full height as he regards us, dabbing at the small cut on his lip with his sleeve. "For she will never be mistress of this estate as long as I have the breath to forbid it."

Connor's eyes are steady on his father as he speaks. "Then prepare to lose another son, for I would rather live the rest of my life as a pauper with my beloved than endure one more day of privilege without her. She is my wife, with or without your blessing."

I put my hand on Connor's chest to stop him from speaking, overwhelmed by all of the trouble I have caused. "Stop. You don't mean that." I look up into his green eyes, but then look away, unable to say what I must. I push past him and rush out the door, the heavy wood and iron slamming behind me. I've barely made it twenty paces when I feel a pull on my arm.

"Don't," Connor says, putting a finger to my lips as I start to speak. "Just listen. For one moment, just listen to what I have to say." His eyes soften as he brushes a strand of hair from my

shoulder. "I meant every word. I can live without the estate and the title, the trinkets and the travel to foreign lands. I can live without my family. But I cannot live another day without you."

Connor pries my fingers open and lets the pendant dangle from its chain, kissing the ruby before tenderly fastening the clasp around my neck once again. "You are my family. The only family that I'll ever need. Whatever happens, we are meant to be together. Forever."

Forever. The word echoes in my ears as the memory fades and the black velvet box comes into focus. My heart is still pounding as I think of the fight, of the look in Connor's eyes as he spoke, of the truth that I now remember in them.

"I had the earrings made for you," Drew says softly. "Before . . ." He doesn't finish the sentence, but we both know. Before Connor was killed. "But they were lost to time."

I look at how the silver shines. These earrings aren't like the pendant—they lack the same weight and age. "So you made these?"

Drew nods sadly. "I did. I only wish they were the originals."

"They're beautiful." I have to say it, because it's true.

Drew leans in, but before he can say anything else, I feel a heavy sense of foreboding. I look up through the window in the practice-room door and see Griffon standing in the hallway staring at the two of us.

"Damn." I pull myself away from Drew, and yank the door open. Griffon doesn't move, just looks at me with a question in his eyes.

"Hey," I say, trying to play this off like it's nothing. "I was waiting for you."

Griffon nods toward the practice room. "Who's that?" No way is he going to let this go.

I gesture vaguely in that direction. I feel like I'm walking on the edge of a very sharp knife. One wrong move and it's going to be bad. "Nobody. Just someone that Kat used to work with." I grab his hand and try to lead him to the door, but he won't budge.

"If he's nobody, then what's that in your hand?"

I look down and see that I'm still holding the little black box. I don't dare look behind me to see if Drew is still standing there. "Uh, some earrings. He's a jewelry designer and he was showing them to me."

Griffon folds his arms across his chest and looks right into my eyes. "I thought you agreed to tell me the truth from now on. No more hiding things. I'm going to ask one more time. Who is that?"

My breath gets shallow and I feel my heart racing. There's no going back now—I have to tell him the truth. "His name is Drew."

Griffon waits without speaking, calm on the outside, but even from here I can feel how upset he is.

I force myself to look in his eyes so that he can see I'm not lying about the rest of it. "Before . . . a long time before . . . his name was Connor. Connor Wyatt."

He seems to lose all color in his face as the name sinks in. After that lifetime he must have done research on Lady Allison, because he knows exactly who Connor was. "Lord Connor Wyatt?" He glances back over my shoulder. "Are you sure?"

I press my lips together hard; the uncertainty of his reaction is killing me. I can only nod.

"I'm out of here," Griffon says suddenly, turning and walking quickly down the hallway.

I catch him as he reaches the outside door. "Griffon, stop, please! Let me explain!"

One hand on the door, he straightens his back and turns toward me. The look on his face is devastating. His eyes are hard, as if he's made a crucial decision in the few moments since he heard the truth. "There's nothing to explain. I get it. You have unfinished business with . . . with him. I can't compete with that."

"Come on, you're being ridiculous." I feel suddenly hot all over, like I'm going to be sick. "There's nothing between me and Drew. You've got to believe that." I reach for his arm to lead him outside, but Griffon shakes me off. "Please," I say. "Let's go outside and talk about this."

Griffon looks at the ground. "There's nothing to talk about."

"It's not like that." I feel desperation rising as I open the door. "Please. Just come outside."

Griffon grunts, but follows me. The sound of cars whizzing by on the busy street calms me just the slightest bit. "Drew's engaged to Kat's boss." I take a deep breath and start again, knowing this isn't coming out the way I want it. My voice drops to a whisper. "He . . . he was explaining some things that I'm starting to remember."

Something shifts in Griffon's eyes, and I feel a jolt of hope running through me. He wants to believe me. He reaches over and lightly runs his finger over my ankh. "He gave you that, didn't he?"

I force myself to answer. "Yes. And he just wanted to give me the earrings that go with it."

I can barely hear him as he whispers, "What else does he want from you?"

"Nothing! It doesn't matter. I don't want to be with him, no matter what our relationship was before. I want to be with you. I love *you.*"

Griffon blinks slowly and his nostrils flare as he considers my words. "I'm not ready to do this again, Cole."

"What do you mean *again*?" My words rush out as I try to keep him here. I can feel him pulling away, retreating from me. "There hasn't been anyone else."

"I don't mean with you." His tone is dismissive, and I feel everything deflate. "I've done this before, and I swore I'd never do it again. If . . ." He pauses and glances at me just for a second. "If you have a history with him, something you have to finish in this lifetime, I can't stand in the way of that. I won't stand in the way of that. Not this time."

In a rush I realize that so much of what he's reacting to has nothing to do with me or our relationship in this lifetime. It's all about the pain he's carried through many lifetimes. "What happened in your past has nothing to do with us," I say. I can hear the pleading in my voice, but I can't do anything about it. "This is about you and me. Here and now."

Griffon waves my words away, but the look of pain on his face is unmistakable. "This isn't about my past. It's about yours. I can't—I won't compete with a ghost."

"How can I make you understand that I'm not interested in Drew?" It feels like there are miles between us, like he's someone I don't even know.

The door to the studio opens and Drew walks out. His eyes flick to Griffon, but then settle on me. "Everything okay?"

"Just go away!" I shout. I thrust the earrings back into his hands. "You've done enough."

Time seems suspended as Griffon looks from me to Drew and back again, his hands clenched into tight fists as he slowly takes a step back. His face is a mask, and I'm so far away I can't read any emotions. After what seems like an eternity, he turns to me. "I'm going to do you a favor and walk away."

I grab for his hand as he turns to walk down the sidewalk, but he's already out of reach.

"You can't go!" I shout, but I'm already talking to his back. "Not now. Please!"

"Think of it this way," he says, glancing over his shoulder. "I'm making your decision a hell of a lot easier."

Ten

Are you sure you want to do this?" Kat asks, looking over her shoulder for traffic.

"I have to. He won't answer my calls, and I have to talk to him. He just needs some time to realize that he made a mistake. That's all." Just turning down Griffon's street makes my stomach churn. I check my phone one more time on the off chance he's answered one of the texts I've sent since yesterday, but the only thing on the screen is the picture of Rayne and me that's been my screensaver for months. I stare at the houses going by, steeling myself for the first glimpse of his.

Rayne leans forward from the backseat. "Peter's been no help at all. He says this is between the two of you." She squeezes my shoulder for support. "Sorry."

"Guys are like that," Kat says. She glances at me as she drives. "I hate to say this, but maybe it's for the best, you know?

You two seem to argue a lot." I don't blame her for thinking this, because I couldn't tell her what had happened the last time, that I'd found out that he was the one who had executed me back then—all she knew was that we'd had a fight.

"It's not for the best," I say. "This is all just a misunder-standing."

"I don't know why you won't tell me what it was about this time," she says. "Maybe I can help."

"I told you, it's no big deal." If Kat even got the smallest hint that Griffon broke up with me because he found me with Drew, she'd go ballistic. I had just finally gotten her to stop thinking I had a thing for him. This kind of information would send her over the edge. I point out the front window. "It's that one there. The one with the brown shingles."

"Nice," Kat says, pulling over to the curb and taking in the immaculate front yard and the big façade. "I thought his mom was a professor at the university."

"She is."

"Well, no wonder they keep having tuition hikes if their pro-fessors can afford houses like this. Not cheap."

I look up at Griffon's window and try not to picture the room behind it. The white board with all of his cryptic equa-tions written on it. His big, comfortable bed. The last time I was here things were so great between us—I never imagined it would all turn out this way. I look down the driveway and see his bike parked in the back behind Janine's truck. "He's here. They both are."

Kat unbuckles her seatbelt. "You want me to come with you?"

"No," I say quickly. She can't hear the things I have to say. "I have to do this alone." I turn and look back at Rayne. "But I'm glad you guys came." I open the door. "Wish me luck."

Rayne leans forward and plants a kiss on my cheek. "Luck. We're here for you."

The curtains are closed as I walk onto the porch, and I can't see any movement inside. As I lift my hand to knock I hear faint reggae music coming from somewhere and take a deep breath. I wonder what Janine has said to him. Or more importantly, what he's said to her.

I hear Janine shout "Coming" from somewhere in the back, and my heart starts pounding in the few seconds between that and when she flings the door open. "Cole!" She seems genuinely surprised to see me and leans over to give me a hug. "Baby girl, it's so good to see you."

Her touch brings a sob into my throat and I have to swallow hard before I can speak. "Thanks." I bite my lip hard to keep from crying. "I'm sure you heard what happened."

She looks right at me. "He won't talk about it. But I can guess."

"I should have talked to him like you said. Instead, he saw Drew at the studio and totally freaked out." I can feel the desperation rising up inside me again, like this is the only chance I'm going to have to set things right. "But it wasn't like that. He didn't even give me a chance to explain." We're still standing on the porch, so I look behind her, but the living room is empty. "And now he won't pick up the phone. Is he here?"

"In the study," Janine says, stepping back to let me in. She gives my hand one last squeeze before letting me go.

I walk through the living room to the back part of the house and stop short in the doorway to the study. Griffon's not alone.

He looks surprised to see me at first, and then his features seem to harden and I can tell he's replaying yesterday's events in his mind. "Hey." He makes sure the word isn't welcoming. "What are you doing here?"

The woman on the couch next to him is maybe ten years older than he is, and with her long dark hair is exotic-looking in a way that's impossible to place. They're hunched over some architectural drawings spread out over the coffee table, and something about the way they're sitting so close tells me this isn't the first time they've met.

"I thought we needed to talk," I say, suddenly feeling like a little kid. I pull myself up as tall as I can. "About what happened."

Griffon sits back and doesn't make any attempt to get up. "I thought we said everything we needed to say."

I glance at the woman beside him. She's watching the two of us with interest. "Can we maybe take this somewhere else?" I ask.

"This is Giselle," he says. "One of my colleagues from the Sekhem that I was telling you about. She's here to work on the new lab setup with me. You can say anything in front of her."

Giselle smiles at him and waves uncomfortably at me. I wonder how many of his lifetimes she's been part of.

"Maybe I *can*," I say, getting a little frustrated, "but I'd rather not."

He seems to take a second to decide something. "Okay." He nods his head. "Let's go in the kitchen."

Griffon leads the way, not once looking back to see if I'm following. There's another guy in the kitchen, dunking a tea bag in a giant mug of hot water.

"Cole, this is Christophe," Griffon says, introducing us. "He's working with us on the lab too." He looks at Christophe. "We need a minute alone, if that's okay. I'll be in there in just a second."

"Nice to meet you," Christophe says with a German-sounding accent as he scurries from the room. Not that I blame him—the negative energy flowing between the two of us is only getting stronger.

Griffon leans against the sink and crosses his arms in front of his chest. Even without empath training, I'd recognize a hostile stance anywhere. "So what else is there to say?"

I throw my arms up in frustration. "What else? How about everything! You're willing to just throw all of this out because of one stupid second that you completely misinterpreted? I already told you that it didn't mean anything to me. Drew means nothing."

"It's not one stupid second," Griffon says carefully. His eyes are firmly on the wood floors. "It's a lifetime together that was cut short. A lifetime that will always make you wonder what might have been. A lifetime you won't be able to complete if you and I stay together."

"That's ridiculous." It feels like he's put a wall up between us, and everything I say is just bouncing off of it. Like he's putting words in my mouth and telling me how to feel. "You're acting like I don't have any say in this at all."

"You don't." Griffon finally raises his eyes to meet mine. I can see his jaw tense as he looks at me. "I'm not giving you one. Whether you're with Drew or not, I don't want to be the deciding factor. I don't want you to look back and think about how things might have been if you'd decided to go with him instead of me."

"So you're just being the hero and stepping aside?" I ask in frustration. I need to remind him of what we have together, so I lean in closer, reaching for his hand, but instead of meeting me, he shrinks back. I stand completely still in an effort to keep whatever shred of dignity is still clinging to me. "It's like I don't matter to you at all."

He bites his lip, and I know he's using a distraction technique before he speaks. "You do matter to me," he says quietly. "That's why I have to do this." He pushes himself away from the sink and I think for a second that he's going to lean in and put his arms around me again. But he doesn't. "We've talked about what makes fate and destiny. Now it's time to go find out for yourself."

Griffon walks back to the study and I'm left standing in the empty kitchen for several long seconds. I want to scream and cry and do whatever it takes to snap him out of this. But deep down I know that none of it will do any good. He's made his mind up about how things are, and nothing I say is going to change that.

Even though I know it's not, the house seems strangely vacant as I walk through the kitchen toward the front door. As I pass Griffon's painting hanging in the living room, I wonder if this is the last time I'll ever see it, the last time I'll ever be here.

Kat and Rayne don't say a word as I open the door, but the car is filled with expectation. I sit down in the front seat and deliberately fasten my seatbelt, the metallic click echoing through the silent interior. I don't trust my voice; my heart is so heavy. I think of a million things I could say, a million things that I want to say to him that will probably stay inside me for the rest of my life. That I'm not Allison anymore. That I want to rewind time and never show the pendant to anyone. As these thoughts race through my head, I come up with the only one I can actually say out loud.

"It's over. Let's go home."

Eleven

Nicole Ryan! Did you know about this?" Mom must be all the way out in the living room, but even with my head buried under the covers I can hear her just fine.

"Crap," I mutter to no one. I lift one corner of the comforter and peer at the clock next to my bed. Kat must be somewhere over Texas by now. She promised she'd tell them before she left. Now I'm the only one left to deal with all of the garbage that she's stirred up.

I hear Mom pounding down the hall seconds before my door flies open. "Did you know about this?" she repeats.

I roll over to face the doorway where she's standing and waving a piece of notebook paper. "Know about what?" This kind of answer is just going to piss her off more, but I need to buy some time to think.

"This. This note from your sister! What does she mean she's meant to be with Owen and she's gone to England?"

I roll back over and face the wall. It's become a familiar sight in the past few days in that, except for some trips to the bathroom, it's pretty much all I've seen. "I guess it means she's gone to England." Not even a week ago I was feeling sorry for her because Owen was leaving. Doesn't take much to turn everything upside down.

"Did you know what she was planning? It's the Fourth of July, for God's sake. The block party is this afternoon—what am I going to tell everyone?"

I shrug, unable to even rustle up any emotion about this. So Kat's on a plane, on the way to live with her boyfriend in London. Not like I'm going to feel sorry for her. Or guilty for not giving Mom a heads-up. Ever since I left Griffon's house, I've felt dead inside, hollow, like all of the emotion has been sucked out of me. I honestly couldn't care less.

Mom bangs her hand on the wall in frustration and I jump just a little bit. "What about school? What about her future? Oh my God, the money we've already paid out for college! How could she just up and leave like this? Your father is going to go crazy." She waits for a reply, but getting nothing, she slams my door and stomps back down the hall.

Now that she's gone, I relax a little bit. I vaguely remember Kat coming in to say good-bye early this morning. At least I think it was this morning. I've spent so much time in this bed that the days are starting to run together. Not that I've been doing a lot of sleeping. Seems like every time I close my eyes, all I can picture is the look on Griffon's face when he spotted me and Drew in the practice room. The pain in his eyes as he finally walked away causes my stomach to clench. I've spent entire days and nights picking apart every word of our conversation, wishing I could do it over again. If I could go back in time and change only one thing, it would be talking to Drew that day at the studio. I'd have shoved him out the door and refused to look at anything he had to show me. I thought I wanted answers about what happened in that lifetime, but not at the expense of what I have in this one.

My door opens again and I brace myself for another onslaught from Mom, but instead a paper bag sails across the room and lands on my leg.

"Get up, already," Rayne says, closing the door behind her. "Your allotted grieving time is over. You need to get the hell out of this house."

I pull the covers over my head. "I can't go out. I never want to go out again."

"Oh, come on." Rayne sits down on the edge of my bed and bounces up and down a little. She smiles at me and points at the bag. "I got you one of those disgusting bagels you like."

My stomach turns at the thought of a jalapeño bagel with salmon cream cheese. "Thanks. But no."

"I ran into your mom on the porch. Boy, is she pissed." Rayne gives me a crooked smile. "Guess she found out about Kat, huh?"

I shrug. "Nothing they can do about it. She used her own money. Happy Independence Day to Kat."

"Yeah, but it'll totally take the heat off you. Nothing you can possibly do will be as big as this. She did you a favor."

"Yeah. I'm grateful. Kat left me here to deal with everything after she promised she wouldn't. She's going to go live an amazing life in London and I'm stuck here." *Without Griffon.* I close my eyes, trying to banish the thoughts that are creeping into my head.

"How long are you going to stay here, anyway? You're missing work, and there was a great party in the Mission last night. Plus, it's the Fourth—you have to come watch fireworks. We'll grab a couple of chairs, go down to Aquatic Park, freeze our butts off, and try to see something through the fog. You can totally hang out with me and Peter."

I look at her, knowing that she means it all in the nicest possible way. Anybody else would seriously piss me off. "Yeah. The three of us will have a great time together. Maybe we can all huddle under the same blanket. Not awkward at all."

"So now that Griffon's gone, you're going to spend the next year in your room? I'm not going to let that happen. You have to get out there—you'll feel better. At least just come with me to the café. If you won't eat, maybe a little coffee will do you good."

An Americano with half and half is the first thing that's sounded even remotely palatable in days. I grab a pillow and hug it to my chest. "Will you go get me one?"

"No. I'm sorry, the To Go window is closed. You have to come get it yourself." She bounces a few more times and then stops, a serious look on her face. "Come on Cole, I'm worried about you. We all are. I know how much this totally sucks, but you have to let him get this out of his system. When Griffon has time to think about it, he'll come back."

I've tried telling myself different versions of the same thing, but the reality I have to face is that Griffon's gone. "He won't," I say. "You didn't see his face. He really means it." He won't let me explain or let himself believe what really happened. Despite the fact that I'm trying to be practical and realistic, tears well up in my eyes.

"Oh, man," Rayne says and scoots up to brush the hair out of my face. "Honey, I'm so sorry. I wish I could fix it. The best I can do is drag you out for a lousy cup of coffee."

"I know," I sniff, trying to get a grip on myself. "I appreciate it."

I look down at my bunched-up sheets, noticing their sour smell for the first time. I don't want the life that waits for me outside of this house. The one without Griffon in it. But I'm starting to make myself a little sick. Maybe just one cup of coffee. Then I can come home, change my sheets, and climb back into bed.

"Just give me an hour," Rayne prods. "You don't even have to come to the fireworks tonight. Just get out of this house. You'll feel better."

"I don't want to feel better," I say, throwing the comforter back. "The only way I'll ever feel better is if Griffon changes his mind, and that's not going to happen. I want to feel every moment of this misery." I sit on the edge of the bed and put my feet gingerly on the floor. "Plus, you know I don't like fireworks."

"If you want to wallow, go ahead. One cup of coffee and I'll let you come running back here." Rayne pulls me to my feet. "But first, do the rest of us a favor and go take a shower."

I tuck the sleeping bag around my feet and settle back into the folding chair. It's almost totally dark now, but the music is still playing from the bandstand up the street and Frisbees are still whizzing by my head on a regular basis. I'm trying hard to share Rayne's holiday mood and not sink back into the depression that's become oddly comforting, like a favorite pair of worn jeans. I glance up at the overcast sky—it's like a blank slate now, but in a little while it's going to explode with lights and noise. Waiting for fireworks shows always makes me a little jumpy. Once they start I'm usually okay, but I get a little flinchy at the beginning.

Rayne leans against my legs. She and Peter are sharing a sleeping bag on a tiny patch of grass we've carved out for ourselves, and even though they've tried to keep the contact to a minimum, I can't help but notice how happy they are together. "You warm enough?" she asks, looking up at me.

"I'm okay. Once in my life I'd like to watch Fourth of July fireworks without wearing a parka and a sleeping bag."

Peter pulls a wool blanket from around his shoulders and hands it to me. "Here, take this. I'm warm enough."

That one small gesture brings tears flooding into my eyes. "No, it's fine. I'm fine." I can feel the sadness well up from somewhere down deep until it seems like it's going to crash over me like a tidal wave. If I stay here, I'll drown. I kick the sleeping bag off my legs. "I'm going to walk around for a little bit."

"But the fireworks are going to start in a couple of minutes. You can't go wandering around down here by yourself."

"You were the one who said I needed some fresh air. I'm just going to go find a little more. There are thousands of people here, nothing's going to happen."

"Are you sure? I feel so bad."

"I'm sure. Don't feel bad. I'm doing enough of that for everyone."

"Keep your phone on," Rayne says as I stand up and zip my jacket tight. "And text me."

"Yes, Mom." I turn around and look at all the people crowding every available space and try to decide which way to go. I really just want to be alone right now, and where better to do that than in the middle of five thousand people? Without a destination in mind, I start to head back toward Fisherman's Wharf. A few people bump me while I walk, but almost everyone is settling in to their small patch of grass or sidewalk to wait for the fireworks to begin.

I've only gone about a block when one lone pop fills the sky with red and makes me jump. There are people crowded on every horizontal surface, but I find a tiny space on a brick wall and squeeze myself into it. The fog above our heads flashes with color as the giant fireworks begin to light up the night. I try to wipe my mind clean of all thoughts and just enjoy the noise and the oohs and ahhs of the crowd of strangers around me. One loud whistling firework ends in a trail of sparks that seem to embed themselves in my brain. The overwhelmingly loud sound of the crackle and hiss as it comes back down to earth fill my ears, and before the panic can take hold, I realize that I'm being pulled into another memory.

The fireworks explode in the dusty street, but I'm so used to the noise now that I don't even jump when one goes off right next to me.

"Throw it!" my brother yells, handing me a small, flaming cylinder.

"Thamun! Stop!" I shout, trying to get everyone out of the way and toss it onto the ground as all of the faces around us light up with color. All the other boys my age squeal and run in different directions, trying to get their own firecrackers to light.

It seems like it took forever for Diwali to get here, and we finally get to stay up late, eating sweets and tossing firecrackers into the street. I feel a little sorry for Kavita because she's stuck inside with the girls cooking and cleaning, so I light another firecracker in her honor and toss it at Varun's feet, laughing as my big brother screams like a girl and runs away just in time to avoid the flash.

In seconds he's back, his dark eyes shining. "Ramesh, look at this one." He's holding a round ball that is almost as big as his head. Varun caresses the side as if it's a pretty girl's cheek, and grins at me. "This is going to be the best one of the night."

"Where did you get that monstrosity?" I ask. I'd never seen a big one that close up before.

"I did a favor for someone," my brother says cryptically. "Get everyone to stand back and I'll light it."

"Thamun!" I shout again as loud as I can, but it seems as if no one is listening. "Look out! Varun is about to light the biggest of them all!"

I hear a hiss as the flame makes contact with the wick, and turn away for just a second to grab one of the little boys who is racing right into the line of fire. Before Varun has time to toss it away, there is a blinding flash and a noise that is loud enough *to rip the ears off one's head. The air is filled with the sounds of screaming, and I'm on my knees, my hands clawing at the dirt that is quickly getting damp with drops of something from above. I can't see anything in my panic, and it takes a few seconds to realize that the deafening screaming is coming from my own throat.*

I jump as the air seems to vibrate with another loud bang, but this one is high in the air above my head. My heart is beating fast with the panic of the firecracker accident. Diwali. I remember my friend Gabi talking about that holiday. This must have been the glimpse of India I've had a few times before. I touch my hands to my face as I think about what happened. What came after that night? Did I survive?

The fireworks are coming fast and furious now, so it must be the finale; I wonder how long I've been gone. I glance around but everyone is motionless, their necks craned toward the sky to watch the clouds flash and change color.

"You're back."

I startle at the words as Drew turns to face me, and anger fills me instantly. "What are you doing here?"

He pauses to let some of the loudest fireworks pass. "Protecting you. Do you have any idea how vulnerable you are when you're in the middle of a memory?" Even though my ankh is hidden by my jacket, I feel the weight of its presence every time he speaks.

"Apparently very vulnerable, if you're any indication." I jump down off the wall and start to walk into the crowd, but Drew jogs to catch up.

"Would you stop running away from me?"

"Only if you'll stop following me."

"I wasn't following you," he says, dodging people as they bend down to pack up their chairs and blankets. "You're in my neighborhood."

I look around and realize he's right. I'd forgotten that the party at Francesca's house was only a block or two from here. I glance out toward the water, realizing that just a few weeks ago, Griffon and I were wrapped up in each other, staring at the very same view. I walk faster.

"Things aren't going so well at home and I just needed to get out of the house. I saw you sitting there," he explains. "I could tell that you were in no shape to be left alone, so I just sat next to you and waited. Is that so wrong?"

I stop and face him, barely able to contain my desire to punch him in the chest. The anger rolls off me in waves, and Drew must sense it because he takes one small step backward. "*You're* all wrong! If you hadn't shown up at the studio the other day, everything would be fine." I clench my fists, trying to keep my voice steady. "Griffon's gone."

Drew raises his eyes to meet mine. "Maybe he sees what you refuse to. That we're destined for each other."

"We are *not!*" I turn and start to walk away. The people around us are already beginning to thin out, and I scan the crowd for Rayne and Peter.

"Wait," Drew says, and reaches out to touch my sleeve, but I shrug him off. Even through the thick fabric I can feel the vibrations between us, so I step back until they become just a dull ache.

"Griffon was everything to me. He's Sekhem," I say, the pride in my voice unmistakable. "Important Sekhem. Not like some selfish, low-life Khered."

Drew's face registers the surprise I'm sure he wanted to hide. "Is that what you think? If that's true, I can only imagine what kind of crap he's been telling you all this time." He crosses his arms over his chest. "There are other facets to life than what the Sekhem have been feeding you. Khered take advantage of the opportunities we've been given in a different way. The Sekhem don't have all the answers. It's not only about hard work and crushing responsibility."

Responsibility. That word has been following me around since the day I had my first memory. "What are you talking about?"

"There are many ways to live in this world, and apparently you've only been shown one tiny side of the benefits that our kind of immortality can bring."

Immortality. I hadn't really thought of it that way before. As pissed as I am at myself for staying and even talking to him, another part of me is just the tiniest bit curious. "And you have another?"

Drew smiles, and I have to look away—otherwise I'd have to admit that it makes him even better-looking. "There's only one way to find out. Have dinner with me."

His arrogance makes me want to hit him again. "Did you not hear anything I said? You've ruined my life. I'm not going out with you."

"Okay, then." He shrugs. "I guess you're going to have to

spend the rest of your life—the rest of your lives—wondering how things might have been."

I start to walk away. Thoughts are tumbling through my head so fast I can barely keep up. Immortality. Responsibility. Khered. When I glance back over my shoulder, he's still standing there with an amused look on his face. Damn him—he's right. I *am* always going to wonder.

"One meal," I shout back. "One hour. And that's it."

Twelve

Drew is waiting out in front of the slightly shabby restaurant as I walk from the bus stop on 24th Street. The sun is still high overhead, and I wonder why he wants to eat at the same time as old people. Probably so that Francesca won't catch him. I doubt he'll even eat anything, but then again, neither will I. I'm here on a fact-finding mission, and that's all.

"You came," he says, turning the full force of his smile on me. "I wasn't sure you'd get the message I left at the studio." I almost miss the glance at the ankh that's prominently displayed around my neck.

"I got it." I look up at the sign on the restaurant. "Salvadorian?"

"Is it okay?" He looks genuinely concerned. "I love the pupusas here."

"I'll let you know." I can hear the irritated tone in my voice, but I can't help it. If it wasn't for Drew, I'd be eating dinner with Griffon. My mind flashes to him and I wonder what he's doing tonight. And who he's doing it with.

The bell on the front door dings as Drew holds it open for me. This place isn't what I expected—fluorescent lighting and small formica tables surrounded by worn red vinyl chairs. Not exactly what I pictured as a restaurant Khered would like. Nice to see that Drew isn't going out of his way to impress me.

"Hello, Señor Drew!" says an older woman as she comes out from behind the counter to give him a kiss on both cheeks.

"*Hola*, Maria," Drew says. They chat in Spanish for a few moments—his accent is flawless, of course. Maria glances at me and he gives her a big smile. "*Esta mi amiga* Cole."

"You are welcome here," Maria says in halting English with a large smile, grabbing both of my hands. For a split second I wonder if she's Akhet too, but all I feel is genuine warmth. "Please, sit down. Would you like a menu?"

I wasn't going to eat, but the smells from the kitchen are making my stomach growl. "Sure."

The chairs scrape the floor as we pull them out and settle down facing each other over the small gray table. Maria hands me a menu and then winks at Drew before she walks back to the counter. Drew doesn't say anything, just sets his phone faceup on the table.

I look over the top of the laminated menu. "Expecting a call?"

"No." He pushes a few buttons and numbers start racing across the screen. "I'm setting the timer. Should the hour start now, or from when I met you out front?"

I try not to smile. "From now is fine."

"Great," he says. "I got a six-minute bonus."

I scan the unfamiliar dishes on the menu, not knowing what to get.

"Do you eat pork or chicken?" Drew asks.

"Both."

"I'd try the pork, chicken, and green chile pupusa platter. It's one of the best I've ever had."

"Okay," I say, ordering his recommendation when Maria comes back to the table with our water.

"I hope you're not planning on stealing food off of my plate," I say when Drew doesn't order anything.

"Maria already knows what I want," he says. He looks around the small restaurant with something that looks like pride. "I used to come here a lot when I first moved to San Francisco. For just a couple of bucks you can get enough food to last you the entire day. After a while, Maria started slipping a few extra things in here and there with my orders." He shrugs. "It was just nice to be in a place where someone noticed you, you know?"

I nod. That's why I like going to the same café every day. We may not be on cheek-kissing terms, but I don't ever have to tell them what name to write on my cup. "How long ago did you move here?"

"Four years ago," he answers. "When I was sixteen. Got off the bus with a backpack and a duffel bag and not much else."

"Hmm," I say, reassessing one view of him.

"Hmm, what?" he asks.

"Nothing. It's just that I thought you were older."

"I'm twenty in this lifetime," he says. "For all that age really matters."

I think about the way Mom and Dad still treat me like a kid. "For a lot of people, it does really matter."

He laughs. "I see your point. The fact that I can't legally drink or even rent a car is a complete joke."

"So you were all by yourself?" I feel old enough to make my own rules, but I don't know if I'd want to land in a strange city alone.

Drew plays with the straw wrapper on the table. "Yep. My parents aren't Akhet, and I got tired of being told what to do. Emancipated myself, got on a boat and then a bus, and finally landed here." He drags the wrapper through a drop of water and it expands like a wriggling worm. "They were pretty angry about it at first, but I know that was because they were scared for me. Can't blame them, really. Things are better now, though. I try to get back to Australia and see them as often as I can."

"Why San Francisco?"

"Something was just pulling me here; it felt like this was where I was meant to be. I didn't know why then," he says, then looks up at me. "But I do now."

It's my turn to study the cracked tabletop, and I'm relieved when Maria comes with our food so that we have something to do. So much of me feels like I shouldn't be here, that I'm betraying whatever might be left of me and Griffon just by agreeing to see Drew, but there's a tiny part of me that wants to understand this thing we started five hundred years ago. To find some answers to the questions my memories are uncovering.

"Enough about me," Drew says, as we both dig into our food. "What about you? Besides teaching at the studio, what do you do?"

"I'm in high school," I say, like that explains it all.

"But what about after? College?" He looks down at my left hand. "Or Juilliard, maybe?"

I pull my arm under the table. "Not anymore."

"I thought you still played."

I shake my head. "Not like before. I . . . can't."

"Well, maybe not right now, but what about next year?"

"It's not going to happen," I say, not wanting to hear him recite all of the possibilities. That's what everyone does when I talk about not being able to play, and I'm tired of it. There are no possibilities. I might as well move on. "My playing career is over, and I just have to face that fact. I'm never going to be the next Suggia or Ma. It's over."

Drew chews thoughtfully, not seeming to mind that I just about bit his head off. "You like Suggia?"

I stare at him. Nobody outside of my music friends has ever heard of Guilhermina Suggia. "Of course. She was only the most groundbreaking female cellist in history. There aren't that many recordings because it was so long ago, but I have a few. But it wasn't just the music, it was the way she lived her life, refusing to settle for anything less than the best, not letting the fact that she was a woman stop her from getting to the very top, even in the days when female cellists were almost unheard of."

"What's your favorite?"

"Recording? Probably 'Kol Nidrei.' It's just so emotional—you can feel what she's feeling as she moves through the piece."

Drew nods. "That's a good one." He pauses and glances around the restaurant, which has been rapidly filling with people as we eat. He leans over the table. "I saw her do the Moór double concerto in Paris. It was life-changing."

I sit back. "In 1913? With Casals?"

"That's the one." Drew finishes eating and folds his napkin over his empty plate. I have nothing to say to that. How can you come up with a response when someone tells you that he saw the cellist you admire more than any other play in concert—a concert that took place a hundred years ago?

I feel almost jealous. "I'd give anything to have been there."

Drew looks thoughtful. "Maybe you were. Even though you don't remember everything about your past, you should stop thinking in the limited terms of one lifetime. If you were alive then, it's possible that your paths crossed."

I consider this. From what I remember I was alive then, and playing the cello, although not at her level. I've been slightly obsessed with Suggia from the minute I heard her name. Is it possible that it's not just admiration, but memory? "That's crazy. I never thought of it that way."

My thoughts are interrupted as Maria comes and takes our plates. As we sit waiting for the check, I can sense that Drew is thinking about something bigger than Guilhermina Suggia. "You can ask me," I tell him.

"Ask you what?"

"Whatever you've been keeping quiet about this whole dinner," I answer.

He grins, and once again I'm struck by how handsome he is. I look out the window instead of at him.

"I do have one question," he finally admits.

"I figured."

Drew clears his throat. "What happened to you after I'd gone? I was taken away . . ."

"By the soldiers," I say. "I remember."

"Right. For some ridiculous, trumped-up charge of treason against the crown." He laughs bitterly. "I never thought they'd actually go through with it."

"But that day in the hallway, as the soldiers took you away . . ." I take a deep breath and look at him before finishing the sentence. "We never saw each other again, did we?"

"No." There's pain in his eyes as he tries to continue. "I was imprisoned in the Tower and executed a few months later."

"I saw what you wrote on the wall. In Beauchamp Tower. *Ad vitam aeternam.*"

For once, Drew looks surprised. "You did? When?"

"Last spring. I was on vacation in London. I didn't know what it meant then; I was only getting flashes of memory. But still, I knew it was important."

He sits back in his seat. "Wow." He's silent for a second. "I remember carving that, thinking that you'd never see it. *Hoping* that you'd never be in the Tower to see it." Drew lifts his eyes to meet mine. "Which is what I wanted to ask you. What happened to you? Did you marry again? Even if I was gone, you should have lived out your life in comfort. There was enough money, and I'd made provisions that should have kept you well into your old age."

"You don't know?" I'd never considered that fact.

He shakes his head sharply. "I've searched, but there are no records. It's like you just dropped off the face of the earth."

"In a way, I did." I look around to make sure nobody is listening. "I was executed not long after you were killed. A few months maybe, as close as I can figure."

Drew's eyes are angry as he brings his fist down hard onto the table. "Damn! That was not the agreement." He starts to reach for my hand across the table, but pulls back quickly, remembering, his eyes searching mine for the truth. "You've got to believe me, I never would have gone if I'd thought for one minute that's what would happen. I agreed to surrender only if they left you alone. Otherwise, I would have fought to the death to keep us together. The king . . . was smitten with you." I smile as he slips into the more formal speech of our first lifetime together. "I guess I figured that his adoration would keep us both safe," he continues.

I remember my thoughts as I sat in the Tower, waiting to meet my fate, hearing the workmen pound at the platform that was to host my death. "I think that's what went wrong," I say, knowing as the images form that I'm right. "All I remember is that the king propositioned me and I refused him. I think that's what got me killed."

Drew's phone vibrates and I look to see it marking the end of one hour. I'm a little annoyed to discover that I'm disappointed. "We can stay," I say without thinking, enjoying being able to talk about this freely, to maybe find some of the pieces that are missing from my memories.

"No. You said an hour, and it's up." He picks up the phone,

his motions exaggerated as he puts it in his pocket and slips his arms into his jacket. Just as we start to get up, Drew puts both hands on the table, and I can see his arms trembling as he locks eyes with me, a sad smile behind them. "At least you remember that much. You refused the king, a gesture that cost you your life," he says, his voice barely above a whisper. "Because that's how much you loved me."

Thirteen

Focusing on not focusing on anything is harder than it sounds. I always play better when I don't think about the notes or the music and just let instinct take over, but with all that's been going on, clearing my mind isn't easy. As the bow glides over the cello strings, I can tell that my fingers are getting stronger and finding the right places on the board more often. When I finish the piece, even I have to admit that it doesn't totally suck. Not stage-worthy yet, but not completely awful either.

"That was nice," Mom says, watching from the doorway. "Best I've heard you sound."

Since your career ended, I finish for her in my head. "Thanks," is all I say out loud.

She takes a few steps into my room. "Are you feeling better?"

"I guess," I say cautiously. I haven't talked to her about

Griffon at all. There's too much I'll never be able to tell her. "Why?"

Mom walks over and sits on my bed, looking around the room like she's never been in here before. "I have eyes. I know something happened between you and Griffon."

I nod, afraid to say anything. Just thinking about Griffon is enough to make me start bawling like a baby.

"You know you can always come and talk to me about things like that. I've been around a while. I might even be able to help."

"Thanks," I whisper. "We broke up." I blink back the tears that form just from saying those words.

Mom leans over and puts her arms around me. At first I pull back—Mom and I don't hug that much anymore—but then I relax into her and feel more relieved than I have in days.

"Want to talk about it?" she asks.

"No," I answer. "It's over. I just have to move on."

Mom pulls back and puts one hand on my cheek. "Oh sweetie, nothing is ever over."

"You don't know that." I sniff and run the back of my hand over my eyes.

"Maybe I do," she says, and this time I'm content to let her have the last word.

We sit quietly until Mom straightens and takes a deep breath. "Dad's coming down for brunch. Are you about done practicing?"

"Dad's coming here?" Despite the fact that he lives in the apartment above ours, he's rarely shown up for a meal since the divorce.

Mom holds my gaze steady, like she's daring me to say more. "Something wrong with that? He *is* your father."

"Nope. Nothing wrong with that. Let me just put this away and I'll be right in."

I set the cello in its case, trying to ignore the heaviness that settles in my chest every time I touch it. I know it's stupid, but I haven't polished the wood in weeks, because I think that maybe some of the fingerprints on it might be Griffon's. We've had no contact at all since the last time at his house, and I know I'm being ridiculous by trying to hold on to even dusty traces of him, but I can't help it.

The table is set for three like it always used to be, but instead of Kat sitting across from me, Dad is shaking out his napkin. Kat hasn't even been gone a week, but since that first outburst, Mom hasn't said too much about it. My contact with Kat has been limited to four texts and two status updates, so I guess her fabulous new life in London is taking up a lot of her time. I always knew that she'd be moving out anyway at the beginning of the school year, but it's still weird, like more than one person is missing from the house.

"Well, this is nice," Dad says, breaking the silence.

Mom shoots him a glance. None of us are supposed to acknowledge that nice, normal family meals aren't what we do every day. "It is. Can you pass the bacon, please?"

"Sure." For a few excruciatingly long minutes the only sound in the room is the clinking of silverware on the plates.

"How's it going at the studio?" Dad finally asks me.

"Fine."

"Did I hear you practicing earlier?"

"The improvement is amazing," Mom answers for me. "I'm not saying she should start booking recitals anytime soon, but we might want to look at getting back into the Conservatory before school starts."

"I'm right here," I say irritably. "And I'm nowhere near good enough to even think about the Conservatory at this point."

"You're wrong," Mom says. "And you're going to be a senior this year. We need to start making some decisions about Juilliard or continuing with the Conservatory program once you graduate."

"I have been making some decisions," I say, although that's a complete lie. "I've been thinking about applying to Cal and maybe UC San Diego." I've pulled those two schools completely out of thin air, but I get a feeling of satisfaction from just saying them out loud.

"To do what? Neither of those schools has a music program worthy of your talent." Mom puts her fork down on her plate; the pretense of actually eating is over. "We've talked about Juilliard since you were a little—"

I cut her off before she can say any more. "Mom, face it—Juilliard is completely off the table, and so is the Conservatory. I was thinking I should look into something else. History maybe, or English lit."

"Why? So you can waste your gift teaching?"

"Is that so bad? I teach music now. What's the difference?"

Mom starts to speak again, but Dad puts his hand on her arm. To my total surprise, she shuts up. "What your mother is trying to say is that it isn't time to give up yet. Applications are still six months away, and a lot can happen in that time."

A knock at the door saves me from having to try to explain myself again. "I'll get it," I say, tossing my napkin on the table. Maybe I should bring Kat up in order to take the heat off me.

I'm totally unprepared to see Drew at the front door. "What are you doing here?" I quickly step out onto the porch and close the door behind me. I try hard not to notice that the vintage Doors shirt he's wearing is just tight enough to show off the muscles in his chest.

"You didn't give me your phone number last night," he says. "So I had to come over and see you in person."

"How did you know where I live?"

"I heard Kat tell Francesca once," he says.

I should have known that no random fact would go unnoticed. Or be forgotten. I lean against the door frame. "I agreed to one dinner," I remind him.

"And I appreciate that," he says. "This is an invitation, not an order. There's someone I want you to meet, but it's going to take longer than an hour."

"Who?"

"It's a surprise." The corners of his eyes crinkle up as he smiles.

I hesitate. An hour-long dinner is one thing, but this sounds suspiciously like a date.

Drew's face turns serious, but his eyes focus on mine. "If you don't want to see me again after this, then I'll go. I'll leave you alone. I promise. But you don't want to miss this."

I look at Drew and then down at the ground. I've spent so much time running away from him, but now I'm wondering why. What else do I have to lose? "Okay," I finally agree. "When?"

"Friday. Eight o'clock." He glances toward the window, and I know that Mom and Dad are watching. "Can I pick you up?"

"I'll meet you." By now, that kind of answer is almost a reflex.

"Cole, let me pick you up," he says, a hint of exasperation in his voice. "I have a car, and it's easier." He hesitates, and I don't fill the gap left by his silence. "The minute you want to come home, I'll take you. I promise."

"Friday. Eight o'clock," I confirm and slip back through the door, my heart pounding for no good reason.

"Who was that?" Mom and Dad are standing by the door when I walk back in.

"God, you scared me! What were you doing? Spying?"

"Nice try. Who was that?" Mom repeats.

"Just a friend. He used to work with Kat. At the store."

"What's he doing hanging around here?" Dad asks, his lips set into a thin line that tells me he's more upset than he's letting on. He glances toward the window. "How old is he, anyway?"

I bite my lip. They're not going to like the answer, but it doesn't really matter after all. "Twenty."

Mom crosses her arms in front of her chest, and I know immediately this is not a good answer. "He's a *man*! Nobody that age has any business hanging around you. You're just a child, for God's sake!"

"Child! Seriously? I'm almost seventeen!" I shout back. It's not like I want to go out with Drew, but this kind of treatment is really getting to me. If they only knew what I've experienced in the past couple of months, how much I remember about being an adult, they wouldn't treat me this way. But of course, I can never tell them. "Who I hang around with is none of your business."

"After what your sister pulled, it's completely, one-hundred-percent my business."

My frustration boils over. I knew this would happen. "Just because Kat got out of here early doesn't mean you have to punish me for it!" I glance up at the clock and reach for my bag. So much for happy family meals. "I have to go."

Dad steps into the hallway, blocking the door. "Where? I meant what I said. I don't want you seeing that guy. I'll get the police involved if I have to."

I walk up to Dad, trying hard not to cry. He's always been the one on my side, but now he's just parroting her talk. "If you do, then you're going to have an empty house a lot sooner than you think." He can't meet my eyes, so I reach around him to open the door. Mom starts to say something else, but I close the door behind me before I have to listen to her.

"Have you been practicing?" Janine asks, taking a bite of her salad as we walk toward the Faculty Glade behind her office.

I grin, finally feeling better after my fight with Mom and Dad. Janine sounds just like I do when I question Zander. "Sort of," I say. "Sometimes, if I'm not paying attention, it feels like other people's emotions are shooting at me from all directions. Other times, when I'm really concentrating, I can't get anything at all." It's a little weird to talk to her now. Like the subject of Griffon is just under everything we're saying, like a death we're not ready to acknowledge.

Janine nods thoughtfully. She's either really good at hiding it, or it doesn't bother her at all. "I've read about that happening to other empaths. You have to be careful not to take on the emotions of those around you."

"How do I avoid it? I can't seem to control any of it."

"From what I've researched, it's a matter of controlling the magnetic field that the brain generates from neuronal activity. That's what you're feeling when you read people. And that's what you're going to have to learn to block as you get more sensitive."

"Mom just thinks I'm an emotional mess," I say. I squeeze my eyes shut. That's coming way too close to Griffon territory. "I mean, I just wish I could tell her about all of this." I think about how it felt to have her arms around me. "It feels like there's so much separating us now. So much I can't say to her."

"Maybe you can someday," Janine says. "I told Griffon's father about us, and he's been able to keep our secret for almost twenty years. You just have to be pretty selective. And the consequences aren't as high as they were in the old days. Not many people get burned at the stake for being witches anymore."

That's what Griffon said the day he told me about being Akhet—that the person who helped him was executed for sorcery. "How's Griffon?" I ask, regretting the question the minute it leaves my lips.

She grins. "He's fine. Busy setting up the lab in the South Bay." She pauses. "He was asked to give a big speech at an energy symposium the other day. It's on the Internet—you should take a look. It's a side of him you don't get to see often." I can hear the proud mom in her talking and see how hard she's trying to keep the conversation neutral. Janine looks around at the grassy area. "How about we sit under that tree over there?"

The sun is blazingly bright, so we settle onto the soft mat of redwood needles at the base of the tree. I take a bite of my apple and watch three women in brightly colored saris walking on the path. The one in the middle is wearing one of emerald green, and the silk is so shiny I can almost feel it on my fingertips.

The darkness is total, complete and unwavering. I suspect I'll get used to it—at least, that's what they tell me. I wonder if someday I'll forget about sight altogether. If one day I won't be able to remember what Mum's face looks like, or the bright green color of her favorite sari. If someday, things will be as dark inside my head as they are beyond my useless eyes.

Spicy breakfast smells drift through the air and I roll over, wondering what time it is. I can hear Mum and Daddy whispering in the other room, even though they think I'm still asleep; if I listen, I can hear what they're saying.

"We can't have Ramesh begging in the streets for the rest of his life," Daddy says. "What other choice do we have?"

"But he's still a child! How can you think of sending him away? Especially in his condition?"

Daddy sighs and I know this isn't the first time they've had this conversation. "He's not a child, Hamsa, he's almost twelve. And it's precisely because of his condition that we have no choice. There are no facilities for blind people in India. His best option for the future is to go to school in England. They can teach him how to get around with a cane and to read with his fingers."

They're quiet for a moment, and I can picture Daddy taking Mum's hand, trying to convince her.

"Read with his fingers? Can they really do that?"

"They can," Daddy says. "I've heard all about it from Vikram's cousin, who knows someone who saw it firsthand. The war is over, and I'm told that the Germans' bombs did very little damage to that part of the country in any case. If he's to have any chance at all, we have to take this opportunity."

Mum's voice still carries worry. "What about the rumors of partition? What if something happens and he's so far away?"

"If there is partition, it won't be violent. Everything will be civilized and constitutional. In any case, he'll be safe there. We have to trust that we're doing the best for him."

Varun's breathing is slow and steady and I know that neither their conversation nor the smells from the kitchen have woken him. A few minutes later, I hear soft footsteps in the doorway. Mum pauses long enough so that I can smell the perfumed oil she always wears, and I know that my eyes are so damaged from the firecracker that she has no idea if I'm asleep or not.

"I'm awake," I say quietly.

"You have ears like a hyena these days," she says. I hear her voice change pitch as she smiles, although I have a feeling that it's more forced than usual. "Food is almost ready."

"I'll wake Varun," I say, throwing the covers off. At first I was glad to be staying home while everyone else went to school, but lately I've been missing it. Even Miss Mehta's dreary history class might be worth sitting through if only to get out of this house.

"Thank you, dear," Mum says. I know that she's wondering whether I've overheard them, but I'm not giving anything away. I'm not sure how I feel about going to a blind school in England. On the one hand, it would be better than staying in the house all day, every day. On the other, it's one of the most terrifying prospects I can imagine. All alone in a strange country, not even being able to see where I am when I get lost. We listened to the war on the radio, and even though Daddy says that they didn't hit that part of England, I still picture myself wandering among bombed-out buildings while airplanes drone overhead like in the newsreels we saw at the cinema. I need some time to think about it, although I know that when Daddy puts his mind to something, it very rarely changes. Varun has been trying to get them to send him away to boarding school for as long as I can remember, but for him, the answer has always been no.

My feet hit the warm tile floor and I feel my way from my bed to my brother's. "Get up!" I shout somewhere close to his ear.

"Stupid!" he says, pushing me backward so hard I fall to the floor, but we're both laughing. As much of an ass as Varun is, he's the only one who's made me feel even halfway normal since the accident. He spent the first few months apologizing daily, crying about how he never should have handed me the firecracker in the first place. I hated it. I'm much happier having my irritating older brother back.

"I'm not stupid," I say, launching myself onto his bed. "I'm going to boarding school in England!"

The three women are almost out of sight now as the world comes back into focus. I shake my head, hoping that it wasn't obvious. I flash back to the night of the fireworks and the chaos after the firecracker blew up in my face. I'd spent the rest of that lifetime blind. Did I go to England? Did I learn braille? I feel the tips of my fingers and wonder if they'd be able to read braille, like I can speak Italian. If I learned in that lifetime, is the sense memory still there?

"Another memory?" Janine asks.

I look at the ground, a little embarrassed. "Yes. India this time. I've been getting more and more of those."

"India. That's interesting. I've never had a lifetime in India."

I glance at her. "I was a boy in India, sometime around World War II. I remember I was blinded. By a firecracker." I think about the memory I just had. "I think that's where I began to feel things more. My eyes were gone, so my other senses must have taken over. I could hear better and knew what people were feeling by the tone of their voices."

"It's possible," Janine says, chewing thoughtfully. "Losing your sight would be a traumatic event. If a person can develop musical skills over many lifetimes, I don't see why you can't develop empathic skills the same way. True empathic skills are simply supercharged intuition, and once you learn to trust in them completely, there's no telling where they might take you."

"Do you think that was my last lifetime? Before this one, I mean?"

"You said it was World War II?"

"Yes. I heard my dad talking about England and Germany."

"So that would have made you . . ."

"Eleven. Right after the war ended."

"Could be." Janine nods. "Depends on how old you were

when that lifetime finished, but sure, that might have been the one before now."

"Freaky," I say, amazed.

"Definitely," Janine agrees. "But that's enough chitchat." She rubs her hands on her pants and holds them out to me. "Now, let's see if we can hone those skills into something worth using in this lifetime."

Fourteen

The minute Drew's foot hits the bottom step of our porch, I'm out the door. It's not that I'm dying to see him again, but I want to get the hell out of here before Mom comes home and I have to explain myself. The vague note I left for her in the kitchen will have to do until later.

"Hi," Drew says, pausing on the steps. He's wearing a black V-neck T-shirt and a dark brown leather jacket that looks like he either kept it from a past lifetime or picked it up at a vintage store. I hate that a little jolt of something runs through me when I see him, but I just pass it off as a leftover from the other lifetime. He flashes me a smile. "You look nice."

I glance down at my jeans and black corduroy jacket. I'll never admit that it took me a couple of hours to figure out what to wear; I was going for a cross between looking good and looking like I don't care. Apparently, "don't care" won out. I'm about to say something about him lying, but at the last second decide to let it go. "Thanks. Where are we going?"

Drew turns and steps onto the sidewalk. "It's sort of a secret. All I'll say is that I promise to get you home safely before curfew."

I instinctively feel for my phone in the pocket of my jeans. I can always call a cab if I need to go home. If doing what he wants for one night is going to make him go away forever, it seems like a bargain. "Okay."

He raises his eyebrows. "Really? Great. Don't comment, just keep your mind open and your opinions to yourself for now. My car's over here." Drew leads me down the block to a low-slung black car with a red stripe down the hood. It looks like it would be at home in a superhero movie or on a racetrack. He walks around and opens the passenger door for me, and I slide into a seat that feels like it instantly surrounds me, adjusting to my every move. The interior is all pale gray leather and totally spotless. I look from the chrome dashboard to the steering wheel with the logo I don't recognize.

"This is your car?" I ask as he eases into the driver's seat. "What is it, a Ferrari?"

"Bugatti," he says, patting the dashboard. "It's a great car for driving around town. Or to Vegas."

"We're driving to Vegas?"

He glances at me as the engine roars to life. "I thought about it, but I figured you didn't have that kind of time."

I look around the obviously expensive car, really more cockpit than interior, and try to decide whether he's kidding or not. "So if we're not going to Vegas, where are we going?"

"You agreed not to comment."

"Fine. I'll just sit here and shut up."

"That'll work," he says. We turn toward downtown, but as much as I want to ask more questions, I sit back and look out the window. The driver of every car we pass turns and does a double take at the Bugatti, but Drew doesn't seem to notice.

I feel the leather seat under my hand. "So your parents are insanely rich?"

Drew settles back in his seat as the car shoots forward. "They are now. I help them out. When I was a kid they were just your average, middle-class couple living in Sydney. Dad's an engineer and Mum stayed home with us."

"Now I totally don't get it. What was all that talk about arriving in San Francisco with just a duffel bag? Kat said that you're a jewelry designer. She didn't say anything about race cars."

"I only design jewelry for fun. As far as most people are concerned, I'm a jewelry designer with an unknown source of family money, and that's fine," he says, almost apologetically. "Even Francesca doesn't know anything close to the truth."

A shadow passes across his face as he says her name that makes me think something's going on there. "So what is the truth?"

"Have you been told anything about the Iawi? About Alexandria and the catacombs?"

"I know that the Iawi are really old Akhet. That's about it."

Drew nods slowly, and I can tell he's measuring out the information he's going to give me. "The first formal organization of Akhet took place in Rhakotis. It's now called Alexandria."

"In Egypt," I say, connecting some of the dots. "Which is why everything has an Egyptian name."

"Right. When people first began to realize that they were remembering their past lives, they wanted a safe place to store valuables to make their next lives easier. We found that in Rhakotis. Some Iawi keep things in other places too, but Rhakotis is the only sanctioned place for safekeeping."

I look up at the lighted windows of the high-rises as we pass through the Financial District. "What kinds of valuables?" I finally ask.

"Small things, mostly. Jewels, gold, things like that. Although the past few centuries have brought more opportunity to save things in other places and go back for them in the next lifetime. We've gotten more savvy about what types of things people find valuable over the years." He leans forward with a smile. "Do you have any idea how much a Honus Wagner baseball card is worth these days? I can buy a couple of Bugattis for the value of one little baseball card."

"That's it? You just sell baseball cards for a living?"

"No. Every lifetime is more expensive than the last, which is why you always need to build on the money you've put aside. Some Akhet skills can come in extraordinarily handy for that. Picking the best of the stock market, knowing which tech companies will probably thrive in the future." Drew laughs. "It's pretty simple, really. I have money. Companies need money in order to start up or expand. I give them what they need, and they give me a cut of the profits." He shifts hard with his right hand. "Raising money is pretty simple once you get the hang of it. We all do it. I'd imagine even your Sekhem friends aren't hurting for cash."

I remember Griffon saying that money wasn't a problem when he had the right-handed cello made for me. But he and

Janine live in a pretty regular house, and he drives a motorcycle. Not a race car. Although Janine does seem to know a large number of powerful and wealthy people.

"They don't live like this."

"I'm sure they could if they wanted to."

I look over at Drew, and he's got a broad smile on his face.

"Why are you so happy?"

His smile is instantly replaced by a more serious face. "Sorry, I forgot. No fun around Cole."

I frown. "That's not true. I'm plenty fun."

"We'll see about that." He reaches into a space behind my seat. "But I did get you a little something. Just for fun."

"I don't want anything else from you," I say. I already feel a little guilty about the earrings I shoved back into his hands after he went to all the trouble of making them for me.

He holds a bag out to me. "Why not? I already said that money's not an issue. It's not a big deal."

I take the bag and place it in my lap. Inside is a black dress and a shoebox. I lift out the dress and the box—I recognize the designer, because Kat is always going on about their stuff. Inside the shoebox is a pair of high-heeled black platform sandals with red soles. Everything is exactly my size. Suddenly, my face feels hot. I shove it all back in the bag and tuck it behind his seat. "I can't take these."

He looks defeated. "Why not? I just saw them and thought about how great they'd look on you."

"I don't want them."

"I'm sorry. I didn't mean to upset you," he says. "I just thought you'd like them."

"I'm not something else for you to purchase," I say, anger rising inside me. "I agreed to go with you one more time and that's it. I'm just fulfilling my end of the bargain."

He looks so hurt I almost feel like apologizing. "Honestly, I didn't mean anything. You used to love it when I got you things before. I just thought you still would feel that way."

"Well, I don't," I say. "I'm not Allison anymore."

He parks the car near a row of warehouses by the piers and turns his steady gaze on me. "Trust me, I know that."

Drew grabs my hand as he helps me out of the low-slung sports car, but I pull it away and manage to climb out myself. Drew glances back at me, but doesn't reach for my hand again.

I look around at the alleys full of trash bins and burned-out streetlights as we approach a plain gray door. "Where are we?"

"San Francisco."

"Funny." I glance at the nondescript brick building with the rickety-looking fire escape climbing up the side. There's no sign out front or over the door. I hear sirens in the distance, but other than that, it's disturbingly quiet out here. I feel for the phone in my pocket. Just in case. "I mean, what is this place?"

"It's a club," he says, ringing a bell that's almost hidden on the right side of the door frame.

"What kind of a club?"

The door opens and we're ushered into a dark hallway by a man in a suit. "A private club," he answers.

"Good to see you again Mr. Braithwaite," the man at the door says.

"Thanks, Max," Drew says. "Anyone special in tonight?"

"The usual suspects," he says. He looks at me, but I don't feel

anything menacing in his eyes. "I see you've brought us someone new."

"This is Cole," Drew says. "She is new. I'm showing her
around."

The man looks approving. "Shewi?"

Drew nods. "Just a few months."

The man looks surprised, but doesn't say anything more.
Drew smiles at him. "Max likes to call himself an ordinary doorman, but he's really the master of ceremonies at this place. Nothing happens here that he doesn't know about. Or approve of."

Max gives a little bow in my direction. "And your friend
here is prone to exaggeration. But welcome to our little home
away from home. Enjoy."

I can hear faint music playing and murmuring voices as we
walk down a dimly lit hallway. Drew slows his pace and turns
to me. "Sorry about that. Most of the people here are Iawi. Some
of them remember lifetimes that stretch back to the beginning of
memory. That's why Max was so surprised that you're Shewi
and so new. Stick with me and you'll be fine."

"Wait. This club is for Akhet?"

He nods. "It's a private club, like I said. There are many
places like it all over the world where people like us can come
and talk freely, to meet up with people and not have to worry
that what we say will be overheard by those who don't understand. You'd be surprised at the people you can meet in a place
like this."

I remember what Janine and Sue said the other day. "I thought
most Khered were more like me. You know, not Iawi."

Drew's brows crease. "Who told you that?" He pauses and

shakes his head. "Never mind. Most Sekhem like to think that you have to be stupid to adopt Khered philosophies. Total propaganda."

A pretty brunette passes us on the way to the door. "Have you brought Francesca here?" I ask.

"No." His eyes shift away from me. "I can't. It's one of the things that makes it hard." He starts moving again. "I really don't want to talk about her right now."

Every time Francesca's name is mentioned, Drew seems to get annoyed. I wonder what he told her about where he is tonight. I'm guessing it wasn't the truth.

At the end of the hallway is a lounge area with a well-stocked bar at the far end. There are groups of people sitting in overstuffed chairs around small round tables and others relaxing in booths that line one wall. I can see other rooms through doorways in both walls and wonder how big this place really is. Several people look up and wave at Drew, and I'm surprised at the mix of people in this place—they seem to range in age from early teens to old enough to be my grandparents. I wonder vaguely if I've ever known any of them, if we've ever been connected in the past.

"Hey, old man! Good to see you." A guy in his late thirties throws his arm around Drew's shoulders.

Drew quickly hugs him back. "Robert! Mate, where have you been? It's been at least a year."

"Italy, mostly. We got a new villa on the Amalfi coast. You have to come by—Abby and the kids would love to see you again."

As he's speaking, I recognize him from the trailers that have been in all the theaters for the past month. The movie he's in with his wife Abby is supposed to be the big summer block-buster. He's a lot shorter in real life.

"Maybe later this summer," Drew tells him. He smiles at me. "Ever been to Italy?"

I shake my head, not wanting to admit that I'm a little star-struck and afraid of saying something stupid in front of an actual superstar.

"Well, that will have to change," Robert says. He places his hand on my arm, and I know he's looking for any vibrations that might connect us. The thought that someone so world-famous is touching me completely blows what's left of my concentration. He squeezes my hand quickly, seemingly satisfied with whatever information he got from me. "Any friend of Drew's is more than welcome."

"Do you want a drink?" Drew asks, nodding toward the bar.

I look at him and feel my cheeks getting red. "I'm sixteen, remember?"

Robert throws his head back and laughs, revealing the perfect smile that has won him so many awards. "She's cute."

Drew smiles, and I'm grateful he's not laughing too. "The rules are a little different here. Physical age is only a number, and not something we tend to worry about. There's no actual drinking age in this club."

"You're still new?" Robert asks me.

I shrug, suddenly feeling like a little kid. "I guess so."

"We were all where you are at one time." He looks around the room. "Don't let anyone push you around just because you're Shewi. Some of the Iawi forget what it's like the first time." He lifts my hand and kisses it. "I find it charming."

"Come on, let's get a couple of drinks and sit down." Drew glances at his watch, and I realize that this is where we're meeting up with his special guest.

We walk to the bar, Drew stopping briefly to greet a few people along the way. Everyone seems nice but vaguely condescending; even the guy who looks like he's about my age treats me like a child once he figures out that this is my first time here.

"We'll have a Scotch and your best chardonnay," Drew says to the bartender. "Is that okay?" he asks me.

"Fine," I say, thinking that maybe one drink will make me less nervous about being here. I turn and lean against the bar, being careful not to look like I'm staring. Everyone in here is well dressed, and there are more diamonds glittering in the dim light than I've ever seen in one place before. Even the people who wouldn't be considered physically beautiful in normal circumstances have something about them that makes you look twice. I glance over at Drew as he's talking easily with the bartender. With his perfect features, I have to admit that he'd probably make a person look three times.

"Drew!" In seconds he's disappeared under a cloud of white faux fur. At least, what I *hope* is faux fur. All I can see besides the jacket are jet black curls and impossibly long brown legs sticking out of a very short leather skirt. When they finally come up for air, there's a bright pink lipstick stain on his cheek. "You're in town! You *are* coming to my show tomorrow night, then?"

"I'm not sure. I've got a lot going on right now." He nods to me. "Portia, this is my friend Cole."

And that's when I realize who she is. I've only seen her in videos and at the music awards, but that's definitely Portia

Martin standing right in front of me. Until she leans over and grabs my face, planting an identical kiss on my cheek. "Any friend of Drew's is a friend of mine," she says.

Despite the perfume and hairy jacket, I can sense that she's being honest, and I can't help but smile back. "Thanks. It's nice to meet you."

Portia makes an expert pouting face. "You want to come to the show, don't you? I'll have two passes waiting for you both at the door if you'll come. We're running previews before the big tour that's coming up. Say you will."

"I . . . um . . ."

Drew discreetly wipes at the stain on his cheek, a lipstick stain most guys would kill to have. "How about I text you as soon as our plans are settled?"

"All right. But I'm going to leave them in your name anyway. At the Civic Center. About nine o'clock. I'll be expecting you."

"No promises," Drew insists.

Portia grabs my hand and gives it a squeeze, and I swear I see her give me a little wink. "So nice to meet you, Cole. I have a feeling we'll be seeing you around."

After she leaves, I stare Drew down. "You're friends with Portia Martin?"

He shrugs, his eyes sparkling in the dim light. "Sure. She's just a person like everyone else."

"Portia Martin is *not* like everyone else."

"Hey, there's a booth free over there," Drew says as he hands me my wine. I slide in opposite him, and it doesn't take long before we're joined by two women and a man, all in their twenties, I guess.

From the introductions, I can't tell what the women do, but baseball is mentioned a couple of times and I figure out that the guy must play for a major-league team. I file his name away, thinking that Griffon will probably know who he is, until I remember that I'm not going to be talking to Griffon anytime soon. It's moments like these that are the most difficult— something comes up that I can't wait to tell Griffon, and when I remember that I'll probably never get to tell him, it hits me all over again.

I sip my wine and try to follow the conversations that are going on around me.

"She's living in Georgia, can you believe it?" The dark-haired woman says with a thick southern accent. "The country, not the state."

"Have you seen her?" Drew asks.

"No. She's still physically a child and hasn't had access to much technology up till now. She contacted me through the site, but it will probably be another five years before she can really join us. I'm so glad she did, though. I've been wondering what happened to her." The woman looks at me. "Have you registered yet? It's so important if you want to find people you've known in the past."

"No." I look to Drew for help.

"Cole is still regaining her memories," he explains for me. "So I haven't told her about the registry yet. Not much point if she doesn't know much about her history."

"Is the registry like a database of Akhet?" That must be what Janine and Sue were talking about that day.

"Exactly," the red-haired woman says. She has a faint British accent. "It's easy enough to find these days. You must be verified before you have complete access, and then you enter information about your past and your contact information in your present. You can find other Akhet you've known over the generations."

"Like Match.com for us. So much easier than going all the way to Alexandria," the man says with a smile. "That was such a hassle."

The southern woman turns, and I see a diamond-encrusted ankh sparkling at her chest. She catches me looking and holds it up to the light. "Pretty, isn't it? I was tired of the old one, so I had this made." She nods to the pendant around my neck. "Yours looks like you've had it for a while."

I can feel Drew's eyes on me as I reach up to touch it. "It was just given back to me after a long time away." I glance across the table. "Drew had it made for me. Centuries ago."

The woman next to me puts one finger on the ruby in the center. "That seems fitting. The ankh isn't just the symbol of eternal life; for us, it's a promise that we'll be together again in another lifetime."

The word echoes through my mind as I run my fingers over the curve of the pendant. A promise I have no intention of keeping.

Fifteen

We're in a cluster of people around the bar when Drew waves to someone across the room. "Excuse us, will you?" he says to the others as he pulls me away from the crowd. "The reason we came here tonight just walked through the door."

"Who is it?" I ask, looking around.

"Right here," Drew says, approaching a guy in his forties with tan skin and a little bit of gray at his temples. He extends his hand. "Mr. Ramirez?"

The man turns and examines Drew's outstretched hand for a moment before taking it and breaking into a smile. "Drew? Please call me Frank."

"Okay, Frank," Drew says, looking relieved. "Thanks so much for agreeing to meet us here."

Frank's focus on Drew is intense, as if he's blocking out everything else in the crowded room. "Not a problem," he says.

His speech is clear, but there is a formality to it that makes me wonder if English is his second language. Frank switches his gaze to me. "This must be the young lady you told me about."

"I'm Cole," I say, taking his hand. There are some Akhet vibrations between us, but I don't sense any past connection.

He must feel the same thing, because he smiles broadly. "Nice to meet you. What did you say your name was?" His dark brown eyes are intent on my face.

"Cole," I repeat, leaning in so he can hear me over the noise in the room.

Frank still looks confused as a slightly younger man joins us, placing a drink on the counter next to him. Frank's gaze softens as he introduces us. "Ah! This is my husband, Robert."

We exchange greetings and then Frank turns to Robert, his fingers fluttering through the air, and I suddenly understand. He's using sign language—Robert must be deaf.

Robert leans toward me, and I'm startled by his clear speaking voice. "I'm sorry, what was your name?"

"Cole," I repeat.

"Cole," he says with a smile. "That's nice." He turns to Frank and makes some deliberate gestures, and suddenly Frank's face breaks into a smile.

"Cole!" he says, turning toward me. "Of course. I don't know why I didn't get that at first."

I look from Robert to Frank as they grin at each other. "I'm sorry," Frank says to me. "I'm deaf. I thought you knew."

"No, I didn't." I'm a little flustered and glance at Drew, who just shrugs like he didn't know either. "It's okay, though." The minute I say it, I squeeze my eyes shut. What a stupid thing to say.

Frank nods with a smile. "It is. I contracted measles when I was a baby in this lifetime and have been profoundly deaf ever since. I'm usually good at reading lips." He tilts his head at me. "But every now and then a beautiful name trips me up."

Robert gestures to an open table and taps Frank on the elbow. "Shall we sit down?" he says, making sure Frank is watching him as he speaks.

"Let's," Frank says, grabbing his drink and leading us to the table. "I hear you're quite an accomplished cellist," he says to me as we sit down.

I look at Drew, wondering how much he said. "Was," I correct. "I don't play much anymore."

"I don't either," Frank says. "Not this time."

"This time?" I ask. "Were you a musician before?"

Frank looks at Drew, and I'm wondering if he's waiting for a translation when Drew says, "I didn't tell her."

Robert laughs, and Frank just nods in acknowledgment. "I was," he says, turning back to me. "My lifetimes have always revolved around music. Two times back, I focused on the cello too. You may have heard of me." Frank pauses, and I can sense he's teasing me. He poses with one arm extended and his chin up. "La Suggia?"

I gasp, picturing the elegant woman in the red dress whose portrait with the same pose has been hanging in my room for years. "*Guilhermina* Suggia? That was you?"

"It was," Frank acknowledges, his dark eyes shining with the memory. "What a lifetime," he sighs. "Casals and I were celebrated throughout Europe, playing for kings and queens. Salons in Paris, impromptu concerts in Prague." He focuses back on me. "Now *that* was a life well lived."

I can hardly believe it, although if I've learned anything over the past few months, it's that anything is possible. How many people get to ask their long-dead idol questions? "What was it like?" I ask. "Being one of the first women to play?"

"Frightening," he answers. "And exhilarating. Empowering." The smile on his face shifts just a little. "And sometimes crushingly lonely." Robert laces his arm through Frank's and absently pats his hand. I remember that Suggia left Pablo Casals after decades together, their competitiveness often given as the reason for the split. She didn't marry until she was in her forties and never had any kids. "I gave up a lot for my music," Frank finally continues. "That kind of singular drive was right for that lifetime." He glances fondly at Robert. "I've since learned to keep more of a balance."

Drew leans forward, and Frank's eyes shift to him. "Cole isn't sure she wants to continue with music. She has an injury that's made it hard to play recently."

"If you're meant to be a musician in this lifetime," Frank tells me, "it will be impossible not to continue in some capacity. Your body and your spirit won't let you quit."

I think about the low-grade yearning I feel inside when I haven't played for a while. About the feeling of peace that I only find with a bow in my hand. "So, what do you do now?" I ask. "Since you can't play music this time?"

Robert looks at Frank with admiration and then answers for him. "He won't tell you this, but Frank is one of the most respected composers in the entertainment industry." He names several blockbuster movies with big, epic musical scores.

I see Frank watching Robert's lips as he speaks. "I write a little music," he says modestly.

"But . . . you can't hear it?"

"Just because I can't hear the notes doesn't mean I don't know what they sound like," he says. "I write each part, hearing it in my mind and in my memories." He sits back and sips his drink. "I do okay."

"A bunch of gold statuettes in our bathroom says that you do more than okay," Robert teases.

Frank looks a little embarrassed. He leans toward me. "You can't let your circumstances dictate your life. Only you can decide. Success is twenty percent ability and eighty percent desire." He smiles. "You can do anything you want. As long as you want it badly enough."

"You look tired," Drew says as we drive up the hill toward my neighborhood.

"I just have a lot going through my head," I say, my body feeling heavy in the seat.

"There's a lot to learn," Drew agrees. "That's why I've been trying not to overwhelm you with things all at once."

"It's okay," I say. "I'm actually glad to be getting some answers." Aside from the basics, Griffon never liked to talk much about being Akhet, and now I'm wondering why. We drive in silence for a minute, images and snippets of conversation from tonight flashing through my mind. "Did you know Frank before tonight?"

"No. Not personally. I found him through the database and thought you might enjoy meeting him."

"It was one of the coolest things that's ever happened to me," I tell him honestly. "Thanks." I feel in my pocket for the card with Frank's information on it and the open invitation to get in touch whenever I want. I can pick up the phone and text Guilhermina Suggia any time I feel like it. The only bad part about it is that I can't ever tell Herr Steinberg. He would just die. But not before he had me committed. I think about all of the people Drew knows all over the world and wonder how many he's introduced to Francesca. I know it's not a good subject with him, but I risk it anyway. "You said that Francesca isn't Akhet," I say.

Drew shakes his head but doesn't speak.

"How do you explain things to her? The money? The people you know?"

"I can't." He sighs and looks directly at me. "Which is one of the reasons why we're not together anymore. I've moved out of that house and bought an apartment closer to downtown. I tried to make it work, but it was just too hard. Too many things I had to censor. It's so much easier to be with people who really understand."

The news gives me a sinking feeling in the pit of my stomach, like a safety net has been pulled away. "You broke up? When?"

"It's been happening for a while. I really care for Francesca,

but it was always going to end badly. I couldn't be honest about
the most basic things in my life, couldn't introduce her to some
of my closest friends." Drew pulls up and double-parks in front of
my house. "I don't want to talk about her anymore." I worry
that my parents will see the car, but suddenly I don't care if
they're mad at me.

Drew glances at the pendant around my neck. "Do you mind
if I touch the ankh? It's been so long since I held it."

I nod, and feel a surge of electricity rush through my body
as his fingers brush my skin. Drew turns the ankh over in his
hand and traces the ruby in the center. "I thought we'd be together
forever when I had this made for you," he says. "The ruby had
been in my family for generations, and it took weeks of working
with the silversmiths to get the design exactly right."

My mind flashes back to the day in the sunroom when he
gave it to me. I remember feeling like I was going to burst with
joy. "If you gave me an ankh way back then, were you already
Akhet?"

"Yes," he says. "I had been several times over."

"But you knew I wasn't."

"I knew you weren't then. But I could feel something extraor-
dinary between us, and I hoped that maybe your awareness
would start before too long." He sets the pendant gently against
my chest and lifts his eyes up to meet mine. "The bottom line is
that I couldn't live without you."

"Turns out I couldn't live without you either," I say, fully
intending the double meaning.

Drew puts his head against the steering wheel. "I'm so sorry.
Despite everything, I couldn't protect you. I couldn't even save

my family." He lifts his head, and I feel the moment shift as his eyes meet mine. The air feels thick with energy, and I know it will only take the suggestion of movement on my part to change things between us. I have to admit that I hesitate, considering it, until someone flips the porch light on.

"I'd better go," I say quickly, grabbing my bag and slipping out of the car.

Sixteen

I break into a galloping run as I round the corner onto Haight Street. Rayne texted me from the café twenty minutes ago, and she's going to be pissed if I keep her waiting much longer. I haven't been the best friend in the world the past couple of weeks—between work and the guys, we haven't done half the things we planned at the beginning of summer, so we made a firm date to hang out today. And now I'm late because Mom made me clean my room.

I slow down to catch my breath. I wish I could tell her about Drew, about the club and about meeting Portia Martin, but I feel like I have to keep all that to myself for now. Telling her about being Akhet is one thing. Spilling all of the Khered secrets must be against somebody's rules somewhere. I'll just add that to the list of bad friend qualities I've been compiling lately.

I see them in the back just as I reach the café window. Rage fills my body as I watch Veronique next to Rayne at the back table, their heads bent together in intimate conversation. Crossing the room doesn't even register, because it feels like only an instant has passed before my hand is on Veronique's arm, pulling her up from the table despite the difference in our sizes. "What in the hell are you doing here?" I know my voice is loud, I know people are staring, but at this point I don't care.

Rayne's hands are on my arm and her voice is pleading. "Cole! Stop! You're overreacting."

With all of my strength, I shove Veronique toward the door. "Get out! And don't come near any of us again or I swear to God I'll get someone to take care of you for good." Griffon might not love me anymore, but I have a feeling he'd still deal with Veronique if I told him what she was doing.

Veronique heads toward the door in the suddenly silent café, and Rayne pushes me out with her.

"We're going to settle this once and for all," Rayne says, pulling the two of us into an empty doorway in the next building.

"I'd love that!" I say, my frustration growing. "She tried to *kill* Griffon. Do you not remember that part?"

"Of course I do. But things are different now." Rayne shares a knowing glance with Veronique that I don't like at all. "We have to tell her."

I pull my arm free and step away from Veronique. Even being this close to her makes me feel out of control. "Tell me what?"

"Our connection," Veronique says calmly. "I knew it from the moment we met, and now I've been able to share the unbelievable news with Rayne."

I stare at them. "I swear to God, you'd better tell me what's going on here."

Rayne smiles, and I can see the excitement in her eyes. "I know who I was in a past life."

I shake my head. "How could you possibly know that?"

"Veronique told me. I could hardly believe it when she said it, but then something about it started to feel right, you know? Like it made sense in a weird way, but then I started to wonder why you'd never felt it too. Or maybe you had, but you were keeping it from me for some reason."

My nails dig into my palms as I clench my fists, trying to keep this under control. "Rayne, seriously—what are you talking about?"

"Alessandra!" She's practically bouncing with excitement. "Veronique recognized my essence! I was Alessandra all those years ago."

I wait for someone to laugh, to break the string of tension that's woven around us, but only serious looks pass between the two of them. "That's crazy!" I say after several seconds of silence.

Rayne steals a glance at Veronique, who hasn't moved a muscle. "We knew you'd say that, which is why we've had to keep it a secret."

I can't believe she's falling for this. "Have you ever felt anything? In all the time we've researched that lifetime, did anything seem familiar? Do you remember anything that might connect you to Alessandra?"

"No," Rayne admits. "But that just means I'm not Akhet, right? It doesn't mean that I wasn't Alessandra."

"She hasn't transitioned yet," Veronique volunteers. She looks up, her face filled with a combination of hope and fear, and I recognize the longing in her eyes. She puts one hand on my arm and before I can pull away, somehow she draws me into a memory.

I stroke the chestnut wood in small circles, careful to get every smudge and fingerprint off the polished surface before stowing the cello away in its case for transport to the next town, the next venue, the next audience. This instrument is the most valuable thing I've ever owned—the most valuable thing any member of my family has ever owned, and I promised my parents that I'd take care of it while I was on tour. I look up at the generic wooden walls of the practice room, and for a split second I can't remember where we are. Closing my eyes, I retrace our steps. We arrived two days ago on the boat, and then took carriages to the ornate theater. I've never seen so many people and horses in the streets of any city we've visited so far, gazing in wonder at the buildings and the shops as we pass. New York City. I start to wonder what the rest of the tour will be like in this amazing country when I hear soft murmurs from the practice room next door. There's a high window separating the two rooms, so I quietly creep onto a chair and pull myself up so that my eyes just clear the frame. Alessandra and Paolo giggle as he closes the door and embraces her. I know I should step away from the window and leave them to the small scrap of privacy they've managed to carve out for themselves, but I can't bring myself to look away. Paolo is so handsome, his dark eyes flashing with wit and intelligence. I can only hope that someday, someone will look at me the way he looks at Alessandra. The

*giggles subside and the mood turns suddenly serious, as Paolo
takes Alessandra's face in his hands, kissing her gently on each
eyelid.*

*"Mi amore," he says, his words coming out short and clipped
as if he's fighting for control. "There will never be anyone for me
but you." He brushes her golden hair away from her face, taking
a strand and twisting it around his finger. "I want to be with you
forever."*

*"And I with you," Alessandra answers, her eyes glistening
with tears. She strokes his cheek with her delicate hand.*

Paolo suddenly drops to one knee. "Marry me, then!"

*I gasp so loudly that it's a wonder they don't hear me. But
they only have eyes for each other.*

*"Marry me!" he repeats. "Make me the happiest man on the
face of the earth." He lifts one hand and kisses it gently.*

*Alessandra is just about to answer when their door is flung
open with such force that it nearly knocks me off my perch.
Signore Barone bursts into the room, his face scarlet with anger.
"What is going on here?" he demands, reaching down to pull
Paolo to his feet by the collar.*

*"Papa!" Alessandra cries. "Let him go! He has done nothing
wrong."*

*But Signore Barone doesn't listen and Paolo crashes against
the wall, music stands rattling as he slides heavily to the floor.*

I squeeze my eyes shut. Only a few weeks later, right here in
San Francisco, Alessandra would lie broken on the concrete
three stories below the rooftop, her life spilling out of her in a
growing pool of red. I open my eyes again and Veronique is

staring at me. I see a desperation in her face that I remember from that boy so long ago.

"Rayne *is* Alessandra. It's the same essence, I'm sure of it." Tears form in her eyes as she speaks. "I've been searching for her since that night on the roof a century ago. I can't believe she's been here this whole time." She blinks hard, and I can see her fighting for control. "I was right all along. Alessandra's essence was drawn to you in this lifetime."

"Rayne is *not* Alessandra," I say angrily. "I've never felt any connection. She's my best friend in this lifetime and that's it." I turn to Veronique, blocking Rayne out completely. This is between the two of us. "Rayne is a seventeen-year-old girl. She's not Akhet, Veronique. She has a boyfriend."

She waves the thought away. "The only reason she has a boyfriend is because she doesn't remember what we were to each other."

I turn to Rayne. "Are you hearing this? Does she really think you'd give up Peter for her?"

Rayne looks suddenly confused, as if something she was sure of is suddenly falling apart. "I don't know. I mean, I love being with Peter. But Veronique has told me so much about that lifetime, about how we felt about each other, about how much in love we were." She seems to draw herself up straighter and glances at Veronique. "We were destined to meet again."

"You're only repeating what she's told you," I say.

"Because she doesn't remember the truth," Veronique says.

I stare at the two of them. Anger is getting me nowhere, so I have to try logic. "Think about what you're asking her to do . . .

to be. You're asking a high-school girl to give up her boyfriend and fall in love with a woman almost ten years older than she is." I realize as I say it that I'm already thinking of myself as older than Rayne. My concept of age and experience is shifting with every week that passes.

"This isn't about age or gender," Veronique says. "I'm not asking her to love me in spite of being a woman. Or even because of it. On a higher level, love isn't about men and women or women and women—all of that loses any sort of meaning." She looks at Rayne and I sense she wants to grab her hand. I think I'd punch her if she did. "Our kind of love is about essences that are indelibly intertwined throughout history, regardless of how they're packaged in this lifetime."

"What if you're wrong?" Rayne says to me. "What if I am Alessandra? I mean, it makes sense. You've been like my sister since the first day we met, and if we were best friends in another lifetime, then we really do have a special connection."

"You're my best friend in this lifetime," I insist. "But that's it. Our connection doesn't go beyond the day we met back in second grade." I see the hurt in Rayne's eyes, but I can't back down. I can't let Veronique's lies start to make sense.

Veronique takes a step forward. "I don't know why you can't see the connection, but I can. The relationship I have with the essence that belongs to Rayne goes beyond love . . . beyond lifetimes. You of all people should understand that. What you and Griffon have is obviously the same kind of relationship."

The words hit like a punch in the stomach. "Griffon's gone," I finally say, clearing my throat, realizing after almost two weeks that it really is true. "Proof that even the strongest connection sometimes isn't enough." I close my eyes and shake the emotion off. "You're just trying to take advantage of her. Rayne's different. She's not like us."

"Neither were you just a few months ago," Veronique says. "A few months ago, you weren't Akhet. Maybe Rayne is ready to transition too."

"What, like you're just going to wave your arms and magically Rayne is going to start remembering her past lives? Wouldn't that be convenient."

"I'm not a child!" Rayne yells at me. As she turns away, I catch a glimpse of something around her neck, hanging from a silver chain. "You don't have to stand here—"

"What is that?" I interrupt, pointing at her chest. The ankh isn't like any I've ever seen before—it has a black stone in the middle and some kind of hieroglyphic writing on the front. "Where did you get it?"

Rayne glances at Veronique and my fury boils up all over again. I can't believe it. "Take it off," I insist.

Rayne puts one hand over the pendant. "You're not my mother."

I grab her by the shoulders, wishing I could shake some sense into her. "I know you think this is some kind of romantic story, but it's not. Veronique is just making this whole thing up to fit some twisted agenda. Don't you remember what Griffon said? We shouldn't even be standing here talking to her."

I see a glimmer of doubt in her eyes, so I keep charging forward. "Veronique also thought I killed Alessandra. Her track record isn't all that good up to now. If you're so sure about what she's saying, call Griffon." I reach in my pocket and hold out my phone. "Call him right now and tell him where we are and what she's said."

"I don't know," Rayne hesitates. She glances at Veronique. "Everything she said made so much sense . . ."

I look into her eyes, willing Rayne to trust me. "Because she's very good at telling lies. That's what she does. Just because she wants you to be Alessandra, that doesn't mean it's true."

Rayne nods slowly, her eyes locked on mine. I don't know if she totally believes me, but I've managed to plant enough doubt to get her out of here. She reaches up and unclasps the chain from around her neck. "I'm sorry, Veronique," she says, her voice barely above a whisper as she hands it to her.

"I'm sorry too," I say, as I put one arm around her shoulder and lead her down the street.

Seventeen

A reggae festival? Since when do you go to reggae festivals?"

We walk out of the tunnel and into Golden Gate Park. The meadow is crowded with people dancing by the stage, pounding away in drum circles, lying on giant blankets staring at the sky, and standing in clumps playing hacky sack. Pretty much all the stuff we usually make fun of.

"You wanted to know what we were doing today," Rayne says, swinging Peter's arm back and forth. "This is what we're doing." I can tell from the edge in her voice that she's still a little bit mad at me.

"But reggae?" I wave my hand in front of my face to try to get rid of some of the pot smoke that's hanging in the air. After all the Veronique nonsense from yesterday, I'm glad to see her with Peter again. It took most of the day, but I finally managed to convince her that Veronique is full of crap. At least I think I did. Rayne is such a hopeless romantic that I can never be entirely sure. I'm just going to have to keep a close eye on her from now on.

"This is what's going on in the park today. Besides, it's free and it's a nice day, so stop complaining." Rayne rubs her arm and winces.

I glance down at her skin. "What's wrong? You're all red."

"I don't know," she says, looking at her arms. They're both a bright pink color. "I must have gotten sunburned without realizing it. It really hurts."

I look closely at her face. "Your cheeks are red too." I put one hand up to her forehead. "You feel hot. Are you getting sick?"

"I don't think so," she says. "But I do have a little headache."

"I have some Advil," I say, fishing around in my bag.

"It's okay," Rayne says. She puts her finger and her thumb on either side of her other hand and presses down. "I'll just do some acupressure. That should work."

I sigh. Rayne always wants to go the holistic route. "If you say so."

Peter puts one arm around her shoulders and I trudge along a few feet behind them. My phone buzzes, so I pull it out to glance at the number. I realize I'm smiling as I open up Drew's text.

What r u doing?

I text him back. *At a reggae fest in the park.*

No, seriously. Where r u?

Seriously. GGPark. With Rayne and her BF.

Drum circles and hacky sack?

I laugh out loud, and Rayne looks back at me. *You must be a regular.*

I rule at hacky sack.

Don't know if I would brag about that.

"Who is it?" Rayne asks.

I glance over at Peter. He still talks to Griffon. "Nobody."

You should know by now that I have many talents.

There's a pause for a few moments. And then he texts again.
I had fun on Friday.

I hesitate, not wanting to encourage something I can't finish. *Me too.*

Do it again soon?

I glance up and realize we've stopped walking. Peter is nodding his head to the music from a band that's on the stage, and Rayne is just looking at me. *Maybe. GTG.*

I slide the phone back in my pocket as we wander around the park looking at the booths full of tie-dye and pipes that are to be used for legal tobacco products only, if the signs posted are any indication.

We start down the hill toward another part of the festival with Peter leading the way, past the merry-go-round and through the playground back to the meadow. I look over and involuntarily glance up at the top of the cement slide that's carved into the side of the hill. At the top of the slide was where my life changed forever—where Griffon first told me about being Ahket.

Rayne untangles her arm from Peter's and reaches into her bag, catching my eye as I watch her. "Maybe . . . maybe that Advil . . . ," she says, but her words sound thick and heavy. I lean over and look at her carefully. Her face is flushed, and I can see through her sunglasses that she's squinting her eyes as if the light is hurting them. I start to say something to her about seeing a doctor when her bag slips off her shoulder. As she bends down to pick it up, she stumbles slightly, her body weaving as she tries to stand up straight.

"Rayne?" I say, taking a step toward her. "Are you okay?"

With immense effort, she turns to look at me, one hand pressing against her forehead. "I don't—" she begins, but her knees buckle and in an instant she's lying in a heap on the grass.

Peter drops to the ground beside her, cradling her head in his lap. "Rayne!" he calls. He rubs her cheek, but she just turns her head and moans, eyes shut tight and her jaw clenched against the pain.

"I'll call 911!" I shout, watching her motionless on the ground. I fumble in my pocket for my phone.

"There are some paramedics in the parking lot," a guy next to us says. "I'll go get them. It'll be faster."

People around us start noticing Rayne on the ground and push back to give us some space. I kneel down by her head, not having a clue what to do.

"Come on, Rayne," Peter says. "You'll be okay. Just hang on, you'll be okay." He repeats that over and over again like a chant as he holds her hand, one thumb rubbing her fingers. "You'll be okay."

It seems like forever, but finally two men in uniform push through the crowd carrying big medical boxes. "Out of the way!" they shout. "Give us room." They bend down, feeling for her pulse and checking her eyes. "Who's with this girl?" the blond one asks.

"We are," Peter says. "Is she going to be okay?"

The other guy speaks into a radio that's hanging at his shoulder, calling for the ambulance.

"What's she on?" he asks. "What did she take?"

I stare at him. They think she OD'd. "Nothing! She didn't take anything!"

He glances over and I know that he doesn't believe me. "Her pupils are huge. The best way to help your friend is to tell us what she took."

I lean in closer to him. "I'm telling you, she didn't take anything! Do something! Don't just sit there!"

Peter puts his arm around me, as much to hold me back as for comfort, I imagine. "Cole's right. One second she was fine, the next she was on the ground."

I glance from him to the paramedic, who nods, although I still don't know if he believes us. I take a deep breath and try to calm down. "She said she had a headache," I say, "and she was really hot."

He reaches for a syringe just as Rayne's eyes roll into the back of her head. Her fists clench and her legs jerk as her body arches up in a tremor. "She's posturing!" he shouts to the other guy. "Where's that ambulance? We need to get her out of here now!"

We stand there watching helplessly as waves of convulsions take over her body until they load her into the ambulance, slamming the doors as they speed out of the park.

We call Rayne's mom on the way to the car, and by the time we get to the hospital she's standing in the waiting room, looking lost. Her eyes are red and frantic, so I walk over and give her a hug. She holds me tight, and I know she's giving me what she'd rather be giving Rayne right now. "They asked me to leave the room," she says. "They're going to have to intubate her, and they don't want me in there." She looks at me and tears well up in her eyes. "She's not even breathing on her own. What happened?"

I squeeze her hand. "I don't know. She said she wasn't feeling well, and then she just collapsed on the ground."

"They said she might be on drugs. Did she take anything? You have to be honest with me."

"She's not on anything, I promise," Peter says. "Cole tried to give her an Advil and she didn't even want that. You know how she is."

"I know," her mom sniffs. "I'm so glad you two were with her." She puts one hand to her mouth. "I can't imagine what would have happened if she'd been alone."

"It just looks bad," I say. "She's going to get through this just fine." I say that to convince all of us, because any other outcome is inconceivable. "Where's Sienna?" Rayne's sister should be here instead of me.

Rayne's mom looks up, momentarily confused. "I . . . um . . . I think she's at work. I should call her."

"I'll do it if you want me to," I say.

She glances at the commotion in the emergency room. "No, I will. She should hear it from me."

Before she can move, a nurse pokes her head out of the emergency room. "Mrs. Foreman? Your daughter is stable for now. We're going to transfer her up to the ICU. You're welcome to come up, but I'm afraid everyone else will have to stay in the waiting room. We have to limit visitors, at least for tonight."

We walk to the doorway as her mom looks at us with panic in her eyes. "ICU. That's bad, isn't it?"

Peter puts a hand on her arm. "It's the best place for her right now. She's going to be okay."

The curtains are pulled back, and through the team of doctors and nurses that surround her, I can see Rayne lying flat on the rolling bed, a tube down her throat and tape on her mouth as one nurse squeezes a bag every few seconds to help her breathe. One hand pokes through the railing they've put up around the mattress, and more than anything I want to grab it, to give the fingers with the chipped blue nail polish a reassuring squeeze, but before I can make a move, they're halfway down the hall.

Rayne's mom hesitates for just a second. "Where are all of her things? Her purse, her phone? She never goes anywhere without her phone."

"I've got everything," I say. "Go with her. I'll bring her stuff home and you can get it later."

"Thanks," her mom says, tears shining in her eyes as she turns to follow the crowd of people toward the elevator.

Eighteen

I hold the soft edge of Mum's sari in my fingers and feel a flood of emotions that aren't mine. Sadness, definitely. That's to be expected, even though I've told her over and over again that I'll be okay. I'm ready to go. I put one hand up to her face, my fingers exploring her mouth as it turns down in the corners and the dampness her tears leave in the corners of her eyes. She sits completely still and lets me.

"Mummy, don't be sad. You'll make it harder."

I can hear her sniff, even though she's trying to cover it up. "I know. You're going to have a wonderful time in England and learn so many things. I'm just going to miss you."

"Me too," I say. "I'll be home soon, though." There's something else—excitement, an undercurrent that's almost giddy. I can tell she's trying to suppress it, but it's there just as clearly as

if I can see it with my own eyes. I hesitate, then lean into her before whispering, "I know you have a secret."

Mum pulls her hand out of mine and I feel her move a small distance away. "Secret? I don't have a secret."

I turn my face in the direction of her voice. "You do. I can feel it."

I hear her gasp. "How can you possibly feel it? The baby is still so small—it will be many more months before it is born."

Baby. Mummy is going to have another baby. That's the secret she's been keeping. Daddy too. I pretend like I knew this all along. "I just can," I say, as mysteriously as possible.

"No secret is safe around you lately." Even though she doesn't say it out loud, I know what she means. Now that my eyes are gone, everything else has been pushed into vivid focus. Sounds are louder, touch is more sensitive. And that small voice we all carry inside is much more insistent.

"Isn't that as it should be?" I smile at her. "And soon you will have a new baby, so you will not miss me as much."

Mum presses me to her chest. Even though all I see is blackness, I inhale the familiar powdery scent and feel her heart beating through her sari. "I will always miss you just as much," she says, and even without listening to the voice inside, I know she means every word.

I blink in the darkness, and for a second I can't tell whether my eyes are open or not, just like in the dream. Lying still, I let my mind wander over what I've just seen and realize that it wasn't a dream, it was another memory.

Gradually, my eyes adjust to the dim light in my room, and I can make out a faint gray light that outlines the closed curtains. I've only been asleep for a couple of hours, but I'm amazed that I managed to doze off at all. In a rush, the events of yesterday come flooding back and I roll onto my side, curling my legs under me. My stomach lurches as I think about Rayne being wheeled out of the room, the bag filled with air the only thing keeping her alive.

Sitting on the edge of my bed, I grab my cell but see only the screensaver, no new texts. I hesitate only a second before I begin typing the letters. Early morning, late night; time doesn't mean much in this kind of a crisis.

How is she?

Peter texts back almost immediately. *About the same. Won't let me see her.* I can picture him sitting in the hard plastic chairs of the waiting room. Maybe if I come, he'll go home for a little while.

I'm coming. Coffee?

Pls. Lots.

I pull on my jeans, trying not to think past getting to the hospital. After scribbling a quick note, I hurry through the quiet house and out the door, holding my breath for fear that I'll wake someone and have to explain why I'm going out so early in the morning. Mom and Dad will argue that there's nothing I can do for Rayne right now. They don't get that I'm not going for Rayne. I'm going for me, because I can't stand not to.

I run up to Haight Street and turn the corner, alternately running and walking a few steps in order to catch my breath. The street is practically deserted—all of the stores still have their metal grates solidly in front of their doors, although the smell of coffee drifts in the air as the cafés get ready to open for the day. The few humans on the sidewalk are hidden in doorways by lumps of rags or tattered sleeping bags, their spare-change cups empty but at the ready by their sides.

Café Sienna is already buzzing with life when I get there. I glance toward the back, half expecting to see Veronique at the table, but for the moment it's empty. I get coffee for all three of us on a brown cardboard tray and load my pockets up with sugar, because I have no idea how Peter or Rayne's mom take it.

The bus stops just outside the hospital, and soon I'm balancing the drinks as I walk through the lobby toward the elevators. The security guard at the information booth doesn't look up as I pass.

Peter's the only one in the tenth-floor waiting room when I get there, sprawled out over a couple of chairs, the unwatched TV blaring in the corner. "Thanks," he manages when I hand him one of the cups. He looks exhausted, but the dark circles under his eyes and the day's growth of stubble make him look somehow even cuter than usual. I take out my phone and snap a picture of his scruffiness.

"What was that for?"

"For Rayne, when she gets better." Because she has to get better. "Do you want some sugar?" I toss the packets onto the table.

Peter takes a sip. "No. I'm not sure I'll even be able to get this down in the first place."

"Is her mom in there?" I nod toward the locked doors of the ICU. Unlike downstairs, here you have to be buzzed in by the nurses.

"Yeah. She's been there most of the night. She tried to get me to go home, but I'm not leaving until I see Rayne. And even then, I'm not sure."

I don't try to talk sense into him, because I know exactly how he feels. We sip our coffee quietly and watch the minutes tick by on the wall clock. I get up and walk over to the window. The view is amazing from way up here; you can see the whole city. I wonder how long it's going to be before Rayne will be able to appreciate it.

"Cole!" Rayne's mom says, walking into the waiting room. Her hair is wild, with only a few strands still contained in their original ponytail. "What are you doing here so early?"

"I couldn't sleep. How is she?"

She sighs. "Stable, finally. They had to take her off the ventilator and bag her twice during the night." Her eyes fill with tears. "I thought we were going to lose her."

I wrap my arms around her neck and she hugs me back. After taking a deep breath, she continues. "She's in a coma right now. Unresponsive, but they still don't know why. They're going to wait until later this morning and then take her down for a CAT scan as long as she stays stable." She looks at Peter. "Do you want to see her?"

He sits up. "Of course."

Rayne's mom goes to sit next to him. "It's not easy. She barely looks like herself, and there are tubes everywhere. But there can be two at a time in the room with her. Do you want me to go with you?"

Peter looks up at me. "Take Cole first. She's Rayne's best friend."

I shake my head. "No way. You've been here all night. You go now, I'll go after." I don't say so, but I need a little more time to get myself together before I can face her.

He stands up, his legs a little shaky. "If you're sure." He rubs his hands over the front of his jeans, and I can tell he's nervous too.

"I'll be right here." I take his still-warm seat, feeling like the job of holding up hope has now been transferred to me. They're only in there for about ten minutes, but it feels like hours before they come back to the waiting room, Peter wiping tears away with the sleeve of his jacket. Rayne's mom has a hand on his shoulder. "It's going to be okay. You were great."

He looks stricken as he takes a seat next to me. He nods. "You should go. It's hard, but she needs us more than ever." Peter takes a deep breath and seems calmer.

"Are you sure you want to?" Rayne's mom asks.

"I'm sure," I say, following her into the hallway. "They don't have any idea what's wrong?" I ask, as we reach the double doors.

She shakes her head sadly. "Not really. They ruled out meningitis last night, which is a relief. As far as they can tell, something neurological is causing her organs to fail one by one. Her oxygen levels were rough all night, and now her kidney function looks compromised." She gives me an encouraging squeeze. "But they'll figure it out, I'm sure of it. And as soon as they do, we'll know how to treat her."

Even as the words come out of her mouth, I know she doesn't fully believe that. She's worried that the doctors won't find the cause of the trouble in time. And I don't blame her.

"We need to wash our hands at the sink right outside the door," she says as we approach the nurse's station. "And then use the hand sanitizer that's just on the other side. They're really worried about infection in here."

We're buzzed through the heavy double doors, and it's like entering another world, dim and quiet except for the beeping of machines and the whoosh of assorted ventilators. The nurses seem to walk on air as they check tubes and type on portable monitors.

"She's down at the end," Rayne's mom whispers. We walk by several people lying in curtained beds, but I can't bring myself to look at any of them. Instead, I focus on a clock that's on the opposite wall, slowly ticking toward six a.m. "Here we are," she says, still quiet but with a forced sense of levity. "Rayne," she says to the figure on the bed. "Cole came by to see you, isn't that nice?"

She leans over and whispers to me. "You can touch her, but just watch the machines."

I nod, unable to trust my voice. The only thing recognizable about Rayne is her hair. Everything else looks alien. She's lying flat on the mattress with a tube coming out of her mouth that's hooked up to a big square machine right next to the bed; it makes a rhythmic pounding sound as it forces air into her lungs. There's tape on her cheeks to hold the tube down, and more tape holding more tubes to the back of her hand. Someone pulled a blanket up to her chest, but wires and tubes snake out from under it to more machines on either side of her head and to IV bags that are hanging on a pole. There's a plastic clip on her index finger with a red light on the end, and I notice that someone has taken off all of her blue nail polish, although her fingers still have a slightly bluish tint, as though they're cold.

Rayne's mom sees my glance. "They're monitoring the color of her fingers," she whispers. "She's been having some circulation problems." She looks on the other side of the curtain. "I'm going to go check with one of the nurses. I'll be right back."

Rayne's mom walks away, and I know this might be my only chance. I take a deep breath and reach for Rayne's lifeless hand, being careful not to disturb the monitor on her finger or the tubes that are stuck into the veins on the back of her hand. I direct my thoughts through my body and into hers, hoping that she's with us enough to understand. *It's okay, Rayne. I'm here with you. Just show me what's going on. I can help.*

I grip her fingers lightly, but I don't feel anything at all. Somewhere in the distance I can still hear the beeping of the monitor, so I squeeze my eyes shut tighter. I hold my breath as I wait, but I get no sensations.

I open my eyes again and look around the room. Through an opening in the curtain around the bed I can see Rayne's mom still talking to the nurse. I watch the lines in the monitors go up and down in rhythm and look at Rayne lying so still on the bed—right here with us, but still so impossibly far away. I'm the only one who can reach her, and I'm doing a crappy job of it. Her mom and the nurse will be back soon; I've only got moments to get through to her.

Taking another deep breath, I try to clear everything else away. In my mind I can hear Janine telling me to relax and get out of my own way, so I close my eyes and focus on that, pushing my thoughts through my chest and down my arms to where my fingers are touching Rayne's. I picture a channel opening between the two of us, just like Janine taught me.

In an instant, I'm bombarded by confusing images—*children riding bareback, their long black hair flowing in the wind as they race along the base of a snow-covered mountain . . . a dance in a fancy drawing room where women in puffy, ornate gowns link arms with men in short pants and stockings as a small orchestra plays off to one side . . . hundreds of people in colorful clothes dancing barefoot on the muddy ground as a band plays loud rock music from a stage half a football field away.* And then there's pain. It's only fleeting, like a radio station that's not tuned correctly, but sputtering and intense. My skin feels like it's on fire, and my fingers ache like someone's squeezing them in a vise. I feel panic rising from somewhere deep inside, like being trapped underwater. I can see the surface and want more than anything to get there, but all I can do is sink farther toward the bottom.

Rayne's mom puts one hand on my shoulder and I gasp, coming back to the present. "Go ahead, talk to her," she says gently. "She'll hear you."

I watch Rayne's face for any sign that I connected with her just now, that what I just experienced is what she's seeing. I take her hand again, ready for more images and sensations, but all I feel is the cool dryness of her skin. I can't control the connections. It's more like they control me, and I feel weak and faint from the effort just now. "I'm here, Rayne," I say softly, leaning in close. "Peter's out in the other room just waiting for another chance to get in here and see you. We can't get him to leave; he looks so scruffy and cute."

I look over at Rayne's mom and she nods encouragement. "One of us is always here," I say. "We're not going to leave you alone. You just make sure you stay with us, okay? Hang in there. I know it's tough."

A nurse has been hovering by the curtain, but now she leans in toward Rayne's bed. "I have to take her vitals now. We need to let her rest."

"Okay," I say. "I'll be back soon." I give Rayne's fingers one last squeeze, and it might be my imagination, but I think I feel the faintest pressure back.

Rayne's mom puts one arm around me as we walk back down the hallway, and I lean into her just a little bit. It feels like my legs are stuck in quicksand and I know I need to sit down soon. "You did great, honey," she says. "I'm sure it really helped."

My mind is racing with the images I saw and the sensations I felt. I was *with* Rayne in there, wherever she is right now. I could feel her pain and her frustration as she tries to stay with us.

"I'm going to go back and sit with her," Rayne's mom says. "See if you can get Peter to go home, at least for a little while."

"I will," I say, pushing back through the double doors. I've got to sit down soon, or I feel like I might pass out.

"Her numbers are looking better," I say as I walk into the waiting area, but I stop cold in the doorway. Peter's not alone. For a second, I think about running out of the room, but I know my legs won't carry me very far.

The two of them look up, and I see damp tears in the corner of Peter's eyes. He glances at Griffon and then at me. "Um . . ."

My legs buckle for real then, and I'm grateful for the chair that's leaning against the wall as I sink into it. I feel like I'm going to throw up, so I put my head down toward my knees, knowing I look like an idiot, but glad to get away from Griffon's eyes.

"Cole," Griffon says with alarm, and I feel his hand on my forehead. As soon as he touches me, he pulls back, obviously remembering that we're light-years away from physical contact at the moment. He kneels down. "You look pale. Are you okay?"

I try to sit up, knowing that I look wobbly. "Yeah." I take another deep breath. The nausea seems to be passing, although my heart feels like it's beating out of my chest. "I'm okay. I just haven't eaten much today, that's all."

"Is there a vending machine around here?" Griffon asks Peter. "She needs a Pepsi or something."

"There's one two floors down. I'll go," Peter says and dashes out the doorway, clearly glad to get away from whatever scene he imagines is about to happen.

Griffon squats down in front of me. "What did you do?"

The creak of his leather jacket as he moves and the faint, spicy scent coming from his body is too much. I put my head in my hands, feeling totally overwhelmed. "What do you mean?"

"Just now. Your Akhet vibrations are all wrong. Faint and out of synch."

Staring at the speckled linoleum floor, I reply, "I made contact with Rayne. For a few seconds I could feel what she's feeling." I stop. How can I explain to him that I could also see images, like her thoughts were somehow transmitted into my head?

"And now you feel terrible? You've got to be careful using your empath skills like that. You don't know what that could do to you."

I look up at him for the first time, taking in the power of his warm, amber eyes. Eyes I'd not quite managed to forget over the past few weeks. His hair is a lot shorter—without the curls he looks older, and I have to fight the urge to reach out and run my hand over the smooth suede at the back of his neck. "What else am I supposed to do? Just watch her die? I'll do anything I can to stop that from happening, no matter what it does to me."

I hear footsteps in the doorway, but it's not Peter. "Is she okay?" Giselle asks, stepping into the room.

Griffon turns. "I think so. Just weak from connecting with Rayne."

Giselle sits down next to me in a hard plastic chair, and I can smell the flowery, soapy scent of her perfume. "So she can really do this? Cole is really an empath, as you say?"

I stare at her. "I'm right here."

Her mouth straightens into a tight line. "Of course. I'm so sorry. That was rude. Are you feeling better?"

"I'll survive." I look at Griffon, wondering why he brought her here. She has nothing to do with Rayne.

Griffon looks at Giselle and then back at me. "We're on our way to the Peninsula," he explains. "We have a meeting with the architects who are designing the new lab." He pauses. "What did you sense? When you were in with Rayne?"

I take a deep breath and try to pick things out of the jumble of senses and images. "She's really confused." I pause. "And there are a lot of images going through her head. Almost like memories, but a lot more random."

"Wait," Griffon says, staring at me. "What do you mean you saw her memories? I thought you could only sense other people's emotions, not read their minds."

"I don't know." I look up at him. "I was connecting with her, and it was like I could see what was going on in her mind and how she was feeling at the same time." I take a deep breath, not sure I can explain something that I don't totally understand. "Not exactly like watching a movie; it was more like the impression of the things she was thinking. Does that make sense?"

Griffon's studying me closely. "Sort of. But I've never heard of anything like this before. What kind of images did you see?"

I close my eyes and try to remember. "Crazy things that don't seem to fit together. A flash of one scene and then a flash of another. None of it makes any sense."

"Like a hallucination?" Giselle offers.

"Maybe," I say, nodding. "Her head is splitting with pain and her skin hurts, like it's on fire."

I see a look pass between the two of them. "Anything else?" Griffon prompts.

"Her fingers. Her fingers ache badly, like they're being squeezed really tight. They're almost blue, and her mom said she's having problems with her circulation."

Griffon stands up in front of me and folds his arms, looking at Giselle as if he's trying to confirm something. "Meningitis, maybe?"

"No." I shake my head. "Her mom said they ruled it out last night."

"Okay. That's good."

"Can you think of any other symptoms?" Giselle asks. "Anything you might have noticed yesterday?"

I think back to the blur of yesterday afternoon. Was it only yesterday? It feels like a lifetime ago. "Um . . . she had some really violent convulsions, and they kept saying that her pupils were dilated. The paramedics thought that she was on something."

"Hmm. Interesting." Griffon looks at Giselle. "What do you think?"

She purses her lips thoughtfully. "If it's not meningitis, then it's still something that's affecting her nervous system."

"How quickly did it start?" Griffon asks me. "Was she feeling sick for a long time?"

"No," I said. "That's what's so weird. For most of the day she was fine. Then she just said that she had a headache and it felt like she had a fever. The next thing I knew, she was flat on the ground."

Griffon paces a little in front of me. I sit as quietly as possible so I don't interfere with his thinking. "Okay," he finally says, more to Giselle than to me. "This is going to sound crazy, but what about ergotoxicosis?"

Her eyes grow wide. "Saint Anthony's fire? Maybe. But we haven't had that in this country for centuries."

"I saw a lot of it in Italy the lifetime I transitioned—all the symptoms are there," Griffon says, shaking his head. "But where would she have gotten it?"

"I seriously doubt that it would appear organically," Giselle says. "Not now."

"Okay, what are you guys talking about?" I ask. They're speaking so quickly I can barely keep up.

"Ergot is a fungus that causes symptoms like you've described," Giselle explains. "It started on rye seeds and was common throughout the Middle Ages. It causes hallucinations, convulsions, and gangrene."

"Ergotoxicosis caused the Salem witch trials—the accusers were actually hallucinating because of the fungus. The convulsions made for a nice show," Griffon says, and I wonder if he got to see that in person.

"And there are rumors that an ergot outbreak in late 1024 caused spontaneous Akhet transitions in thousands of people in Germany," Giselle says. "But we haven't seen it in any part of the world for decades."

"Wait, something can *cause* a person to become Akhet?"

Griffon gives Giselle a sharp look. "It's only a theory, and most Akhet don't believe it. An unusual number of Akhet transitioned that year, and the only thing they had in common was a critical case of Saint Anthony's fire. But it's never happened again."

I feel a momentary panic as I remember what Veronique said about Rayne being ready to transition. "Could someone make the fungus? Like in a lab?"

Giselle shrugs. "I suppose so. There has been talk of people trying to synthesize the ergot mycotoxin, but as far as I know, nobody has ever succeeded. Why? Who do you know that would do this to your friend?"

"Veronique," I say quietly. I don't want to believe she'd go this far. But I know she would.

Griffon's head snaps around. "What?"

"She's been seeing Rayne again," I explain. "She has this idea that Rayne is the essence of Alessandra. I told her that it wasn't true, but she's completely convinced."

"And she's a microbiologist, so she has the skills," Griffon finishes for me. I can feel his anger as he speaks. "Plus, she's just crazy enough to try it. Why didn't you tell me?"

"You haven't exactly been around," I snap at him. "But it doesn't matter. What does matter is, what do we do now? If it is what you think, is there a cure?"

"Not exactly," Griffon says. "And if it goes untreated, convulsive ergotism can be fatal."

Fatal. "So why are we just sitting here? What can we do?"

"Hang on, there are treatments. Vasodialators and anticoagulants, along with Ativan to stop the hallucinations."

"How are we going to tell the doctors? There's no way they're going to believe a couple of teenagers diagnosing a disease that disappeared centuries ago."

Giselle reaches into her bag and pulls out a laminated medical identification tag from a hospital in Switzerland. "I've got this one."

Of course. She's a doctor too. "What are you going to say?"

She clips the tag onto her jacket. "That I'm a friend of the family and that I've seen this in rural outposts on my trips with Médecins Sans Frontières. All I have to do is point them in the right direction—once they do the research, they'll figure it out for themselves."

Giselle stands up and strides through the ICU doors like she owns the place. Peter's still not back, and I'm acutely aware that Griffon and I are alone in the waiting room. At that moment my phone buzzes, and I can tell from his glance that Griffon hears it too. I check the display, but put it quickly back into my pocket. Not a call I want to take right now.

A flash of understanding passes across Griffon's face. "It's Drew, isn't it?" His eyes, which had been so soft and concerned, turn hard and gleaming.

"Does it matter?" I say, putting every ounce of hurt and frustration I feel into my words. "You've already decided how things are going to be."

"I just saved us both pain and aggravation because I already know how it would end." His mouth is set so tight he can barely speak.

"And what about what I want? You took that totally out of the equation."

I see a flash of indecision in his eyes, but he quickly turns away. "Look, I came here for Peter," Griffon says evenly. "And for Rayne." I can't see his face, but the silence that follows that sentence says volumes. He didn't come here for me.

Nineteen

My pocket is vibrating. I sit up straight in the chair, blinking in the dim light of the waiting room. I've been staring at the same four walls for two days now, only leaving when my parents demand that I come home because of the ridiculous notion that my staying here might somehow be doing Rayne some good. The hope that I had when Griffon first diagnosed the problem is starting to fade with every passing day, and whenever I think of the hostile words we said to each other even as Rayne might be dying, I feel sick to my stomach.

I glance over at Peter's chair, but for once it's empty. The only other people in the waiting room are an older couple quietly eating lunch out of plastic containers, and I wonder where Peter could be.

My phone vibrates again and I pull it out of my pocket. I told

Drew the basics of what happened to Rayne and I know he's concerned, but I can't deal with talking to him right now.

Suddenly, I need to move, to feel like I'm doing something, even if that something is totally useless. I'm not sure where I'm going to go, but I can't sit here any longer. I'm pressing the elevator button when Rayne's mom comes rushing down the hall.

"Cole! Wait!" she calls, slightly out of breath. "Rayne wants to see you."

"She—what?" I must have heard her wrong.

I see tears in her eyes, but she's smiling underneath it all. "She asked for you. She's awake, can you believe it? She can't talk because of the ventilator, but she has a notepad to communicate."

"How?" I manage.

Her mom shrugs happily and gives me a quick hug. "The doctors figured out that it's some crazy disease that they thought died out a hundred years ago and gave her some medication for it. It's a miracle. They say that if she continues to improve, they'll take her off the ventilator tomorrow or the next day. Do you want to see her?"

"Of course," I say, following her through the double doors. I can't believe they listened to Giselle. There's a change in the room, like a heavy cloud has been lifted. As soon as I pull back the curtains around her bed, Rayne looks straight at me, her eyes a mixture of pain and relief. She lifts one hand and motions me toward her bed.

"Go on," Rayne's mom says to me. She leans over the bed to talk to Rayne. "I'm going to get some of those lemon swabs the nurse said you can have, okay? I'll be right back."

Rayne nods with a small but decisive motion.

I stand next to the bed, amazed at the change in her, feeling suddenly awkward. Rayne points to the notepad that's on the table by the foot of her bed. I pick it up and hand her the pen that's lying next to it. Her fingers are still not working right, so she grips it awkwardly in her fist as I hold the pad up near her face.

You did, Rayne writes in a sprawling, nearly unreadable print.

"'I did'?" I say. I look at her and she nods toward the pad. "I did? What did I do?"

Felt u. She puts the pen down for a second and I can sense her exhaustion. It takes a moment before she can continue. *Here.*

"I've been here the whole time," I tell her.

Fixed this. Rayne has to put the pen down on the bed; the effort is taking too much out of her. Her eyes are wide open, expecting an explanation.

I look around, but all of the nurses are busy with other patients. I lean down close to her face. "I just helped figure out what was wrong. Griffon diagnosed what it was and told them what to give you to fix it."

Rayne points to the floor, and I know right away what she means. "Yes," I say. "Griffon was here. Peter too—I'm sure he's still around here somewhere."

Rayne looks at me with her eyes wide open, and I can almost hear her question. "No. Everything's still the same with me and Griffon. But that doesn't matter. What matters is that he figured it out and you're going to be okay."

I see one lone tear trickle down her cheek as she closes her eyes, exhausted from the effort of communicating. "I should go find Peter for you," I say, even though I know she's already asleep. I reach up to brush the tear away, but something catches my attention as my finger touches her skin. I pull back, startled, and then tentatively reach out to touch her one more time, to make sure I'm not imagining things. But I feel it again, and I hold my hand there to make sure there's no mistake.

The vibrations coming from her are the same ones that I've learned to recognize in others over the past few months. I stare at her, sleeping fitfully, and can't believe it's happened. The one thing in all of this craziness that I never even considered possible has actually happened. Veronique, for all her desperation and manipulation, actually did it.

Rayne's Akhet now.

Even as I'm listening to Zander butcher my favorite Chopin piece, I have one eye on my phone propped up on the music stand, willing it to ring. Rayne and her mom both insisted I leave the hospital and get on with my life, but my mind is still back there with them. I must have left five messages for Janine on the ride between the hospital and the studio. She hasn't called me back and it's killing me to not talk about Rayne with someone. I've given her until five o'clock, and if she doesn't call by then, I'm going to Veronique's lab alone. If it really was ergotoxicosis, then I know exactly where Rayne got it and why.

I touch my jacket pocket to make sure Veronique's business card is still safe inside. Thank God I kept it from last year when she introduced herself at one of my concerts; otherwise I wouldn't have a clue where to find her.

We're finishing up a particularly screechy section when my phone finally jumps to life. I grab it and look through the window in the practice-room door around the hallway and down toward the lounge, but there are parents and students everywhere. I glance at Zander, who looks so bored he's barely conscious. "Do you care if I take this?"

"Whatever," he says, dropping the bow and grabbing his phone out of his pocket. He's immersed in a game before I can even answer mine.

I turn my back to Zander, even though he's not paying any attention. "Janine! Thank God!"

"I must have gotten half a dozen messages from you," she says. "But you were talking so fast I barely understood anything. What's going on? Is Rayne okay?"

"I think so," I say, trying to stay calm and make sense. "At least she will be. Did Griffon tell you what Veronique did?"

"Yes, but I can't believe it. The whole link between ergotoxicosis and Akhet transition is just a myth, a theory that some Iawi use to explain a particular period when there was a lot of activity. It's crazy to think that someone would actually try it."

I hesitate. "Well, it must have been ergotoxicosis, because the medicine they're giving her seems to be working. But that's not why I called." I look over my shoulder at Zander, but he's still totally absorbed in his game. And even if he was listening, he wouldn't understand anything anyway. "Veronique was right!" I whisper. "It worked. Rayne transitioned! I could feel the vibrations when I went in to see her."

There's total silence on Janine's end.

"Did you hear me?"

"I did," she says slowly. "But do you realize what you're say-ing? If this is true, it could have enormous implications for the world. For the future."

"But I'm sure about what I felt. Rayne is Akhet. It's in-credible!"

"Look, I'm not saying I don't believe you, but creating Akhet is impossible. It's something that happens to the essence organ-ically. Maybe you were just excited to see that she was getting better."

"That has nothing to do with it." I feel fear gnawing at my stomach. I never thought she wouldn't believe me. "I know what I felt. I'll take you with me so you can see for yourself. I may be Shewi, but I'm not an idiot."

"I believe you," Janine says quickly. "I'm sorry. It's just so hard to get my head around it. Don't talk to anyone else about this, okay? We need to find Veronique and see what she's done. Do you have any idea where we can find her?"

"Her lab's in Mission Bay," I say. I reach into my pocket and pull out the card. "The University Annex. I can meet you down there in forty-five minutes." I read the address to her.

"Got it," Janine says. "I'm going to get some people to go down and check it out. Stay by your phone and I'll let you know what we find out."

Just sit by the phone? That's my role in this? "But I think I should—"

"Stay there," she insists. "Leave this to Akhet who have a lot more experience than you do. It could be dangerous."

More dangerous than standing on a rooftop three stories up with a gun aimed at my head? I got through that episode with

Veronique okay, and I'm a little irritated at Janine's patronizing tone. "I can handle it," I say firmly. If I hadn't called her, they wouldn't know anything about this.

"The best thing for you to do is sit tight. I know it's hard, but you've done your part. I'll call you back," Janine says with a clipped tone, and my phone goes dead.

"I'll call you back," I mimic out loud.

That gets Zander's attention. "Fight with the boyfriend?"

"No," I say, but I notice my hands are shaking as I put my phone back in my bag. I glance at the clock. Only five minutes left in our lesson, but there's no way I can concentrate now. It feels like big things are happening while I'm forced to sit behind the scenes and wait. I want to confront Veronique, want to do something horrible to her like she keeps doing to the people who are close to me. She's a selfish, crazy Akhet scientist, and I want to be there when they take her down. Instead, I'm stuck in the studio waiting by the phone. "How about we cut this lesson a little short?"

Zander shoves his phone back in his pocket. "Works for me."

"Go to the lounge and get a juice box," I say. "And walk really slowly. Like, five minutes' worth of slowly."

He shoves the music in his backpack and closes the cello case. "I got this." We stand up and I hold the door open for him.

He leans toward me. "And if you ever need relationship advice, I'm your man."

I stare at him, slightly disgusted. His head barely reaches my shoulder. "Just. Go."

Twenty

The sky is streaked with orange as I finally step off the bus. It's actually not all that far from the studio, but this part of the city seems like it's worlds away. Despite the fact that it's after regular working hours, there are still people coming out of the green-glassed building.

I cross the street, rehearsing the words I've practiced all the way over here. I'm sure there's a guard or a doorman or something—they're not going to let just anyone walk into a university research facility. Pulling the heavy front door open, I run through my story in my head one more time. I'm almost disappointed to find that the front desk is empty. The few people I see on this floor are just rifling through their tote bags for their keys or tapping on their phones on their way to the exit. Nobody is paying any attention to a sixteen-year-old girl looking lost in the lobby. All of the doors—including the elevator—have slots for card keys, and I know I'm not going to get very far without one. I hear a ding behind me as the silver doors slide open and an older man in a black button-down shirt walks out of the elevator.

"Ooh! Hold that, please," I call, and scurry across the lobby.

He stares into his phone as he holds the door open for me. "Thanks," I say breathlessly. "I'm here to see my cousin..." I begin my story, but he's already halfway across the lobby floor, heading straight for the front door. As the doors slide closed, I punch the button for the fifth floor and wonder if Janine and the other Sekhem are already here. I didn't have enough money for a cab and the busses were running their usual rush-hour-slow, so it took longer than I'd hoped to get here.

The hallway is quiet and deserted as the elevator doors open—I must have beaten them here anyway. I stop, looking at the numbers on the doors. In my mind, I hadn't gotten any further than this; I figured I'd get to the lab and watch as the Sekhem dealt with Veronique. I didn't count on being here all by myself. I turn back to the elevator, thinking that they can't be very far behind, when I see my reflection in the brushed metal doors. I look small and young, like someone who's lost in a much bigger world. Except that I don't feel like that person anymore. I feel like someone who needs to start making things happen. To show Janine and the Sekhem that I'm not just some Shewi who needs their help to do everything.

I turn and face the empty hallway again. There are nothing but identical doors on each side, marching toward a window that looks out over the bay. Veronique's lab number means that her room must be down toward the end. As I take a few cautious steps in that direction, I start to think about what I'm going to say when I get there. *What the hell were you thinking?* seems like a good place to start, but I'm going to have to trust myself this time. I'll figure something out.

Two rooms down from the end of the hallway, the door that matches Veronique's number is open just a crack. It's too small to see through, so I push it with my finger and it inches open a little farther. I can feel my heart pounding in my chest, and I take a deep breath to try to calm down.

"Hello? Veronique?" I call, pushing the door open all the way. I don't see anyone, but the lab is completely trashed. Papers and broken glass litter every surface; two stools have been over-turned, and another one is lying on a black countertop. Entire drawers have been pulled out and emptied onto the floor. It feels like the room is still in motion—as if the papers have just fin-ished fluttering to the floor. I jump back, scared that someone might still be here, but a quick glance around tells me the lab is empty. I take a few cautious steps into the room, glass crunching under my feet even though I'm trying to avoid messing anything up. The Sekhem sure worked fast—they must have been in and out before I even got off the bus. I wonder if they found what they were looking for. And if they took Veronique with them.

I peek around the island in the middle of the room and see a pool of reddish-brown blood on the floor. She must have put up a hell of a fight. How did they get her out of here without anyone seeing them?

I hear footsteps pounding down the hallway, and for a split second a jolt of fear races through my body—they must have come back for something. Janine told me to stay out of this.

What are the Sekhem going to do when they find me here? Before I can react, the door is thrust open, and I don't know who is more surprised, me or Griffon.

He takes just a second to recover at the sight of me, standing in the middle of the mess. "What happened?"

"I'm not sure. I think the Sekhem had to take things further than Janine thought; there's a ton of blood on the other side of this counter."

Griffon grabs my arm and pulls me back toward the open door. For an instant I get a sense that he wants to protect me. It makes me both irritated and grateful. "This wasn't the Sekhem," he says, his voice rising with alarm. "I'm the first one here— everyone else is coming up behind me."

I feel a shiver run down my back. "You mean this was someone else? Who? Nobody else knows."

He takes in the room at a glance. "We don't know who else Veronique told. She's insane—she might have talked about this to almost anyone." Griffon runs his hand over his newly short hair with a pained expression on his face.

I can sense his anxiety. "What do you mean?"

"If you're right, and Rayne transitioned—"

"I *am* right," I insist.

Griffon ignores my interruption. "Then this might be a very big deal." He looks down at my hands. "Did you touch anything?"

I shake my head. "Just the door. I got here just a few seconds before you did."

That seems to calm him some. "Good. That's good."

"Shouldn't we call 911 or something?"

"No." Griffon looks at me like I'm stupid. "We'll handle this ourselves. The university won't even know that anything was wrong by the time we leave tonight." He looks back down the empty hallway. "You should go before everyone gets here."

"I don't want to go. This is as much about me as it is about you."

Griffon looks surprised. "It's just easier if you stay out of this."

"But what about Veronique? What if they found what they were looking for?"

"We have people all over—we'll be able to figure out who did this. And to stop what she's created from getting into the wrong hands." He hesitates. "Look, Cole, it's just better for everyone if you stay invisible for now. Once you're in the Sehkem, there's no turning back. You need this time to transition and develop your skills. That's what I'm trying to give you—more time. Now quit being so stubborn and take it."

I'm about to protest when I stop. I can see the truth behind his words and how intensely he believes in them. He's trying to do this for me. "Okay. For now. But . . ." I'm about to ask him to call me when I remember where we are, who we are to each other now. "Make sure Janine calls me."

"I will." He looks relieved. "Now go."

I run back down the hall and push the elevator button. The one on the left opens almost immediately and I get in, pushing the button for the ground floor. Before the doors can close, I hear the other elevator ding and a rush of footsteps as people get off. I push myself into the corner as I see the backs of several men rush down the hall. Just before the sliding doors meet, Giselle stops in midstride as if I'd shouted at her and turns to look directly at me. I catch my breath as the elevator jerks and starts down, my reflection barely recognizable in the metal doors.

"Staying in tonight?" Mom asks as she passes my doorway.

I look up from my laptop. "Yeah. I'm tired."

She leans against the doorframe. "It's been a tough couple of days, hasn't it?"

I laugh, thinking about how much she doesn't know. How much she'll never know. "I haven't been sleeping much."

"Well, now that Rayne's on the mend, that should get better. Do you have any lessons tomorrow?"

"Not until eleven," I say.

"Good, you can sleep in. I'm going to go watch the late news if you want to come sit with me."

"Maybe I will in a minute," I say. I turn back to my search as she walks down the hallway. I'm trying to see if Veronique belonged to any clubs or hung out with anyone that might give a hint about who might have beaten us to the lab. For a brilliant young biochemist, she has a surprisingly small Internet foot-print. I'm scanning through some entries about her research in college when I hear Mom shout from the living room.

"What?" I say from the doorway.

"Quick!" she says. "Come in here!"

I rush to the living room in time to hear the reporter say "... cause of death is unknown at this time." He's standing in a marshy field lit by spotlights, and I can see airplanes taking off somewhere behind him. The headline scrolling down below reads "Body of Young Scientist Found Near Airport."

"Authorities say a search of her laboratory has so far turned up nothing, although that is the last place where she was seen earlier this afternoon. Anyone with information about this case is asked to contact the San Francisco police department." The reporter signs off and the screen flickers to another story.

"That was Veronique!" Mom says. She looks stricken. "They said that they found her body this evening, but they don't say what happened."

I stare at her, unable to think of anything to say. There was a lot of blood at the lab; I should have seen this coming. I wonder if they got what they needed from her. "I don't believe it."

Mom puts one hand to her mouth. "Me neither! She was such a nice young woman. They were just here a few months ago—remember, she played piano for us? So talented . . . it's such a waste."

I nod slowly. I know I should be feeling relief—Veronique's gone and she won't be bothering us again, at least not in this lifetime. But all I feel is numb.

Mom looks up at me. "I wonder if the boyfriend had something to do with this. He was nice enough, but I always felt that he was a little shifty. Most of the time, things like this have to do with people you know." She shakes her head sadly. "Still, it's such a shame."

"It is," I agree, not knowing what else to say. It's much safer to have Mom thinking that this is some sort of domestic-violence case. Not that she would ever guess the truth—that as crazy as she was, Veronique unlocked the secrets of Akhet transition. And that knowledge got her killed.

Twenty-One

Janine isn't telling me the whole truth. I can't read her all that well over the phone, but even so, I'm sure there's something she's hiding when she calls this morning about Veronique. She said all the stuff I'd expect her to say—that the Sekhem are on top of it, that I should just sit tight and wait for news, but there's something deeper behind her words. It's been over a week since we've had an empath lesson, and I'm thinking it's time to schedule another one—I'll be able to find out more if I see her face-to-face.

I'm checking my phone again when I see Drew walk in the front door of the studio. I duck my head and pretend I don't see him through the glass of the practice-room door, focusing on the piece in front of me and my fingers on the strings. I glance up again and see him walking back toward the exit, surprising myself by opening my door and calling out to him. "Drew!" The instant the word is out, I regret it. I don't want to encourage him. But I need to feel connected to other Akhet right now, and he's about the only one left who actually wants to see me.

He spins around and looks at me sheepishly. "I was just leaving you a note." He nods toward the front desk. Rebecca waves a piece of paper in my direction, her eyes following Drew's every move. I walk over and grab it from her.

"It's an invitation," he says. "To a party at my new place on Friday. I figured coming here was better than stopping by your house." He looks right into my eyes. "And you haven't been returning my calls."

I glance over and see Rebecca hanging on his words. I walk back toward the open door of the practice room and motion for him to follow. No harm in being seen with him here this time. I fold the invitation in my hands. "Sorry about that; it's been kind of crazy lately."

"How's Rayne?" He seems genuinely concerned.

"Better." I hesitate. Janine said not to tell anyone about what happened with Veronique. Even though I'm sure Drew had nothing to do with it, I decide to listen to her. "Looks like they figured out what kind of infection it was and how to treat it. I'm going to the hospital as soon as I get out of here. I think they're going to let her go home soon."

"Good! I'm really glad." He nods toward the invitation. "Well, Portia Martin's coming back into town for a show this weekend, so I thought I'd have some people over," he continues. "A little housewarming dinner at my new place. I'd love it if you'd come."

I glance back at the closed door, but everyone seems to be

minding their own business. "Some people? Like the people who were at the club?"

Drew grins and sits down at the piano bench. "Yes. Mostly Khered. It'll be a good opportunity for you to meet other Akhet. People who might be able to help you in this lifetime."

I've been thinking about Frank and the different Akhet I met with Drew that night. I know what Griffon and Janine think about them, but they all looked so content and happy. Still, accepting the invitation feels like some kind of betrayal. "I'm not sure I can make it."

Drew pokes at a few of the piano keys. "Too bad." He looks up and smiles at me. "But I understand." He puts his hands on the keyboard and plays a few chords, expertly and without hesitation. This isn't his first time at a piano.

He nods toward the cello. "Have you been playing?"

I shrug. Not like he has any stake in it. "A little. It's a right-handed cello that . . . that they made for me." It feels wrong to even say Griffon's name in front of Drew.

"Cool." Drew plays a few riffs. "We should play together sometime."

I shake my head.

"Not in front of anybody. Just for fun." Drew's fingers hover over the keys, and then I hear the first few bars of "River Flows in You."

I take a step toward the piano, my heart pounding at the familiar notes. "Stop."

Drew lifts his hands off and the sound vibrates through the small room. "Okay," he says slowly. "Why?"

"Just . . . not that song."

"You don't like Yiruma?"

"I do. It's just . . ." My mind leaps back months, back to when things were normal and my biggest concern was what to play at the next concert. I exhale. "That was the song I was working on with my partner before the accident. Before . . . all of this started." That was a lifetime ago.

Drew's concern gives way to a smile. "It's one of my favorite contemporary pieces."

"Mine too."

He reaches over and grabs my chair, turning it to face the wall. "There," he says softly, sitting back down at the keyboard. "Don't play it for me. Or the people out there in the studio. Play it for the wall." He strikes the first note. "Play it for you."

"I can't."

"How do you know?" Drew closes his eyes and plays the introduction while I stand there, not moving except for a slight swaying to the music that I can't control. When he gets to my part of the piece, it feels hollow and empty without the cello, like a dance partner who's all alone in the spotlight. He pauses and then starts over, the notes of the introduction filling the room, and my fingers itch to follow along, to balance out the soft, high notes of the piano with the mellow, rich sounds of the cello strings.

I sit down and pick up the cello, thinking that I'm just going to follow along in my head, show my fingers where they should go and what they should do. Which is why I'm as surprised as he must be when the first notes reverberate out of the cello and into the air. I face the wall and close my eyes, feeling nothing but the strings under my fingertips and the waves of music as the cello notes wind and twist with the delicate sounds of the piano. It's like being in another world as the music surrounds us in the tiny room, softening the hard corners and weaving together the fabric of the song, strong and solid, while at the same time so fragile that it disappears through your fingers like the smallest puff of smoke.

Too quickly the song ends, and tears are falling from my eyes onto the dark wood of the cello. I wipe them away, but I can feel Drew watching me.

"Right," he says, and I can hear the emotion in his voice as he clears his throat. "We're going to miss you on Friday."

I feel the air pressure change as he opens the practice-room door, and by the time I turn to look, the hallway is empty and Drew is gone.

The rest of the morning is torture, and I can barely focus on anything until I'm standing outside of Rayne's room. They moved her out of ICU and onto a regular floor, and my prayers are answered when I push open the door and see that the bed next to hers is empty. I need to tell her what's going on before she starts having memories, and I need to do it in private.

"Rayne?" I call, knocking on the door frame.

"Hey! Get in here!" she calls from the other side of the curtain. Her voice is raw from the ventilator, but otherwise she sounds almost back to normal.

"How are you?" I squeal, bending into her outstretched arms as she squeezes my neck tight. The Akhet vibrations I'm getting from her are unmistakable, and relief rushes in. Despite everything I'd insisted to Janine, there was still a nagging corner of doubt that I might have been wrong.

"SO much better!" she says. "My circulation is still funny, so they've still got me hooked up to some drugs, but that's nothing compared to how it was."

"You're right," I say, pulling the chair in the corner up to her bed. "Because it was bad."

Rayne's face gets serious, and I can hear the noises from the hallway in the silence between us. "You have to tell me everything. Griffon was here with Peter, but he's being weird. He keeps staring at me and touching me on the arm, but he won't tell me anything, even though I know he had a lot to do with fixing this mess."

"Hang on," I say, and get up to close the door. I sit back down and look at her face. She looks the same, open and trusting, but I know everything has totally changed. Janine said not to tell anyone, but Rayne isn't just anyone. She's the pin on which everything else pivots. There's no other option, so I tell her everything. Everything except the fact that Veronique's crazy plan worked. Everything except the fact that she's now Akhet.

Rayne doesn't say much until I'm done, just nodding her head here and there, like pieces of a puzzle are falling into place. "So Veronique's actually dead?" she asks with tears in her eyes.

"Yes," I say, finding that I feel surprisingly unemotional as I describe what happened and the news reports that followed later that night. At one point I had so much hatred for her that all I wanted was to see her dead, but now I just feel empty. "Don't waste a tear on her, though. She almost killed you."

"I know," Rayne sniffs. "But she didn't mean it. She only did it because she loved Alessandra and thought there might be one last way to be with her again."

Alessandra. I have to find out if Veronique was right. I lean toward Rayne. "There is something else," I say. I try to think back to the day at the slide when Griffon told me about being Akhet and what he said. But I was ready for it then, ready for some sort of explanation about what had been happening to me. Rayne doesn't have a clue. "Have you noticed anything different lately? Has anything changed?"

Rayne is about to answer when we hear footsteps in the hall.

"Hey there! So good to see you!" Rayne's mom says, pushing the door open and setting a bag down on the tray at the foot of the bed. "I brought Rayne some food from El Balazo, but there's plenty to share. What are you two all huddled up about?"

"Nothing," I say, sitting back in my chair. Rayne looks at me with a question in her eyes. "We can talk about it later, it's no big deal." In a way, this is better, because once I tell Rayne, it can't be undone. Her world is going to change soon enough—I might as well let her have a little more normal.

Twenty-Two

I didn't know this many people could fit into Janine's office.

That's my first thought as I open the door to find it full of adults I don't recognize. "Sorry!" I say, glancing at the clock. I'm sure she said to come at two, but a faculty meeting must have run over or something. I start to back out the door when Janine stops me.

"Cole, come in! We were waiting for you."

I pause. That doesn't exactly give me a good feeling. "You were?"

"Yes. Sit down." Janine indicates an empty chair over by the sofa. Her face is impassive, and I'm getting nothing from her movements about why I'm here. This must be what a trip to the principal's office feels like.

As I walk into the room I spot Griffon, and the familiar jolt runs through me. I keep thinking it's going to get better, but it doesn't—that combination of longing and loss hits me every time. He's not sitting down, but leaning against the windowsill in the far corner looking tense, like he might get up and leave any minute.

I take my seat and decide not to offer up any guesses about what's going on here. There's the guy Christophe who was at Griffon's house that day, along with Janine's friend Sue and two other men that I don't recognize. Giselle is nowhere in sight.

"We've been discussing the situation with Veronique and Rayne," Janine says. "And the others felt that it was time to bring you into our little group. See if there are ways you can help us out."

"Okay," I say, in my best noncommittal voice.

The Asian guy with long, dark hair leans forward. "We heard you were invited to a Khered gathering."

I see Griffon flinch, and Janine tilts her head in irritation. "Tetsuro! Seriously." She turns to me. "Sometimes even centuries of living can't force some people to learn manners. Or patience."

I start to rise out of my chair when I realize what he just said. "You mean Drew's party? You've been *watching* me?" I suddenly feel creeped out as I look around. How did they do it? I didn't tell anyone about the invitation.

Janine puts her hands out and tries to calm me down. "It's okay. Just a little harmless poking around—nobody has a hidden camera on you, I swear. Things are just a little tense right now, and it's best to keep tabs on everyone's whereabouts."

I sit back and fold my arms across my chest. "I don't like anyone poking around in my business."

"We're sorry. It's as much to keep you safe as anything."

Suddenly I get what Griffon was saying about time. It feels like in one split second I don't belong to myself anymore. That whatever I do is part of something bigger. I look at him, but he won't meet my eyes.

"Let me make some introductions," Janine says. "You've already heard from Tetsuro. He and Christophe have been working on fuel cell technology in Switzerland with Griffon, but just transferred down to South Bay. This is Eric." A blond guy with glasses gives a little wave from the sofa. "And you've met Sue."

Sue smiles at me. "What Tetsuro was trying not-so-tactfully to say is that your new connections in certain Khered circles, along with what we know are impressive developing empath skills, could be the perfect combination to help us with some research."

And then I get it. They don't have any idea who trashed the lab or who killed Veronique. Despite Janine's assurances, they've come up empty, and somehow they think that I can help. "You want me to spy on Drew and his friends?"

"'Spy' seems a little heavy-handed," Christophe offers. "We prefer to look at it as observing with a goal."

I stare at him. "Call it whatever you want, I'm not sure I can spy on anyone, or that it's going to help you at all."

Janine leans forward. "Griffon says that when you connected with Rayne, you were able to go much deeper than before." She watches my face, gauging my reaction to her words. "That you were able to actually see images rather than just feel emotions."

I nod. "I did. For a few seconds. But I have no idea how. And it made me feel really sick." I can see an exchange of glances around the room.

"Telempathy is a skill that so far exists only in legends and rumors," Sue says. "To be able to master it would be something immensely valuable to the Sekhem."

I remember the feeling of weakness and nausea after I made contact with Rayne. "I'm not in a big hurry to try it again."

Sue holds up both hands in a gesture of surrender. "No one is asking you to," she says. "None of us expect you to go that deeply at the Khered gathering. Just poke around a little, see if you can get any information from casual contact with the other guests. We need to find out who did this, and every minute that goes by puts everyone in more and more danger," Sue says. Her mouth is set into a grim line, and I can feel the intensity in her gaze. "Anything you can give us is valuable at this point."

"But they killed Veronique," I say. "So she won't be able to do something like this again. The worst of it's over, right?"

I see wary glances flit across the room. "Not exactly," Janine says.

Christophe clears his throat. "We have reason to believe that they didn't go to the lab looking for Veronique. Someone got word of what she had been working on and went to get the formula. Veronique was just collateral damage."

"When we searched the lab after the break-in," Sue says, "we found evidence that files and samples had been taken. Which ordinarily wouldn't be of too much concern; ergot fungus in its standard form isn't going to do much damage. Even if it were spread as an epidemic, once it's identified, it's fairly easily treated, as you've been able to see. But Veronique was able to somehow synthesize a totally unknown form of ergot, one that has the capabilities of transforming the very essence of a person. As you've discovered, Veronique's research did what nobody through time has been able to do—to create an Akhet from an ordinary Khem."

"But how is that a threat?" I ask. "I suppose I get why some people would choose to be Akhet—the kind of immortality it brings. But I don't see the harm."

Janine smiles. "And I love that you don't see it."

"The harm is that the people who now have this knowledge in their possession aren't good people," Sue says. "And if you give the formula to the worst of the worst Khem, you can create a group of Akhet who exist not to help the world, but to destroy it in pursuit of their own fortune and power. A group who will get stronger and smarter with each passing lifetime, who will use that immortality to take risks like the world has never seen before."

Janine leans forward. "Worse than any single rogue Akhet out to settle a score." I can tell by the way she's looking at me that she's thinking of Veronique. "Imagine a Kim Jong-un or a Charles Manson who was given the formula. Think about what they could do with Akhet abilities and memory." She's silent for a moment. "Now think about hundreds of them. Thousands of them. Think about what that could do to the balance of world power in a very short time. Think of how much money that knowledge would be worth."

I'm silent. In a few sentences, this has gone from being

something personal with Rayne to having implications far beyond this lifetime. "So what can I do?"

"We think that there were Akhet involved, either people who knew Veronique or who heard about her work through others," Janine says. "And we think it's someone with ties to San Francisco, because they were able to get to the lab quickly and seem to know the area."

"And you think that Khered are immoral enough to pull off something like this?"

I see glances shift around the room again. "Not all Khered," Eric volunteers. "But the perpetrators are more likely to be Khered than Sekhem."

"But what would they be doing at Drew's party?"

"From what we can tell, it's going to be one of the largest gatherings of Khered in recent weeks," Sue says. "Not just local Khered, but Akhet from all over the world. And our intelligence has picked up a lot more activity in and around the city in the past few days."

"We think that whoever was in charge of the break-in at the lab is still local," Janine says. "We can only hope that they won't be able to pass up a chance to make some more widespread connections, maybe make some under-the-table deals."

"And you already have an introduction into that world," Sue says.

"All we're asking is that you go to the party and see if you can use your skills to find out if anyone has some inside knowledge of the break-in at the lab, or if anyone has been talking about it who might have more information than is available to ordinary Akhet," Christophe says.

"We're not even asking you to make deep contact with the others," Janine says. "Griffon told me how much it took out of you when you did it with Rayne, and we don't want you in any danger."

"We will have some security for you," Sue says. "Another Sekhem who has ties to the Khered world will be there to make sure nothing happens. She's one of our top security people, so you don't have to worry."

"Why do I need security?"

"Probably you don't," Janine says. "But if the people involved in this are at the party and they figure out you're reading them . . . they might not be too happy about it. Giselle is just a safety net that hopefully we won't need."

"Giselle?"

"She's part of our security team—I think you met her." Janine says. "She's one of Griffon's colleagues."

Suddenly I'm a little less confident. "I met her," I confirm. "If Giselle, Christophe, and Tetsuro are supposed to be working on the fuel cell lab, why are they involved in this?"

"Because they're local now," Sue says. "And they're valuable members of the Sekhem." She glances toward the window. "And Griffon trusts them, which is no small thing. We need to keep this incident as quiet as possible."

"So you guys are it?" I ask. I look around the room. I don't know how to put this, but they don't seem like they can take down a group of rogue Akhet.

Janine grins like she knows what I'm thinking. "No. We're just the Sekhem you're going to deal with directly. There are many more sections in place that you don't need to worry about."

Everyone waits for me to say something else, to tell them that I'll go along with the plan. Despite what they've said, I'm not really worried about my safety, although I wish the security detail could be someone else. It's just that the whole thing feels like a betrayal. As much as I don't want to be with Drew, not the way that Griffon thinks, I feel like going to his party to serve the Sekhem's agenda is wrong. I look up at Griffon, who's staring out the window.

"You're awfully quiet," I say to him.

"What?" he asks, turning back to the room.

"You haven't said a word. Everyone else here has their reasons why I should do it, but you're just sitting there."

He looks like he's been caught. "It's your decision," he says, his eyes everywhere in the room but on me. "I'm not part of this."

"Then why are you here?"

There's a slight pause. "Good question," he says, getting to his feet and walking out the door.

A few people start to say something, but before I can think, I'm out the door behind him. I want to know why he's hesitating, why he won't come straight out and tell me to go.

"Wait a minute," I call. He's already to the stairs, but he stops when he hears my voice.

"What? You were right, I shouldn't have been in there."

"But you were. You sat there and listened to all of it." I catch up to him. I want so badly to slide my fingers through his. To have him put his arms around me once more so that this time I'll know it's the last time. "Is it the truth?"

"You should be able to figure that out," he says, staring at the wall. "You're the one with the empath skills. You can tell when someone is lying from ten feet away."

"I want to hear it from you." I force myself to keep going. "You're the only one I feel like I can really trust."

His eyes flick toward mine for just a second. "It's the truth. Everything they said. We've never had a situation like this before, and despite appearances, everyone's running scared."

"And why Giselle? Why are they having Giselle babysit me at Drew's apartment?"

"Because she's the best." As he says it, a shadow crosses his face, and I know I'm not imagining it. Giselle and Griffon have a past together.

"Do you think I should do it?"

Griffon hesitates and glances at the closed door of Janine's office. "No." His golden eyes widen and he looks directly at me for the first time. "It's too dangerous. Even with Giselle there. This thing is way out of your league."

"Out of my league?" I repeat, crossing my arms in front of me. "You just don't think I'm good enough to help the Sekhem. That I still need to be protected by people who are bigger and smarter and stronger than I am." I can feel my words tumble over each other as I speak, the anger building in my body. "Protect the poor innocent Shewi girl because she can't help herself. That's what this is about."

"That's not . . ." Griffon starts to say something, but instead pushes past me in frustration and takes the stairs two at a time.

I stand at the top watching him go until I hear the outside door slam on the bottom floor, giving me a sense of satisfaction I haven't felt in a while.

I can hear everyone talking as I open Janine's office door, but they all fall silent as I enter. I look around at their expectant faces and realize it's not just about me anymore.

"I'll do it."

Twenty-Three

I look out the window and watch the buildings go by on Market Street. It would be so easy to just stay on the bus, riding until it doesn't go any farther and I'm the last person on board. But I already told Drew that I'd come and the Sekhem are expecting my help, so I pull myself out of my seat and push the red stop button.

After jumping to the pavement, I head toward the Embarcadero, looking in shop windows as I pass. I've been thinking all week about what to get Drew for a housewarming present, because it's not like I can stop at a store and get him a nice bottle of wine like a normal dinner guest, and he can obviously buy anything else he needs. There's a flower stand on the corner that's still open and I stop to take a look, but bringing him a bunch of flowers would be weird.

"Can I help you?" An older woman in an apron appears at my side.

"I don't think so," I say, backing away.

"Is there a special occasion?"

"Housewarming," I say. "But it's for a guy, so flowers won't really work."

"How about a plant? A house isn't really a home until there are some plants." She leans around a big bucket of sunflowers and pulls a small pot of ivy off a shelf. "This one is guy-proof. Doesn't take a lot of care and actually likes to dry out between waterings. He'll have to try to kill it."

I look around. It's getting late and I can't think of a better idea. "Okay. I'll take it."

"I'm sure he'll love it."

I continue down the street, feeling a little ridiculous with the plant in my hand, like I'm taking it out for a walk or something. I turn right and head toward Mission Street, checking the address on my phone as I go. I almost never come this far downtown, and I'm not sure I have the right place when I stop in front of the tallest building down here that has the right street numbers in gold over the front door.

I walk through the glass doors into what looks like the lobby of the fanciest hotel in town. The lighting is low, but it reflects off the different colored marble on the floors, where several clean-lined couches and chairs wait patiently on a large, ornate rug. I feel eyes on me and look over to see a man in a suit behind a large marble counter staring at me, because a girl in jeans carrying a pot of ivy is so obviously out of place here. I duck back out the door and grab my phone.

I hesitate before I pull up his number. Maybe this is a sign I shouldn't be here at all. I take a deep breath and push Talk.

Drew answers in one ring. I can hear music and voices in the background. "Hey! Are you on the way? I can come and get you."

The sound of his voice makes me stop for a second. Nobody else in this whole city would be as glad to see me as Drew seems to be. "No . . . I'm not sure . . ." I look back through the glass doors. The snooty guy in the suit is watching me. I crane my neck in order to see the top of the gigantic building. "I'm not sure I have the right address."

He recites the numbers for me again, and they definitely match what's on the building. "Is there a guy at the desk down there?"

"Yeah. He looks mean."

Drew laughs. "That's Larry. Just tell him you're here to see me and he'll send you up. I'll be waiting as soon as you get off the elevator. Hurry."

"Okay." I walk back through the doors and up to the counter before I lose my nerve. "I'm here for . . ." I look at the address again. "The apartment number he gave me is GPH." I glance up hopefully.

Larry raises his eyebrows and looks pointedly at my plant. "GPH stands for Grand Penthouse."

I swallow. Of course. Bugatti, penthouse; I should have known. "Right. Drew Braithwaite."

He looks down at something on the desk. "Your name?"

"Cole Ryan."

Larry slowly runs a pen down a list and looks up again. "Take that elevator all the way down to the left. I'll call it for you."

"Thanks," I say in the sweetest tone I can manage. The

doors open as soon as I approach and close silently behind me as soon as I enter. There are no buttons on the wall. Just some mysterious slots and what looks like a camera mounted in the ceiling. I think about waving, but figure that Larry is already watching me and I don't want to give him the satisfaction. The elevator shifts slightly and I realize it's rising fast. Quicker than I'd thought possible, the doors open again, and instead of a hallway, I'm in what looks like Drew's apartment. Or somebody's apartment, but not the one of your typical twenty-year-old guy. The place is huge, with oversized brown suede couches and chairs set in groups around the room, with sophisticated lighting and what I think they refer to on the design shows on TV as "window treatments." Not a discarded T-shirt or written-on whiteboard in sight. All the furniture is just a stage for the wall of windows that are opposite the elevator. I barely glance at them before I start to break out into a sweat. We're so high up that you can see forever—over the buildings and the hills to the horizon, where there's still the faintest hint of an orange sunset. I swallow hard and pull my eyes away from the view.

"You're here!" Drew says, walking to meet me. He leans forward like he's going to give me a hug, but decides against it and just clasps his hands behind his back. "What do you think?"

"It's amazing." There are people all over the two rooms I can see from here, sitting on couches and perching on the arms of the chairs. Like at the club, they are all different ages, but everyone has something about them that makes you look twice. Not to mention that they all look expensive. I scan their faces and wonder if any of them are the person the Sekhem are looking for. If maybe somewhere among these well-dressed people is the one who's willing to risk it all for ultimate power. My heart sinks just a little as I realize there must be at least thirty people in these two rooms alone. Even if I was great at it, I'd never be able to read all of them in such a short time.

"Come look out the windows," Drew says, interrupting my thoughts. "They're the best thing about this apartment and the reason I bought it in the first place."

I instinctively put my hand on the wall behind me, just to feel something solid. "Maybe later."

Drew glances at the windows and then back at me. "Are you afraid of heights?"

I nod quickly. "A little."

"Views are overrated anyway. When you've seen one group of buildings, you've seen them all. I know that what you'd really like to see are the fabulous appetizers made by my wonderful caterers."

"More my speed, I think." I glance back to the windows. "How high up are we?"

Drew smiles. "Sixty-fifth floor."

I can tell my smile is all teeth and no feeling. "Great."

"Is that for me?" Drew asks as we walk farther into the apartment.

"What?" I look down at my hand. I've forgotten all about the ivy, which now seems like the dumbest idea I've ever had. "Oh. I'd like to say no, but I can't come up with any other reason I'd be carrying a plant around." I hand it to him. "Happy housewarming."

"It's perfect." Drew sets the little plant in the silver wrapping on a glass table, where it looks totally out of place. "The designer didn't put nearly enough plants in here." He beams at me. "I love it."

"I'm glad."

He leans over to a large round platter of appetizers. "Ooh, you have to try one of these." Drew hands me a tiny triangle of bread with something on it. "Totally rare. You'll love it."

I take a bite and it tastes like the ocean threw up in my mouth. I quickly spit the leftovers into my napkin and look around for something to take the salty edge off.

Drew laughs at my reaction. "So much for my special Almas caviar. Do you need a drink?"

I nod quickly, hoping that I'm not going to be sick here in front of everyone, and almost as fast, there is a glass of white wine in my hand. I take a swig and it washes away some of the salty fish taste. "Sorry. I've never had caviar before." I shudder a little at the memory.

"I'm guessing the raw oysters are probably not going to be your favorite either." He looks around the coffee table. "Crab cakes?"

I nod and eat one quickly. "Now *these* are good."

"Good. Take a couple and let's go into the other room. I promise I'll keep you away from the windows."

I can feel Drew's hand hovering over the small of my back as he leads me into the living room, but he doesn't actually touch me. I'm a little annoyed that I even notice.

"So, we've been missing you lately," a blond woman says to Drew, pulling him to the side. "You've been hiding yourself away."

A guy standing with her nods in my direction. "And now I see why." I can tell they're both a little drunk already.

"I've been busy," Drew says, smiling at me.

"Too busy for your oldest friends?" The woman pouts at him and then turns to me, waving her hand lazily. "Drew and I spent many years in Paris together." She leans down and stage-whispers, "Not this time. A time before." She leans back, tilting her head toward the ceiling. "Oh, the salons in the Saint-Germain-des-Prés. Late nights at Chez Ma Cousine. Paris in the twenties was really something to see. It would have been a shame to miss it." She glances at me. "Or did you miss it?"

"I don't know." In the Clarissa lifetime I would have been in my forties in the nineteen twenties, so it's possible I was there. "I don't remember."

The guy nudges me in a way I've come to find familiar with Iawi Ahket. "Ah, Shewi." He leaves his hand on my arm a beat longer than necessary, I'm sure to try to find out if we've been connected before. I quickly try to block out the rest of the room and focus on him to see if there is something dark in his essence, but all I feel is a happiness that borders on giddy. Or that might just be the wine. "Such an interesting time," he says, pulling his hand away from me, breaking our connection. "So much to discover."

"It's true," I agree, giving him a smile. He has no idea I was reading him, and that makes me feel a little more confident.

Drew leads me farther into the living room, where several people pull him into a large group and he greets some new arrivals with hugs and cheek kisses. I look around but don't feel comfortable just plopping down somewhere, so I hover on the edges. Someone laughs on the other side of the room and I see Giselle, perched on the corner of a low table, drink in hand, talking to an elegant African-American woman. She doesn't look my way, but I can tell from her body language that she sees me. And that she wants me to see her.

Every few minutes there are more people coming off the elevator and into the room. There's no way I'm going to be able to read each person individually, even if I had all night. I think back to the guy on the bridge that day, and how it seemed like there was a spotlight on him, separating him out from the hundreds of other people in the crowd that day. I wonder if I can do the same thing here. Janine says that empathy is just a higher form of intuition, and that if I allow my conscious mind to be free, my instincts will be my guide. Maybe I'll be drawn to the people who need to be seen.

There's a barking laugh to my right, and I turn back toward Drew. A couple of the people next to him are talking about a party that happened in France a few weeks ago, and I'm trying to listen in when my phone buzzes with a text. I reach into my pocket and pull it out.

You look beautiful. I'm so glad u came tonight.

I glance up, startled, and catch Drew's eye from the middle of the group. He smiles and raises his eyebrows, and I can't help but smile back. I quickly type a reply. *Me too. Except for the fish eggs. Ick.*

I watch him and grin when he twitches as the text comes through. He holds his phone up to the guy who's talking. "You're going to have to excuse me a second. I have to get this."

"Thanks for the save," he says, leading me away from the group. "Sit down with me over here?" he asks. The suede couch is big enough for ten people, and I instantly recognize Portia at one end of it, talking to a girl who looks like a Russian model, all skinny limbs and hard angles.

"Ah, Andrew!" An older woman wearing a lot of makeup pats the seat next to her. "Is this the young lady you were telling me about?" I can see Drew shaking his head just a tiny bit. I'm sure she sees him, but completely ignores the signal and grabs my hand, pulling me close to her. I feel that she's Akhet, but I don't sense any past connection between us or anything dark that would make me want to read her further. "So nice to meet you, dear. I'm Sonia." As soon as she says her name, I recognize her throaty voice; she's the actress who starred in all of those old movies that Dad loves to watch.

"I'm Cole," I say, wishing I could get her autograph, but knowing it would not only be awkward here, but would require an explanation that I couldn't give Dad.

"Cole?" she repeats. "What kind of a name is Cole?"

"It's really Nicole. I never liked it."

Her face brightens as if I've handed her something she recognizes. "Now, that's a lovely name, dear. I knew a Nicole back in France. Beautiful girl." She seems far away for a few moments, lost in thought about people who are probably long dead. She focuses her eyes on me again. "And who are your people?"

"I'm sorry?" I feel a little panicky. Has she already figured out I'm working for the Sekhem?

Drew leans in. "Cole's Shewi, Sonia. Don't hassle her."

Sonia scowls at Drew and smacks him lightly on the hand. "I never hassle. What I meant was, who else have you met since you transitioned?"

"I only know a few other Akhet," I explain, hoping that's vague enough to get her off the subject.

"Mostly Sekhem," Drew says, and I wince.

Sonia waves her bony hand in the air. "Dreary." She turns her attention back to me, grabbing one of my hands in both of hers. "Who are these Sekhem?"

"Just a guy," I say quickly, hoping I can steer the conversation away from Griffon. The last thing I want is to draw attention to the fact that I know Sekhem.

"Isn't his mother Akhet too?" Drew says. I watch his eyes, but all I see is curiosity, not malice.

The skinny girl's head snaps around as soon as he says that. "You said you know a Sekhem whose mother is also Akhet?"

I nod, suddenly on the alert. I glance at Sonia—she's still holding my hand in hers, and I get a distinct feeling that she doesn't like this girl.

"Griffon and Janine?" the girl asks. Their names seem to hang in the air. "I believe their last name is Hall in this lifetime."

I search her face for some sort of deception, some indication that she knows more than she's letting on. "Yes. That's right. They live in Berkeley."

There is a flash of pain or guilt behind her eyes, and she looks from me to Drew. "How is Griffon?"

"Fine, I guess," I say slowly. I glance at Giselle, but I can't tell if she's paying attention. This girl is way too interested in Griffon for it to be anything casual.

"Good." She nods her head. "Good. I'm glad he's well. I knew he was in the area, but I haven't made contact with him in this lifetime."

"I'm surprised," Sonia says, a touch of annoyance in her voice. "You seem to make contact with *so* many people."

I relax a little bit and give her a tiny smile. Sonia doesn't like her because she thinks she's a slut, not because she's dangerous. "So you knew Griffon before?"

"In Italy," she says. "It was just as his awareness was starting. In the middle of the seventeenth century."

"I lived in Italy too," I say in Italian. "But later. In the late eighteen hundreds." I glance at Drew, knowing that I haven't told him the whole truth about me and Griffon and how we were connected in the past. I wonder if he can tell.

She doesn't look surprised at all, but answers in the same language. "Is he married? Does he have a family?"

I smile. "He's only seventeen. No kids that I know of."

"Of course," she says. "It's so difficult to keep track." She looks me up and down so pointedly it feels like I'm suddenly naked. "So you are the same physical age? Are you with him?"

I can feel my face get hot. "I . . . um . . . we went out a little bit," I finally manage.

The woman looks off into the distance. "Back then he was a wonderful lover and a loyal partner. I can't imagine that's changed much."

I stare at her. A wonderful lover? Who throws out information like that as if it's no big deal?

"But not one who forgave easily," she continues. There's a pause. "Please tell him Chiara says hello the next time you see him."

"I will," I say, knowing that her message will never be delivered.

"Well," Drew says, looking uncomfortable. "It's always interesting to see how people connect." He nods to a long table where the caterers have set out plate after plate of food. "Looks like it's time to eat."

It's not until I'm halfway to the table that I realize we were all speaking Italian.

Twenty-Four

. . . so then she says, 'Don't I know you from somewhere?' and I didn't have a clue what to say!" Everyone laughs as Sonia finishes her story.

We're sitting in several large groups around the apartment, our dirty plates taken away almost magically by the caterers. For the first time tonight, Drew isn't next to me, but I see him looking over at me from across the room, making sure I'm not sitting here all by myself. So far I've seen only a few indications that various people are hiding small things like the rift between Sonia and Chiara, but nothing big and revealing like Janine and the Sekhem are looking for.

The man on the couch shifts position as he talks to the woman next to him, not paying any attention to me. As an experiment, I reach out and put one hand next to his back to see if I can read him, if I can find any connection between this random stranger and Veronique, but immediately I'm drawn into a vivid memory of my own.

Ground fog lingers in the early morning light, and I pull the blanket tighter around my shoulders. I bump into neighbors rushing through the streets as I hurry back into our cabin. My chest pounds as I scan the familiar faces, but none bear the features I'm looking for. I pull the heavy wooden door open, hoping against hope, but Mama is the only one to greet me.

"Quickly, child," she says, gathering whatever she can grab and stuffing it into the wooden trunk. "Most of the others have already started out. We don't want to be left behind. Your father is almost finished loading the wagon with supplies for the journey, and Elias said that the army is setting fire to everything that's left and that they're getting closer by the hour."

I look around at the four walls that have been my home my entire life, memorizing every crack in the chinking that holds the logs together. The small wooden pallet that I've slept on since I was old enough to leave my mother's side. The table and chairs that Papa made as a wedding present for Mama. How can we possibly choose what to take and what to leave to the flames? I pick up Sadie from the small shelf above my bed and tuck her into a tiny corner of the trunk.

Mama plucks the dingy cloth doll from her hiding place and holds her out to me. "Aren't you too old for dolls? What use will she be in the new settlement?"

I snatch the doll and place her gently back in the trunk, smoothing the black yarn hair and delicately beaded dress that Mama sewed over many hours bent in front of the fire. "Sadie is not for playing with anymore," I say firmly. "But I cannot

leave her to them." *Just picturing their white, hairy hands on
my treasure makes me feel physically sick. Even worse, what if
one of the soldiers gave her to his own yellow-haired daughter
to play with? The thought makes me shudder.*

*Mama smiles as though she's reading my mind. "Very well.
Sadie may come. But the rest is only for necessities. It is a very
long journey to the new settlement, and we have no need of
luxuries in the wagon."*

*I hear Papa trying to calm the horses outside as the crowds
rumble by in their wagons and on foot. I know Mama hears
them too as she looks around the room that suddenly seems so
small. The dishes are still stacked on the shelves, the crooked
flower vase I made Mama from river clay is on top of the
hearth, and the beautifully woven blanket hangs in the window.
None of these things will be coming with us.*

*Mama shuts the trunk with an air of finality and takes one
last look around the room. "Help me with this," she says, taking
one leather handle as I grab the other. She leaves not even a
backward glance on the place, looking only forward as we step
into the weak morning light.*

I'm disoriented for a few seconds as the memory fades, and
I'm left with nothing but questions. Without knowing where or
when that lifetime took place, I'm sure it's one I haven't explored
before. Who was I? Where were we going? I close my eyes for a
second and try to fix what I saw in my memory. Mama had
light brown skin and long black hair that was caught in a bun at
the base of her neck, and was wearing a long red dress that
looked like something out of *Little House on the Prairie*. I
remember the pounding in my chest as I watched the people

fleeing the village. I was searching for someone, but I have no idea who.

I look over at the man next to me. He's tall, with jet-black hair and a distinct, but not unpleasant, nose. He's still deep in discussion with the woman on his other side and hasn't even noticed our connection, but he has to be the reason for such a random memory—he must have something to do with that life-time. I'm about to tap him on the shoulder when he and the woman stand up and cross the room to get more drinks.

Giselle wanders over from another group and sits on the arm of the sofa next to me, smiling and talking to people she knows. Sonia starts another story and Giselle turns to me while the focus isn't on us.

"Are you enjoying the party?" she asks, taking a drink of her wine.

"It's been great," I say. I glance at the guy. "Do you know who he is?" I ask, nodding in his direction.

Giselle squints across the room. "That's Will Alvarez. He's a writer—screenplays, mostly. But I don't know the woman." She looks down at me, a mild look of interest on her face. "Did you get something from him?"

"Yes," I say, looking back in his direction. "But not like that. It was more personal."

"Well, your skills are just developing. We can't expect miracles from the beginning." I know that Giselle is trying to talk in code, but there's no mistaking the condescending tone of that last statement. She takes another sip, and the way she looks away from me tells me that she doesn't think I can do this. That all of the attention I'm getting from the Sekhem is for nothing.

Everyone around us laughs as Sonia finishes another story, and I see an opportunity in the silence that follows. All of the talk tonight has been about mutual friends and other parties in other lifetimes. I see Drew walk into the kitchen and I decide it's time to focus on some current events. "Hey," I say quickly, before conversation can start again. "Did you hear about the woman they found dead out by the airport last week? I heard she was Akhet."

The entire group is silent, looking at me and, I'm sure, wondering why I'd bring up something like that. At least that's what most people would think. But anyone who's involved would be immediately uncomfortable. I sit up, alert, watching the faces around me.

"I heard that too," a woman volunteers. "Veronique something. Not anyone that I knew, though."

Sonia leans into the group. "Was she Sekhem?"

"Rogue," another woman says. I watch her carefully, but I don't see any signs of agitation. "I heard she'd been involved in some retaliation earlier this year. Sanctioned by the Sekhem, but what are they going to do about it?" Everyone laughs softly.

A guy near me sips some coffee. "How did she die? She didn't go anen, did she?"

"No. She was killed," the first woman says. I don't recognize the new Akhet word, but it must mean something like suicide. I wonder how many Akhet choose that option.

"How?" Sonia asks. "I hope not strangulation. That's a horrible way to go."

"Were you ever strangled?" a man asks her.

"No. But I know someone who was. Dreadful. I prefer

something quick and unexpected," Sonia replies. "Give me a car crash or a well-placed bullet any day."

"How about a massive heart attack? Or an aneurysm?" Portia Martin asks.

Sonia waves the thought away. "Too painful."

"But not for long," Portia says. "I once had an aneurysm in my sleep—woke up with a headache, and in a few seconds that was it."

I can feel the conversation picking up now that we're off the subject of Veronique. I don't see anyone who seems even a little bit interested.

"Has anyone gone the lingering disease route?" a blond woman asks, and many people shake their head in sympathy. "I did that last time, and I'm telling you, never again. If I get sick this time, I'm going anen before things get too bad. Hard to believe that in this day and age euthanasia is still illegal. It ought to be a sacrament."

The conversation turns to everyone's favorite way to die, and I know the subject is lost. Giselle leans down. "Nice try."

I shrug. I should go circulate a little bit, maybe see if I can find out more about Will Alvarez. I start to stand up but lose my balance and bump into Giselle, spilling her red wine on her white jeans.

"Oh, God! I'm so sorry," I say, reaching for some napkins on the coffee table. She probably thinks I did that on purpose.

She stands up quickly. "It's okay."

"Let me get this," I say, pressing a wad of napkins into the stain. As I touch her, I suddenly feel detached from my body for a few seconds, and sense something dark, something deep down that Giselle doesn't want anyone to see.

Giselle brushes my hand away and everything comes back into focus. I look up at her, trying to keep my expression neutral. It could have been anything, something about her past that she's not proud of, something in another lifetime that she's trying to suppress. But out of everyone here, Giselle is the only one I've found who seems to be hiding something big.

"I'm going to find some club soda to take this out," Giselle says.

"Again, I'm so sorry," I say. I don't think she can tell what I know.

She gives me a tight smile. "My fault for drinking red wine in white pants. Don't worry about it."

I watch her walk into the kitchen, wondering what I'm going to say to Janine. If I'm going to say anything to Janine. I'd hate to look like an idiot if it's nothing.

Next to me, Portia looks at her oversized diamond watch and tosses her napkin onto the coffee table. "Ooh! Look how late! I'd better get going. Early call tomorrow."

I glance at the clock that Drew has over the mantle. Almost midnight. "Damn. I should go too. My parents are going to kill me."

Portia smiles. "Ah, curfew. I remember it well."

I sigh. "Now that my memories are coming back, being treated like a kid is starting to really suck."

"We all go through it, if it's any consolation. It doesn't last. Soon you'll be able to do whatever you want." Drew walks across the room and joins a couple of people by the giant windows.

Portia looks him pointedly up and down. "Speaking of doing whatever you want—I think you should definitely be doing *that*."

I bump her in the shoulder and she laughs. "I'm not going out with Drew," I say.

Portia leans in close. "Then I think you should tell him that. He's barely taken his eyes off you all night."

"Why aren't you . . . you know, with Drew?" It would be perfect—the pop star and the handsome young gazillionaire.

Portia looks over at him and seems to be deep in thought, her eyes so dark brown they seem almost black. "We have our own history," she says. "Sometimes there's no going back." She looks at me. "You two have a history, don't you?"

I look over at Drew and nod. Sometimes when I see him out of the corner of my eye I get flashes of Connor and the life we had together, and it gets hard to separate memory from reality. "Yes. A few hundred years ago. I only remember pieces of it, though."

She follows my gaze. "Sometimes it takes more than one lifetime for things to work out as they're supposed to." Portia stands up and stretches so that I can see her flat stomach and tiny little belly ring. I'm not surprised to see the ankh charm hanging off it. "Promise me you'll come to the show tomorrow night. You two blew me off last week, so you kind of owe me."

I think about what it would be like to see Portia on stage after talking to her all night at a dinner party. Rayne was dying to go to the show, but it sold out in minutes when the tickets went on sale months ago. "Can I bring someone?" She only got out of the hospital two days ago, but she'd kill me if I let her miss this opportunity.

"Sure," she says. "As long as Drew doesn't mind, it's fine

with me. I'll see you all backstage at the show." Portia leans in and gives me an air kiss on the cheek. Usually I hate that kind of thing, but with her, it seems to work. She walks over to say good-bye to Drew, and I stand up and gather a few plates that are left on the table.

"Leave those," Drew says, walking back toward me. "The caterers will get them."

"Okay," I say, feeling useless.

"Did you meet anyone you liked?"

"Everyone was great," I say. "I do have a question, though. Does 'anen' mean that someone killed themselves?"

He smiles. "Good catch. Anen is when an Akhet decides to end this lifetime. You won't see very many extremely old Akhet; when these bodies break down, most decide to trade them in."

I hadn't thought much about that. "I guess you don't worry so much about death, knowing there's another lifetime waiting for you."

He looks at me with a serious expression. "Depends on what's waiting for you in this one."

I look away, knowing exactly what he means, a pang of guilt in my chest that I can't return his feelings.

The crowd around us is definitely thinning out. "I guess I should get going." I reach for my bag hanging on the back of a chair.

"Do you have to?" he says. "It's not that late."

"Tell that to my parents. They're already mad at me . . ." I was going to say that they were mad about him, but somehow that doesn't seem right. "We already fight about where I go and what time I come home."

"Sorry," he says. "They didn't like it that I came to your house that day."

I shake my head. "No, they didn't. They think you're too old to be hanging around me." I have to laugh at how ridiculous that is, with everything I know.

His smile is slightly sad. "Under normal circumstances, I'd agree with them. When I turned eighteen, you were only four-teen. If you were my daughter, I'd probably go after the guy with a restraining order. And a baseball bat."

"Lucky for you, my dad's not much of an athlete." I look up at Drew's face. Even though there are the barest hints of laugh lines at the corners of his eyes, he seems ageless. He smiles, and I pull my gaze away and look around the room. "Well, thanks for inviting me. I had fun."

"I'll see you tomorrow, right? Portia said that if we don't come to her show, she'll disown me."

"Um . . . sure. I told her I was bringing Rayne. Is that okay?"

"Whatever you want," he says. "Is she well enough to go?"

"For a Portia Martin concert, she'll go if we have to wheel her in on a stretcher." I smile. "I think she'll be fine, for a couple of hours at least."

Drew looks around at the small groups of people still left in the living room. "How did you get here, anyway?"

"Bus," I say. "They're still running. It's a weekend schedule."

"There's no way I'm letting you get on a bus this late. Give me a second to settle up with the caterers and I'll give you a ride."

"It's okay, I've—"

"I'm not taking no for an answer. I'll be right back."

Drew disappears before I can say anything, and I'm left

alone in the quiet room. Music is playing softly on the stereo in the corner and the lights are dim, but the place seems even bigger now that it's almost empty. Giselle is sitting on the couch drinking coffee and talking to some other women. I'm sure she has orders not to leave until I do.

I glance out the floor-to-ceiling windows that line the walls and take a couple of steps toward one. We're so high up that even though I know the other skyscrapers are huge, they look tiny from here. Over to the right I see the Bay Bridge, a river of lights flowing along the entire span. There are a few ships' lights on the water, and it's clear enough that I can see the lights of South San Francisco disappearing in the distance.

I feel Drew behind me right before he speaks. "Amazing, isn't it? Almost like being in an airplane."

"We're so high up, it feels like one could hit us."

"No chance," he says. "We're not in the flight path."

I take a few steps toward the other window and put my hand on the glass to steady myself. We're at eye level with the very tip of the pointy Transamerica Pyramid a few blocks away, and the lights of Marin blink in the distance. "You really can see everything from up here."

Drew stands next to me and looks out into the distance. "I love being this high up, looking at the tiny dots of light from the cars and buildings way down there. Makes me feel powerful. Alive."

He's standing so close I can feel the warmth of his body against mine. I'm startled to realize I enjoy it, that the sensation of him close to me is familiar, almost comforting. My mind pulls away from the dark, empty space I've been nurturing inside since Griffon turned his back on me at the studio.

I think back to another time and another place. A different face with kind green eyes, but the same essence, the same vibrations between us. I remember the taste of his lips on mine and the softness of his touch on the back of my neck. I close my eyes and see the desire on Connor's face as we come together, completely swept up in the moment until time seems to stop except for the feel of his fingers on my skin. The desire that can't be dampened by centuries apart.

"Lovely to see you again, my boy," Sonia says, coming over to say good-bye. Drew backs away from me just slightly as she gives him a kiss on both cheeks. "It was wonderful to meet you, my dear," she says to me.

"You too."

I glance at Drew, wondering what will happen if he gives me a ride home. I can picture us parked in front of my house and me not making the same choice that I made the other night. "Sonia, wait," I call as she heads for the elevator. "Do you think you could drop me off in the Haight?"

She hesitates, looking at Drew. "If you'd like."

I turn to him. "It's just easier—there are still people here, and this way you don't have to leave."

"It's no trouble—"

"I'll just go with Sonia," I insist, knowing I'm going to get an earful in the car from her. I quickly give Drew a kiss on the cheek, avoiding his eyes and the disappointment I know I'll see there. "I'll see you tomorrow," I say as I run to the elevator that Sonia is holding for me.

Twenty-Five

Can the patient have a cupcake?" I ask, swinging the bag in front of Rayne as she opens her door.

"Ooh, yes!" she says, grabbing it out of my hands. "The patient is so bored she's about to go crazy. Peter was supposed to come over this afternoon, but he's stuck in Berkeley."

I follow her down the hallway and into the kitchen. "So how are you feeling? Besides bored."

"Pretty good. Tired, mostly."

"Is that it? No other symptoms?" I search her face, trying to see if she's been having any memories.

"Not really. Just taking lots of naps. By the way," she continues, "where were you last night? I was texting but you never answered."

I take a deep breath. I can keep lying to her, or I can finally tell her the truth. "I was at a party. At Drew's house."

Her eyes grow wide. "Drew? From the Marina party?"

"Yes." I look down. "Nothing's happened," I say quickly. "It was just a party with some other Akhet people."

"But what about Griffon?"

I think about what he said to me in the hallway of Janine's office that day and feel my anger rise. "What about him? He's gone, Rayne, and he's not coming back. Not to me, anyway. I have to move on." I think about the easy way he has with Giselle. "I'm sure he will."

"I thought you loved him." She looks almost like I've broken up with her instead of Griffon.

"I do—I did. But I also have a history with Drew. We were married once, remember? I need to find out if we're meant to go back to that place, to be those people again."

"But you haven't even kissed him? This time, I mean."

I shake my head. "Not even close." It's not a total lie.

"This whole thing is so insane," Rayne says. "How was the party?"

"Interesting," I say. I look at her eager face, and wish I could tell her everything. But I can't, not yet. Rayne doesn't know she's Akhet, and telling her now would ruin the whole night. "You should see Drew's apartment. It's on the top of the tallest building downtown and decorated by a designer. Looks like it belongs in a magazine. It's crazy."

"So, are you going to go out with him again? What is he, like, twenty-five? Your parents are going to freak out."

"He's only twenty," I say. "And they already did. He came by the house the other day to ask me out and they saw him on the porch. Luckily Mom was asleep on the couch by the time I got home last night, and I snuck into my room without her having a clue."

"I take it back," Rayne says. "I thought nothing you could do would top Kat's leaving, but this might do it."

"Which is why we're not going to tell them. I have a bribe for you if you cover for me."

"You know you don't have to bribe me. But I'm listening."

"Remember Portia Martin is playing tonight at the Arena?"

"Yeah. I also know that the tickets sold out in minutes. I tried to win a pair on the radio for weeks."

"What if I told you that not only can we go to the show, but we have backstage passes?"

"No freaking way!" Rayne pushes me on the shoulder. "How did you . . . ?" She's quiet for a second. "Did Drew get them for you?"

"Indirectly," I say. "I sort of sat next to Portia at dinner last night. I promised her we'd come, so you can't say no."

"Wait, wait—you sat next to *Portia Martin*? She knows who I am?"

"Yep. And she said that she'll be personally hurt if we don't come tonight, as long as you're feeling up to it. Drew said that he'd pick us up, but I can't do it at my place. Can he pick us up here?"

"Um, *yeah*." Rayne licks some cupcake frosting from her fingers. "Hurry up! If we're going backstage at Portia Martin's show, we have to start getting ready now."

"So I'm forgiven?"

Rayne smiles at me. "There was never any question. You

don't have to resort to bribery. Although I have to say, I kind of like it when you do."

I'm trying not to be impressed, I really am. When Drew came to get us in a Mercedes so new it still had the dealer tags on it, I tried to pretend like it was no big deal, even when Rayne leaned over and whispered to me that he was possibly the most beautiful man she'd ever seen in real life. When we were ushered into the very back of the Arena and straight into Portia's dressing room, I acted like I did this kind of thing every day. Even when Portia leaped up off the couch and gave us all big hugs, I shrugged it off like I was just visiting a friend at her house. But now, standing just a few feet off the main stage, watching Portia up front with the lights beating down and thousands of fans screaming at her feet, I know my smile has pretty much taken over my face.

"I got you some water," Drew says into my ear as he hands each of us a bottle.

"Thanks!" Rayne just grins and waves her backstage pass at me like it's all unreal. We found a stool for her to sit on while she watches, and other than looking a little tired, she's doing okay.

As we wait in the wings, Drew stands behind me, not so close that we're touching, but close enough so I can feel the Akhet vibrations between us. I check my phone again for anything from Janine. I feel so helpless, like I failed them all.

"Expecting a call?" Drew asks, nodding to the phone.

"No," I say, tucking it back into my pocket. "Just habit."

"Good," he says. "Tonight you should forget about every-thing else and just enjoy yourself."

He's right. How often do I get to be backstage at an Arena show? Portia finishes her song and waves to the crowd as they pound on the floor and scream for more. Her backup dancers race by us for a costume change, their muscles glistening with sweat, grabbing water as they head deeper backstage. The stage lights dim and a hush comes over the Arena.

Drew's been leaning against the wall, but as soon as Portia starts speaking into the microphone, he snaps to attention. "Crap! She's not going to, is she?"

Because the speakers are pointed away from us, I don't catch everything she says. "What?" I look over at Rayne, who just shrugs.

Drew runs his hand through his hair. "I helped her out on a couple of songs on the last album. But she promised she wasn't going to make a thing out of it."

I look up and see Portia turned away from the audience, her arm extended in our direction.

"Guess I don't have a choice," Drew says. "Will you ladies excuse me for just a minute?" Plastering a smile on his face, Drew strides confidently out onto the stage and grabs Portia's hand. She says something to the audience and everyone cheers as Drew walks over to the grand piano that's off to one side and sits down.

All I can see is the top of his head as he bends over the keys, and in seconds, the first bars of Portia's newest hit come burst-ing through the speakers. Portia stands motionless next to the piano, one lone spotlight illuminating her figure, the rest of the stage bare. The crowd is silent as she begins singing about losing her love to someone else, the sense of loss and longing transmitted perfectly to every single heart in the massive space. She sings to the audience, who wave their arms in slow motion, and turns to Drew as she reaches the part of the song where she talks about finding someone just like the one she lost. Even though it's just Portia and Drew and the piano, no flashing lights or glittering backup dancers, it's the most beautiful moment of the whole night.

"What's up with that?" Rayne leans over and whispers in my ear. "I didn't know Drew could play."

"I think there's not much he can't do." I watch as the song finishes and Drew stands up and waves to the crowd. Everyone is on their feet, screaming for more as Portia wraps her arms around him and plants a kiss on his lips. She said that they had a history, but now I'm wondering just how long ago that history ended.

"Sorry about that," Drew says a little sheepishly as he joins us backstage. There are beads of sweat on his upper lip that he rubs away with the sleeve of his shirt.

"That was amazing," Rayne says, a flicker of awe in her eyes. "I love that song. Why didn't you tell us you played on it?"

We flatten ourselves against the wall as the dancers rush back onstage and the lights come up for the next song. "We were just messing around in the studio one day, and that came out," he says. "We had no idea it was going to take off like it did." He glances at me, a faintly guilty look in his eyes. "She usually has one of the guys in the band play the piano part. I honestly didn't think she was going to do that."

I smile. "You were great."

Relief washes over his face, and I realize just how much he cares what I think.

"I'm glad," he says. "It didn't matter that thousands of people were out there. What mattered was that you were back here. Every word, every note, was for you."

There's a pause, and it feels like time stops for just a moment. Everything seems to come into sharp focus as the music and the stage are pushed into the background. I see the way Drew's hair is damp at the ends from the heat of the stage, and the outline of the ankh he wears through the thin fabric of his shirt. I see the way we were back then, how safe and protected I felt with Connor's arms around me and how unbelievably broken I felt when he was gone.

I want to be part of something like that again—to feel that level of devotion again. Drew loves me even though I've given him every reason not to, and eventually he'll stop giving me second chances. Someday soon, he's going to stop asking.

I reach up and put my arms around his neck, pulling him to me and pressing my lips against his in a kiss that I hope holds both an apology and a promise.

Drew pulls back, surprised, and looks into my eyes for confirmation that it wasn't an accident, like somehow I tripped and fell into him. I smile, almost embarrassed now. He throws his head back and laughs, picking me up and spinning me around, giving me a kiss that's both tender and insistent. I put one hand on his chest, and his heart is beating so loud and so fast it drowns out the Akhet vibrations between us.

As he sets me back down, I look over at Rayne. She's

watching it all with a smile on her face, and I know that any sins against Griffon have been forgiven. "Nice," she mouths, and I roll my eyes at her.

We're walking through the parking lot after the show when my hand bumps Drew's, and instead of moving apart, he wraps his fingers through mine, watching my face to see that it's okay, that things have changed enough between us to hold hands in public.

I glance up at Rayne, who's walking ahead of us through the rows of cars, her head bent and the light from her phone reflected in her face; texting Peter, I'm sure.

"You don't have to worry," I say, leaning into him. "I'm not going to run away."

Drew laughs and squeezes my hand tighter. "I guess I'm not totally sure of that." He brings my hand up to his lips and kisses my fingers. "It's just so hard to believe that you're here, that you're with me now. It's been so long."

"I thought the kissing might have convinced you," I say.

"I might need a little more convincing," Drew says, leaning in and kissing me deeply. I can feel his hunger inside, an overwhelming desire so intense it scares me.

I hear a phone clatter to the ground, and we look up to see Rayne slumped against the hood of an old car from the '50s. She's not completely unconscious, but looks dazed and not totally aware of us as we rush over to see if she's okay.

I recognize the look in her eyes, seeing but not seeing, and know she's someplace else. "I think she's having a memory," I say.

"What are you talking about?" Drew grabs her by the

shoulders and eases her onto the ground next to the car. As he lets go of her arms, he turns to me. "Why am I feeling Akhet vibrations from her?"

"I'm okay," Rayne says thickly. She tries to stand up, but her legs are wobbling under her. "I just had the weirdest flashback." She rubs her forehead. "I've been getting them a lot lately. I think it's from the stuff that Veronique gave me."

"It is, sort of," I say, helping her up. "What did you see?"

She squints. "I was driving an old turquoise blue car on a country road somewhere. It had these huge fins on the back like it was the '50s. It was really hot, so the windows were down, and I was blowing cigarette smoke out into the air."

I look at the car she's leaning against. It's red, not blue, but it has the same huge fins in the back. "Was it like this car?"

Rayne looks at it thoughtfully. "Yeah, it was, kind of."

Drew stares at me, taking it all in. "You don't mean... how...?"

I exhale. I should have done this long before now. It's not fair to keep either of them in the dark, even if it's for different reasons. "Let's find Drew's car. I think we have a lot to talk about."

Twenty-Six

So Rayne's fine with it?" Janine asks, leaning back in her chair as I tell her a carefully edited version of last night's events.

"More than fine with it," I say. "Thrilled is more like it. I wish you could have seen her face when I told her. I thought she'd be pissed about what Veronique had done, but I don't think I've ever seen her happier."

Janine laughs. "That's one way to look at it," she says. "I'm glad you finally told her."

"I had to. She was starting to have memories, and I couldn't let her think she was going crazy."

"You can always send her to me if she has questions you can't answer," Janine says.

"I will. I just hope she can keep the whole thing from her mom. She was so excited; I know that was her first thought, and her mom is totally into all that hippie stuff—psychics and auras."

"At least she has you. Not many people get that kind of an advantage when they transition."

"Thanks," I say quietly.

"What did you tell Drew?"

"Everything," I say. "Well, almost everything. I left out the part about spying on his party, because there was just no good way to put that."

"And what did he say?"

I look away, thinking about the hurt on Drew's face as I told him what had been going on. "He was kind of pissed," I admit. "He didn't like that I'd been keeping such big things from him. But we weren't together when it all happened," I say. "It's not like I owed him anything."

Janine raises her eyebrows at the past tense, but thankfully lets it go. No way do I want to talk about my relationship with Drew right now. Whatever it actually is. He kissed me when he dropped us off last night, but I could tell he was hesitating, holding something back.

"You're right," Janine agrees. "You don't owe him anything."

Her eyes are so honest and kind—I feel the guilt welling up inside. I've been thinking about it for the past two days; I have to tell her. "You know how I said that I didn't get anything from anyone at Drew's party?"

"Yes. You said that nobody there seemed to be hiding anything big." She tilts her head toward me. "Don't worry, it's what we expected. We're trying some other avenues of information."

"Yeah. Well, that wasn't totally true. I did see something, but I'm not sure what it means."

Janine sits up straight. "Why didn't you tell me?"

I take a deep breath. "Because it's Giselle."

Her eyes widen. "Giselle? Our Giselle?"

"Exactly," I say, feeling validated by her reaction. "*Your* Giselle. Which is why I didn't say anything in the first place. I knew you wouldn't believe me."

"That's not fair," Janine says. "Of course I believe you. It's just that it's extremely unusual for Sekhem to turn like that—I can't remember a single case in all of my lifetimes. You caught me off guard, is all. Did you sense that she knows more about this than she's letting on?"

I struggle to find the right words, because I'm not sure what I know. "All I sensed was something dark in her essence. It's hard to explain, but it's like a shadow over the sun, a place that she doesn't want anyone to see."

Janine considers this. "She did volunteer to go with you to the party." She looks me in the eyes. "Do you remember her trying to steer you into or out of conversation with anyone? Did she do anything that would have made you suspicious?"

"I don't think so," I shake my head. "She mostly stayed out of the way, on the other side of the room, the whole time. I sort of . . . spilled wine on her, and it was when I was helping with the stain that I felt that she was hiding something."

Janine studies me. "Do you think that you could read her better if you had more time? If she's involved in any of this, we have to know. It's been a week since Veronique was killed, and every second the trail gets colder."

I remember the look in Giselle's eyes when I saw her at Veronique's lab that day. Was it guilt? Did she know I sensed something? "If I do, I'll have to be careful how deep I go, because if I get sick like last time, she'll figure it out. She saw how I was after connecting with Rayne."

"Is it something you can control?"

I was able to at Drew's party, but that was with a room full of people. "I don't know."

"Let's find out." Janine takes out her phone and sends a quick text. She waits, then looks up at me. "She'll be here in an hour."

"Why do Griffon and Sue have to be here?" I ask, pacing her office. I'm nervous enough about this without him in the room.

"Because otherwise it'll look suspicious," Janine answers. "This way, it'll just be like I called another meeting, and these are the people who could come on short notice. Don't worry— I'll back you up if you go too deep and start to get sick. Just do your best."

There's a knock on the door, and Janine motions to the couch. "Sit over there, and I'll make sure Giselle is sitting next to you."

I try to sit back and look casual, but my heart is beating out of my chest. What if Giselle figures this out? Nobody actually came out and said it, but if she's head of security, then I'm sure she's got a weapon on her. I have to trust that Janine knows what she's doing.

Sue walks into the room, and I can see the strain of the past few days on her face. "I've only got about half an hour," she says, checking her watch. "I've got another meeting in the city—our intelligence says that there are some deals going down that might have to do with the theft at the lab." She collapses next to me on the couch and pats my knee. "How are you doing, dear?"

"Fine," I say, wondering what to do next. If Giselle isn't next to me, then this whole thing's a bust.

"Sue, why don't you take my chair?" Janine says, getting up from the chair she usually sits in. "It's so much more comfortable."

"If I get any more comfortable, I'm going to fall asleep." Her laugh is brittle. "I haven't been getting much rest lately."

"Even more reason." Janine gives her a hand to help her up.

"If you insist," Sue says, settling into the chair while Janine perches on the edge of her desk. As I suspected, Griffon takes the chair farthest away from me when he comes in, leaving Giselle to take the seat next to me when she shows up a few minutes later.

"So, what's this about?" Giselle asks. "I thought we had a good update last night."

"I wanted to include Cole in our meeting," Janine says. "Let her in on where things stand."

"She's not part of the Sekhem," Griffon says. His tone is angry, dismissive. "Not officially." I can't look at him because I'm afraid my anger will overflow, and I need to concentrate and not blow this opportunity.

"True," Janine says in a calming tone. "But she's helping us in a way that nobody else can."

"Like I was saying, there has been some interesting movement with some of the players from North Korea," Sue says. "I don't know if it's about the Akhet formula specifically, but there's more activity in that sector since the break-in. We're checking it out now."

As Sue talks, I cross my arms so that my elbow is just barely brushing Giselle's. I take some deep breaths like Janine showed me and try to block out everything that's going on around me. Giselle moves a little bit, but not enough to break the connection. I try to focus on where our bodies meet. It takes a few frustrating moments, but soon I can sense the same darkness that I felt before, as if there's something she's trying consciously to hide. I can hear people talking in the room, and I feel Giselle's heart rate speed up and familiar emotions wash over me. They're coming from the place she doesn't want anyone to see, a place that she's pushed as far from the surface as she can. She shifts in her seat and pulls her arm away from mine, breaking our physical connection, but I think I have my answer.

"Do we have someone watching customs?"

I pull my awareness away from Giselle and see that it's Griffon speaking. I watch her eyes as she studies him, her pupils large and her breathing shallow. I know without a doubt that this is what she's been trying to suppress all this time. Giselle isn't hiding a connection to whoever broke into the lab and killed Veronique—she's been trying to hide the fact that she's in love with Griffon.

"Of course," Sue says. She turns to Giselle. "What's going on with the analysis of what was left in the lab?"

I can see Giselle pull her attention away from Griffon. "We've been able to isolate the mycotoxin," she says, her voice steadier than I'd thought it would be. "And it's like nothing we've ever seen before. It has similarities to the standard forms of ergotoxins, but the makeup is different. What we haven't been able to do is figure out exactly how she did it. There are still some pieces missing."

"So you can't replicate it?" Sue asks.

Giselle shakes her head. "Not with what we have."

"It doesn't matter what's in it," Griffon insists. "What matters is who has it."

"We know," Sue says. "Trust me, I've got every available detail working on it. I've called in everyone with ties to the most likely suspects."

"But what if it's someone we don't suspect?" he asks, his frustration visible. "What if it's someone who's flying completely under the radar?"

"We're using profilers and surveillance everywhere we can," Janine says. "It's not like there's going to be an entire generation of evil Akhet in the next few weeks. It's going to take decades for the formula to be administered and for the abilities to take effect."

"By then it'll be far too late," Griffon says quietly.

The meeting breaks up quickly after that; there are no good answers to the questions everyone has.

"I'm going back to the South Bay—do you need a ride?" Giselle asks Griffon. Her voice is casual, but now I'm aware of the intent behind the words.

"No," he says. "I have a few things I need to take care of at home. I'll meet you tonight." I try to gauge his words, but either he doesn't know how she feels about him or he's not reacting.

I pull my bag over my shoulder. Griffon rushes out the door ahead of me, and I'm sure that's to avoid any more awkward conversations between the two of us.

Janine looks at me questioningly. "Everything's fine. I'll call you later," I say, leaving her alone with Sue.

I decide to walk to the BART station, because it's a nice day and I'm not meeting Drew until dinner. I push open the doors of Janine's building to see Griffon sitting on his motorcycle by the curb out front. I glance at him and turn to walk down the street when he calls me back. I take a few more steps. I don't want to talk to him right now. I kept it together during the meeting, but the less contact we have, the better for both of us.

"Wait!" he calls again.

I can't exactly ignore him, so I turn and take a few steps back. "What?" I ask, glancing down the street to show him I have somewhere else to be.

"What was all that in there?"

"All what?"

"You were reading Giselle, and Janine set it up." He shakes his head. "Neither of you is as sly as you think you are."

"Maybe you should ask Janine about it."

"I'm asking you," he says. "What's going on?"

"If I tell you, you have to keep it to yourself." I sigh and force myself to look at his face. There are dark circles under his eyes, but aside from that, he looks as good as always. "I felt something dark in Giselle's essence, something that she was trying to hide, and we needed to figure out what it was."

Griffon looks surprised. "You thought Giselle had something to do with the theft of the formula? I could have told you both you were wrong. I've known her for centuries—she'd never go to the other side."

"Maybe you're a little too close to the subject to see it clearly," I say.

Either he doesn't get my implication or he ignores it. "So what was it? What did you see that made you change your mind?"

I hesitate. He's not mine anymore, but that doesn't mean I want to help Giselle. "It's not my secret to tell."

"Fair enough." Griffon nods to the bike. "I'd give you a ride to the station, but I don't have an extra helmet."

I look down at the single helmet strapped to the side and wonder what he did with mine. "That's okay. I'll be fine."

"I can walk with you if you want."

I glance at the crowds of people on the street. I remember shopping on Telegraph with him before, eating pizza and buying records. The difference between where we were then and where we are now is almost unimaginable. Part of me wants to say yes, to have him walk down the street by my side again, but I know it won't mean anything in the long run. I have to keep my promise to Drew. And to myself. "No. Thanks. I'm just going to go alone."

He hesitates for just a moment. "Okay. Guess I'll see you around."

I try not to watch the familiar motion of him straddling the bike and pulling the helmet onto his head. My heart is heavy as I watch him stand up, kick the bike into gear, and rev the engine. That sound is always going to mean long rides up the Great Highway to me, feeling free and confident as I sat behind him. He flips up his visor and looks at me. "You were right, back at the hospital. When you said I didn't give you any choice between me and Drew."

Even now, the memory of that conversation hurts. "I wasn't with him then."

"But you are now." Griffon doesn't flinch at the words.

I pause, choosing my words carefully. "You left," I say to him, watching his face. "Drew stayed."

Griffon nods his head slowly, flips the visor back down, and guns the engine, pulling the bike away from the curb and into the stream of traffic.

Twenty-Seven

This time, Larry the security guard waves me through the lobby and toward the elevators. He must have buzzed Drew, because he's waiting for me as the doors open.

"Hi," I say, stepping into the apartment and trying to gauge his mood.

"Hi," he says, hesitating just a second before he leans down and kisses me. He closes his eyes and shakes his head, holding one palm up against my cheek. "I want so much to be mad at you. But I don't want to waste precious time on pointless emotions."

"Good," I say, reaching up to kiss him again, surprised at the relief I feel.

Drew steps back and takes both of my hands in his. "But no more holding things back, okay? Promise me you'll tell me what's going on. No more secrets?"

"Right," I nod. "No more secrets from now on."

"So, where do you want to eat?" he asks, keeping one of my hands in his and leading me into the living room.

"Doesn't matter to me."

Drew sits down on the big brown couch and pulls me down with him in a long kiss. We don't say anything as we finally pull apart, each wrapped up in our own thoughts. I look at Drew's hand in mine. His arms are tan with a sprinkling of blond hairs. I picture them gliding through water, the sun glinting down on the surface as the waves break into spray. "Did you ever surf?"

"Of course," he says, laughing a little. "Still do when I go visit the folks. Why?"

I shrug. "There's just so much I don't know about you. Like, what did you do when you left home? Where did you go?"

"I went where all good Akhet go when they come of age. First I went to Alexandria to retrieve some things, then it was on to New York and then here."

"So you were loose in the big city as a sixteen-year-old with a huge amount of money?"

"I told you, it wasn't a huge amount then. Just enough to get me started." He smiles, and I can tell he's remembering things I'm probably not going to get to hear about. "I actually did eat a lot of my meals at Maria's place in the beginning, out of necessity. But yeah, it was fun."

"How did you get all of your money to Alexandria? I mean, most of the time you don't know when you're going to die. You can't exactly stop time and say 'hang on, I just have to go to Egypt real quick and stash some things.'" My mind flashes back to the hillside in England where fires were crackling over the screams of the condemned. There's no way he would have had time to hide things before the soldiers took him away during that lifetime.

"If you have the means to get to Alexandria, you stash things there whenever you can, over your entire lifetime. Most recently, I kept most of my money in a safe-deposit box in New York. My 'grandfather' left it to me," he says, putting air quotes around the word. "It's so much easier now to pick up where you left off. Used to be, you had to basically start over each time."

I play with his fingers, trying to remember what he looked like as Connor, but all I get is a fuzzy picture of blond hair and green eyes. His image is hiding in the corners of my mind, like a ghost. "How did we meet?" I finally ask.

Drew props himself up on one elbow against the back of the couch so he can look at me. "We met at the store. You know that."

"No, not this time. The last time."

He looks concerned and a little hurt. "You don't remember?"

"No. I've had flashes of things from that lifetime, some from when I was little on a cliff overlooking the ocean, and others from . . . from the bad time at the Tower. But I have no idea how we met, or any of it." At this point, I can't put any of my lives together in a linear way. It's like a bad music video where you see scenes that don't make much sense out of context.

Drew leans over and kisses me lightly, obviously remembering the time before. "We met at court," he says.

That thought nudges something in my mind. I remember the cool stones of a drafty castle surrounded by tall shade trees. "At some kind of palace?"

He smiles. "That's right. Arundel in West Sussex." He strokes my arm absentmindedly as he speaks. "Your mother was one of the many ladies-in-waiting to Mary Howard. Caused quite a scandal at the time, too—your mother's stock was considered too common to be a lady-in-waiting, but Mary insisted. You were with her at the country house—just a kid really, only about fourteen at the time, but old enough to catch my eye." He pauses, his eyes far away. "You were so beautiful then, too—pale skin scattered with freckles and the most amazing rust-colored hair. Anyone who saw you for the most fleeting second back then would never forget."

I nudge him in the ribs. "So you have a thing for younger girls."

"Only you," he says, nudging me back. "Although I didn't do anything about it until much later. I arranged to have you visit my sister as often as I could—luckily you two got along—just to have you near me. I courted you in baby steps—bringing you small trinkets when I traveled, telling you stories about the people in faraway places."

"I can't imagine it took a lot of convincing," I said, remembering how free and romantic he always seemed.

He glances at me. "It took enough. It wasn't easy to earn your trust. And then when I finally was able to make you mine, my family strongly disapproved."

I get up and walk cautiously toward the window, looking out over the city, thinking about the memory of the garden shed and his father's anger when he caught us together. "I do remember that part. Your father hated me."

Drew sighs, walking up to put his arms around me, pulling

me toward him. "My father didn't even know you. They had a match already picked out for me—had done since I was a child—and a beautiful upstart wasn't part of his political agenda. Someone in your position was suitable as a courtesan, yes, but not as a wife."

I watch the cars as they stream across the Bay Bridge. For once, I'm not afraid of how high up we are. "What did we do?"

"Snuck around a lot at first," he says. "It took a series of threats to convince my parents that I wasn't going to back down."

"Sounds familiar," I say, wondering what Dad would do if he knew I was here.

He laughs. "It is funny how some patterns repeat themselves. Eventually, we got married in secret, and you made me the happiest man in England. I didn't need my parents' approval or a title." He leans over and kisses my cheek. "All I needed was you."

I think about the grand houses and the servants that surrounded us. "So we were poor?"

"No." He laughs. "I said I didn't *need* the title. They eventually gave it to me anyway. Parents have a way of forgiving their kids for a lot."

Drew pushes my hair away from my neck and runs strong thumbs up and down either side of my spine. The sensation causes me to melt and eases the tension inside just a little bit.

I turn and wrap my arms around his waist, his blue eyes dark and intent on me. "I'm glad we get to try again."

As if to test this theory, Drew leans in and kisses me deeply, pressing me against the window, his hands on my hips. My skin comes alive wherever he touches me, and I feel heat radiating as we come together. I close my eyes to see the shadowy memory of another time, the two of us in a cold stone room lit only by a flickering fire, with a rugged wooden bed surrounded by heavy linen curtains.

I slip underneath the silken coverlet, my cheeks flaming with heat, and I wonder if Connor notices in the dim light. There is nothing between us now but thin fabric and a layer of nervous excitement that feels palpable in the drafty room.

"You look beautiful," Connor says, approaching the bed. "No bride in history has ever been as lovely as you were today." He kicks his boots off onto the floor, and I sit motionless, watching him, the candles lending flickering shadows to his ruggedly handsome face.

Drew's hand is trembling as he brushes the hair away from my face, and he inhales sharply. "Through all the years, through every century, I've never stopped loving you." He buries his face in the curve of my neck, tracing the line of my shoulder with his lips. I reach up and tentatively touch his chest, a gesture that feels strangely familiar. For all that's new between us, there's a rhythm to his touch that my body recognizes, our hands tracing patterns that became familiar over weeks and years.

Instead of casting my eyes demurely to the ground as Connor disrobes, I watch with a growing intensity as each article of clothing falls to the floor and he finally stands before me totally unashamed. I pull my eyes away from his body and up to his face, and I can see that he's fighting for control as he slips between the covers.

"We can't have you with an unfair advantage," he says, a

*hint of mirth in his voice. He reaches for the ribbons at the top of
my nightdress, inhaling as it falls open around my shoulders.
His breath is hot as he kisses my neck, and my body takes over,
arching up to meet his in the cocoon of bedclothes that for the
moment is all I know of this world.*

I press my hands against his chest and Drew responds reluctantly, pushing himself away from me. His face is flushed and
his eyes are shining, and I'm wondering if somehow I pulled
him into my memory, or if he was just having one of his own.
"We should stop," I say, my breathing ragged.

"Mmm," he says, his lips on my neck again. "We should. But
I don't want to."

The stubble on his chin is ticklish as he runs it along my
collarbone and I laugh out loud. "There's no rush. I'm not going
anywhere."

Drew puts both hands on the window above me and looks
down into my face. "I wish I could be sure of that." He bends down
and snatches another kiss. "But maybe a dinner break will do
us both good. I want to take you out to the best restaurant in
the city."

I honestly haven't felt like eating in days, but I know how
things will go if we stay here. "Okay. I told my parents I wouldn't
be home until curfew." I look down at my jeans. "But I'm not
dressed for anyplace nice."

Drew holds up one hand. "Hang on," he says, rushing out of
the room. In a few moments he comes back with the black dress
he bought me and the platform sandals in the shoebox. He holds
them out tentatively. "I never returned these."

I look at the gorgeous dress and then back to the slightly

dirty, crumpled clothes I've been wearing all day. I can tell from his face how badly he wants me to wear the things he picked out. I still feel weird about it, but I suppose it's the least I can do. "They are nice."

"You can change in the spare bedroom back there," he says. "I promise I won't peek."

I grab the box and dress on the way to the bedroom, not saying a word. After I shut the door, I lay the dress on the bed and position the shoes under it. I can only imagine how much these must have cost. I run my hand over the heavy fabric, just as flashes of another memory race through my mind.

I touch the soft velvet bodice with one finger, almost afraid of such finery.

"For you, my lady," Connor says, nodding at the exquisite gown and slippers that are spread across the bedclothes.

I cover my mouth with my hand, trying to stifle my smile. "Another gown?" I say. "It's beautiful!"

"We've been invited to a midwinter ball at the palace," he says. "And a lady shan't be seen in the same gown twice in one season." He pushes my braid aside and brushes his lips against my neck, and I realize how much pleasure it gives him to provide for me. I feel the heat from his body as he presses close to me. "Although nothing you can put on will ever surpass your natural beauty."

I blink as the memory fades, the image making me giddy and uncomfortable at the same time. I carefully drop my own clothes to the ground and pull the stiff new dress over my head, reaching around to pull the zipper up as far as I can. I sit on the bed and slip my feet into the shoes, much higher than I'm used to, but when I stand up and look into Drew's full-length mirror, it's like there's someone else looking back at me. Someone older and more sophisticated. I take a few tentative steps in the heels before pulling the door open and walking carefully down the hall. "What do you think?" I ask, striking a pose in the doorway.

"Amazing," Drew whispers. "Beautiful."

I turn sideways. "Can you help me get this zipper up all the way?"

"Of course," he says, his fingers tracing my spine as he fastens the dress. I turn, and he runs one finger down the chain to the ankh that's hanging just above the neckline. "Just a second," he says, walking toward his bedroom and returning a moment later with a familiar black velvet box.

I lift the ruby earrings out of the box and slip them into my ears. "I never did say thank you," I say, tilting my head toward him. "How do they look?"

"Beautiful," he says again. Drew seems lost, and I wonder if he's remembering as well. Looking into my eyes, he runs a finger over one of the earrings, then pulls my hair away from my face. "Have you ever thought about wearing your hair in a braid? It's so long and thick . . . it would be gorgeous."

I pull back and shake my hair out. "No," I say, suddenly uncomfortable. "I like it down now."

"Right," Drew says, forcing a smile. He kisses me on the neck. "You're gorgeous no matter what you do. Now that you look so good, I'm going to jump in the shower and get ready. Where should we go? Coi? Or that new seafood place on Polk?"

"Whatever you want," I say as he disappears into the bedroom. I run my fingers down the smooth skirt, knowing that it's more expensive than anything I've ever worn. A feeling of exhaustion settles in, leaving a heavy weight on my chest. I can't blame that on the dress or the earrings, so I just figure it's because of all that's been going on with Rayne and Veronique's death.

Drew's tablet is sitting on the table, so I sit down on the couch and pull it into my lap. I wait until I hear water running from behind the partially open bedroom door before I bring up the search box and type in Griffon's name. It only takes a second to find the lecture Janine was talking about—it's on a site I've heard about that puts up important talks from famous people. My finger hovers over the link, and I can't decide whether I want to click it or not. Eventually, I do. I was always going to.

The title above the square screen reads "Griffon Hall: Smart Energy to Save the Planet." There's a blurb about him over to the right—how the wunderkind physicist is out to save us from ourselves with an invention that will change the world. Once the little loading circle disappears, there's Griffon standing on a brightly lit stage in front of hundreds of people. He's wearing a dark purple button-down shirt, and as he moves I can see the smallest flash of the black cord that hangs around his neck. My heart skips a beat as he begins speaking, walking casually up and down the stage as if he were in his living room, gesturing and smiling, his dimples flashing as he makes a point and the audience laughs. I'm so busy watching this confident, almost adult version of Griffon speak that I have no idea what he's saying. Before it's over, I click on the red X in the corner and the screen shrinks down to nothing. A completely perfect metaphor for our relationship.

I'm still staring at the blank screen when Drew pokes his head into the living room. He's holding up two shirts. One is the same deep purple color that Griffon was wearing. "Which is better?" he asks.

"The green one," I answer without hesitation.

As we're waiting for the elevator, I catch a glimpse of us in the hall mirror, and I have to admit that we look good together. The green shirt sets off the blue in Drew's eyes, and the dress and heels make me look less awkwardly young beside him. Almost like we really do belong together.

"So, where are we going?" I ask, as we wait for the car to be brought around to the front of the building.

"Coi, I think," Drew says. He slips the valet a folded bill as he opens the door to the Bugatti for me. I watch him as he walks around to the driver's side, saying something that makes the valet laugh. He's always so in control of every situation. "I have a quick stop to make first," he says, easing into the seat next to me. "Is that okay?"

I settle into the soft, buttery leather. "Fine by me." I'm determined to enjoy this night. No worrying about Veronique or the stolen formula. No thinking about Griffon. Or Giselle. Just me and Drew in his fancy sports car, cruising through San Francisco.

The sun is making long shadows as Drew pulls out onto the Embarcadero, still crowded with joggers and tourists even though it's almost dinner time. "Have you been to the Ferry Building lately?" Drew asks. "There are some great restaurants in there now."

"No," I say, looking out the window as we pass it. I realize with a jolt that this is where we landed in my past lifetime, the dock where the ferry unloaded all of our belongings, including my broken cello. "Not this time."

Drew glances at me, but doesn't say anything. We drive in silence, and I watch the people on the sidewalk as we pass. I realize we're headed toward the Marina. "Where are we going?"

"There's something I might want to buy," he says cryptically, one hand on the shift knob. "But I want your opinion first."

I can't imagine what he would need my opinion about. "Why?"

"Because it might involve you someday." He smiles at me quickly. "You'll see."

I don't have long to wonder as we pull into an empty parking space down by the Marina Green. Drew opens the door and helps me out, something I actually appreciate in this dress and these heels. I look around at the boats and the water. "Here?"

"Here," he says, grabbing my hand and leading me along the sidewalk past a small stone building. We cross a narrow white bridge onto a dock that bobs the slightest bit with the current and see a man in a suit waving in front of the biggest boat in the marina. "There he is."

Drew walks up to the man and pats him on the back. "Sandoval, this is Cole, the one I was telling you about."

Sandoval gives a little bow in my direction. "Nice to finally meet you." He winks at Drew. "I see what you mean."

I look at him. "What?"

"Nothing," Drew says with a smile. He gestures toward the boat. "So . . . what do you think?"

"I . . . think you want to go for a boat ride?" I answer, a little confused.

Sandoval laughs so hard I can see the fillings in his back teeth. "A boat ride. She's hilarious." He makes a sweeping gesture. "This is no ordinary boat. It's a superyacht. Five cabins, three salons, and a Jacuzzi tub on the upper deck."

"Okay." I turn to Drew. "What's going on?"

"I was thinking about buying it," he says, practically bouncing with excitement. "But only if you like it."

I crane my neck to see the top of the boat, where a little room is all lit up and I can see the top of a metal steering wheel. "This thing's huge."

"Not so big," Sandoval says. "Only thirty meters. But big enough to take you anywhere you want to go. Shall we take a look?"

"Do you mind if we go alone this time?" Drew asks.

Sandoval shrugs, but looks a little disappointed all the same. "Absolutely. You know where everything is. I'll be here if you have any questions."

Drew walks me along the side of the boat until we come to a small ramp. "All aboard," he says, holding my hand as I totter on my heels. I can see a big deck off the back of the boat, but Drew steers me inside. "All the best stuff is down here. Can you manage the stairs?"

It takes a little bit of effort, but I make it down the curving staircase and into a room lined with shining wood. A grand piano is at one end, along with a flat-screen TV and an assortment of couches and chairs in little groups around the huge room. Another deck is visible through sliding glass doors at the other end, completely furnished with built-in sofas lining the edges and a full dining table and chairs. "Check it out," Drew says, leading the way past the piano and into another room. This one has the biggest bed I've ever seen, perched up on a wooden pedestal.

"I think I'd need a ladder to get up there," I say, looking at all of the expensive-looking furnishings.

"No you won't," Drew says, lifting me up onto the bed and then sinking down beside me. I lean back against the massive pillows and see a window above my head. Drew takes my hand. "Can't you picture us cruising to the Caribbean, lying here in the darkness and watching the stars rush by over our heads?"

"You're really going to buy this?"

"Only if you want me to," he says, his eyes shining. "But think about it: we could just take off anytime to amazing places and keep everything right here with us." He raises his eyebrows. "There are four other cabins, too. Maybe we'll just keep our kids out of school and let them use the world as their classroom."

I sit up so fast I almost hit my head on the headboard. "Kids? What kids?"

Drew puts one hand out and laughs. "Well, not now. But someday. You always said you wanted a big family; wouldn't this be great for family trips?"

Kids. I don't remember that from our time together, and I can't imagine wanting to have kids anytime soon. He's already years ahead of me. "I guess." I look around the bedroom and start feeling anxious amid all the expensive furniture and shining glass. "But how much does something like this cost? It's got to be millions."

Drew lies back down with his hands clasped behind his head. "Doesn't matter. What's the use of having money if you can't do anything fun with it?"

I cross my legs on top of the comforter, knowing I'm totally out of my depth. "But think of what you can do with that kind of money. The people you could help with the millions that it would cost to buy this thing."

He looks over at me. "This 'thing' is something I thought we could share. A place where we could start our lives together." He rolls over and traces his hand along my thigh. "You still think I'm just some selfish Khered, don't you?"

"No. I don't think that," I say, but I'm not convincing either of us.

"Look. I pay my share of taxes. More than my share. You won't catch me with some sneaky offshore accounting—I pay every dime I owe. And I support plenty of charities, like most of the Khered I know. But that doesn't mean that we can't use some of the rest of the money for things that give us pleasure." He pauses. "Plus, just think of all of the people we're supporting if we buy this yacht."

"How is buying a million-dollar yacht supporting anyone?"

"Well, there are the boatbuilders and interior designers. And the captain and crew that we'll have to hire. Not to mention the cook."

I look around at the cabin that's twice as big as my room at home. Maybe Drew's right. I take a few deep breaths and try to calm my heart, to loosen up the tightness in my chest. Maybe

I'm reading too much into this—he just wants to buy a beautiful boat for the two of us, and I'm being an old woman about it. And it's not like he wants to start cranking out kids tomorrow.

"And then there's Sandoval," Drew continues. "He gets a massive commission if I buy this boat." He pulls me down to him, and I can't help laughing as he pokes me in the side. "He probably thinks we're down here doing it right this minute."

"Okay, okay," I gasp. "I give up. Buy the crazy superyacht." I lie next to Drew and put one hand up to feel his cheek just as he bends down and gives me a tender kiss.

After a few moments, Drew pulls away and scoots to the end of the bed. "Let's see the rest of this bad boy before it gets dark."

He lifts me off the bed and onto the ground. If it were up to him, I'd rely on Drew for everything, including getting in and out of my own bed. Instantly sorry for such a snarky thought, I stand on tiptoe to give him another kiss on the lips just as my phone rings.

"Let it go," Drew says as I root through my bag looking for it. "This is our night."

"I can't," I say. "I told Janine to call me if anything happens."

But it's not Janine's number on the screen. I glance at Drew, hesitating, but pick it up anyway. "Hello?"

"Cole," I can hear the strained urgency in Griffon's voice. "Rayne's gone. They've got her and we need your help. Right now."

I can barely understand his words. "What are you talking about? Who's got her?"

"Kidnapped," he says. "We think by the same people who took the formula and killed Veronique."

My breath catches in my throat. "Why would anyone want to hurt Rayne?"

"Because she's proof, Cole. She's the only proof they have that Veronique's formula works." He pauses, and I can hear some commotion in the background. "We got one of the kidnappers. Which is where you come in—we need you to find out what he knows, and we don't have much time. I'll text you the address."

Drew is looking at me with concern. "Change of plans?"

"Change of plans," I confirm, my legs shaking as we hurry toward the stairs.

Twenty-Eight

Is this right?" Drew asks as he turns onto Broadway.

"That's what it says." I show him the address on my phone. The drive has made me impatient, and even though I know it only took a few minutes to get here, it feels like hours since I got Griffon's call.

"There's nothing but mansions up here." He glances out the window and back at me, concern in his eyes. "You don't have to do this, you know. This isn't your fight."

I stare at him, wondering how he could possibly think that. "Of course it is. Rayne's my best friend, and I'm the *only* one who can do this. Unless they get some information from this guy, we might never find her." I look away from him and at the addresses on the houses we pass. "They must be in there," I say, pointing to a huge white three-story house with big bay windows and a turret on the top. I unbuckle my seatbelt before the car is even fully stopped. "You can just let me out."

"I don't think so," Drew says. "I'm not letting you go in there alone." He parks on the street in front of the house, blocking the driveway, and we're barely up the front steps when the big wooden-and-glass door opens. "They're in the basement," Giselle says, pointing to the back of the house. We walk quickly along the main hallway together, and I take in the Persian rugs and oil paintings on the walls.

"Is this a Sekhem house?" I ask. I thought most Sekhem didn't live like this.

Giselle glances at Drew. I wonder how she explained her presence at his party. Friend of a friend? "No. Just Khem. But someone who is sympathetic to the organization. And who has a safe room in the basement." She looks over her shoulder as she leads us. "Easier to keep things quiet that way."

We walk down a curving staircase to the bottom floor of the house. I don't know that I'd call it a basement, what with its carpeted floors and big-screen home theater over to one side. "In here," Giselle says, her tone all business. She pushes a picture aside and punches a code on the keypad behind it, which unlocks a bookcase to reveal the safe room. She holds up one hand to stop Drew. "You can't come in."

"I'm not leaving Cole," Drew says. He grabs my hand.

"It's okay," I say to her. "He's with me."

"Sekhem only," Giselle insists.

Griffon appears in the doorway. There's no emotion on his face when he sees us, although I watch his eyes take in my dress and heels. "Peter's upstairs in another part of the house. You can wait with him there."

Drew opens his mouth to protest, but I squeeze his hand. We have to do whatever it takes to get this done, and there's no time to argue. "It's okay. Nothing's going to happen. Just go up and I'll be there in a little while." Drew must realize he's not going to win, because he bends down to kiss me once, glares at Griffon, and then lets Giselle lead him away.

Griffon opens the door wider and motions me in. The room is more stripped-down than the one outside, and it definitely looks like a place where someone could hole up for days in an emergency. There are metal shelves stocked with supplies lining one wall, and a few chairs and a single bed pushed against the other. In the middle of the room is a small wooden chair with a dark-haired man sitting in it. One hand is tied to the chair back, but the other hangs loosely at his side. His eyes are open and scanning the room, but nothing else about him seems to be moving.

"His shoulder was dislocated in the struggle," Griffon says, seeing my glance at his arm. "And Giselle administered a nerve block to keep him immobile." Griffon's face looks drawn and worried. "He can see and hear, but he can't speak. Doesn't speak English anyway, from what we can tell." He gestures at the man standing behind him. "You remember Christophe?"

"Of course."

Griffon glances at his phone. "Janine should be here any minute, along with some other Sekhem. We need to find Rayne quickly. See if this guy knows where they're taking her, along with any other information he might have." A look of concern crosses his face. "Are you sure you're okay doing this? I saw what it did to you last time—"

"I'll be fine," I say, with more assurance than I actually feel. I picture Rayne alone in a dark place, not knowing where she is or who she's with. She must be scared out of her mind. I feel my anxiety start to rise again and pull my thoughts away from wherever she is. I have to calm down or I won't be able to do this. "How did it happen?"

"We were walking up Haight toward the Red Vic when four men jumped out of an SUV and dragged Rayne into it." He runs his hand over his hair. "It was so fast; we were taken totally by surprise. I managed to grab this one as he was climbing back into the car. They took off without him."

"How did you get him back here without people noticing?" I ask. Haight can be crazy at night, but a kidnapping might make people look twice.

"Giselle knows an array of defense techniques," he says. "She was able to incapacitate him enough to get him in her car and over here. He's not Ahket."

I look at the guy, whose eyes are locked on us. "What did you tell Peter?"

"As little as possible. He knows that it has to do with Rayne's sickness, but that's about it. He's really freaked out."

"I bet." I walk over to the man and his eyes widen, but his body doesn't move. "How long does the nerve block last?"

"A couple of hours, usually. It can vary, which is why we restrained him too."

I run my hands over the smooth fabric of my dress. I'm already sweating and my stomach is rolling. I look toward the closed door. "Should we wait for Janine?" I'd feel so much better trying to connect with him if she were here too.

"We don't have time," Christophe says, typing something into his phone.

Griffon looks at me and his eyes soften a little bit. "You can do this. You've done it before. Just focus on what Janine taught you and ignore everything else."

I nod, breathing hard through my nose. I take a few deep breaths and clench my hands into fists. At least this time I don't have to try to be sly about it; it doesn't matter if this guy knows whether I'm reading him or not.

I take a step closer to the chair, and he flinches almost invisibly. I start to wonder what he's feeling, if he's afraid, but I force my thoughts away from there. It doesn't matter, and any empathy in the wrong direction could get in the way. There are beads of sweat on his forehead and I can see his breath coming rapid and shallow. I put my hands lightly on his shoulders and breathe deeply, centering myself and trying to block out Griffon and Christophe, the safe room, and everything else that's going on upstairs. I focus on the place where my hands meet his jacket, on the energy that's flowing between the two of us.

Griffon's right—he's not Akhet, and he doesn't understand that I'm reading him. At least not yet. What I feel isn't fear exactly, but a sense of disappointment. He knows that he messed up, and if the people in charge find out, they'll kill him. I try to stay calm as I focus on a deeper level, on the place where we physically connect, and imagine energy flowing through that point between our bodies.

Within seconds, I see flashes of the kidnapping, and I flinch with his memory of blinding pain as he's grabbed from behind and wrestled to the ground. He wants to cry out but can't. His brain is working, but everything else is shut down.

"Where did you take her?" Christophe asks loudly, his face inches from the kidnapper's, frustration edging his voice. I hear the question, but all I get is the tone of it. The disruption completely severs our connection.

"Not helpful!" I shout at him. "Besides, he doesn't understand you."

"He knows exactly what I mean," Christophe says, pushing the guy backward. Because he has no muscle control, the guy flops around like a doll.

Griffon grabs Christophe's arm. "Leave them alone."

I close my eyes again, trying not to let frustration wash over me. I'm looking for any clues about where they would have taken her, who's waiting for her. I know he's got to be thinking about it, about who's waiting for them and what they're going to do when they find out he's gone. I clear my thoughts completely and open myself up to the impulses from his body again, trying to sink back to the place we were just a few minutes ago, when I catch a fleeting sense of a big, gray-concrete hotel. I can see people standing out front in a small curving driveway waiting for cabs or smoking cigarettes around a small round ashtray. A wave of nausea hits me and I drop my hands and sink to the ground, the folds of my expensive dress settling in around me.

Griffon rushes over, but I hold out my hand. "I'm okay," I say quickly. "Just give me a minute." I close my eyes and breathe through the sick feelings. My arms are so heavy that my hands drag uselessly on the floor. Once the worst of it passes, I open my eyes. The bright fluorescent light is painful, and I can feel a headache forming.

"There's a hotel; I think it's somewhere in the city," I say slowly, closing my eyes again and describing what I saw. "Across the street is a parking garage, and above that is a big park. People are doing that slow-motion karate stuff on mats, and there's a kids' playground." I sit perfectly still and allow the sensations and images to wash over me again. "There are lots of signs with Chinese letters on them." I open my eyes and look at them. "I think it's in Chinatown."

"I know that park," Griffon says, his voice rising with excitement. "It's Portsmouth Square. Right across from the Hilton. Are they at the Hilton?"

"Maybe," I say, but something about that doesn't feel right. It's like my attention is being drawn somewhere near the hotel instead. "But I don't think so. It's someplace next to the hotel. On the same side of the street, but on the right. Something smaller. Maybe a restaurant or a liquor store?"

As I'm trying to gather my thoughts, the door opens again and Janine rushes in, followed by Giselle. Janine's eyes are calm as she takes in the scene. "Are you okay?"

I nod. "Just a little weak."

"Did you get anything?" Janine looks hopefully at the three of us.

"I think so," Griffon says. "Chinatown, next to the Hilton, across from the park. We don't have anything exact, but that's as close as we're going to get." He seems to have taken charge as he nods to Giselle and Christophe. "You two stay here." He turns to Janine. "How many people have we got outside?"

"Seven. And I can get more on the way there."

"Great." He turns to Christophe. "Let me know if there's anything else."

"I'm going with you," I say, struggling to my feet. None of this would have happened if it hadn't been for me. I want to be there when it ends.

"No way," Griffon says harshly and turns to go. "You're in no shape to come with us."

"You can't make me stay! I'll get Drew to take me."

Janine puts a hand on my arm. "It's dangerous, and we need you here," she says, gently but urgently. "Your job is to get as much information as you can. Christophe will send us anything important when we're on the move. There are plenty of people outside whose only goal is to bring Rayne back safely. They're all well trained and they know what they're doing."

"But—"

"You don't want to be a liability," Janine says.

"Let's go!" Griffon demands, holding the door open. Janine takes one look back at me and follows him out the door.

As the room is secured again, it's eerily quiet. Christophe is tapping on his phone, and Giselle is pacing silently in the corner. I collapse into one of the chairs along the wall and put my head in my hands. Not only has connecting with this guy used up all my energy, but I'm frustrated and angry too.

Giselle walks to the shelving units. "Do you want some water? There's enough here to last us for weeks."

I look up at her. "Thanks. That might help." I squint into the light. "And a couple of Advil if you can find any."

After rooting around in her bag, she hands me some pills and a bottle of water and then looks at the guy in the chair. "You could really see all of those things? Just by putting your hands on him?"

I nod, swallowing the little orange pills in one gulp. "Yeah. Not like a movie, though. It's more impressions and feelings that I have to piece together. It's kind of hard to explain."

"But fascinating," she says. She looks genuinely interested. "Can you do that to anyone?"

I look at the ground, remembering reading her at the meeting. She has no idea. "I think so. As long as I'm in contact with them, I can."

Christophe nods at the guy. "Did you see anything else? Other than where they're taking her?"

"Just that he thinks they'll kill him if they find out he got caught," I say.

A look of concern passes over Giselle's face. "I could tell. I only saw them for a second, but these guys were professionals."

Griffon said that they were on their way to the movies, which means that Giselle was with them. I can feel jealousy flare up, knowing it has no place in this situation. Now is not the time to worry about who Griffon's out with. I glance at my brand-new shoes; and I'm hardly one to talk. "Do you have any idea where they're from?"

Giselle nods to the guy. "Our best guess is that this one's from North Korea. But that doesn't necessarily mean that all of them are."

"And he's not Akhet."

"The guys who took Rayne are just the boots on the ground," Giselle says. "The ones who do the dirty work. I'm sure that there are rogue Akhet behind all of this. There have to be." My face must give away my feelings, because she keeps talking quickly. "Look, they're going to keep Rayne alive. They have to—if they're going to try to make a profit off the formula or give it to others, they need to have proof that it works. And that it won't kill you."

"Reassuring," I say, meaning every bit of the sarcasm.

I can hear Christophe's phone vibrate and we both turn to look at him. He checks the text. "It's just my sister," he says. "We're having trouble with my mother."

"Not now, Christophe," Giselle says irritably.

"I know. Let me just answer her." He turns and taps a few things out on his keyboard before putting the phone away.

Time seems to drag in the stuffy little room, and I wish we had some way of knowing what was going on. I'm feeling stronger after my empath connection. The guy's head is lolling on his shoulder, but I don't think he's asleep. "Do you think I should try connecting with him again? See if there's any more information?"

"Let's see what happens in Chinatown first," Christophe says. "If they find her where you said they are, then it's not necessary." His phone rings and he takes it out of his pocket. "It's Janine." He pushes the button and listens for a second. I study his eyes, looking for clues, but his face is so impassive, I can't tell what he's hearing.

"Okay, thanks," he says. "I'll keep you posted." He turns to us. "They're not there."

"What?" I say desperately. I search my mind for what I'd seen. "They didn't find the right place? Because it's a small shop or restaurant right by the hotel. I can practically see it. On the right as you're facing it. Call them back—"

Christophe puts a hand out to stop me. "They got the right place—a cigar store two doors down from the hotel. They found Rayne's phone on the floor in a storeroom." He looks at me and my heart sinks. "Smashed to pieces. But there was nobody there."

Twenty-Nine

Giselle grabs me as I lunge for the kidnapper. "They're not there!" I shout, wanting nothing more than to pound my fists into him, but she pulls me back and spins me around.

I look frantically from Christophe to Giselle, panic completely taking over every rational thought. "What do we do now? I was sure that was where they were taking her. That's what I saw."

Giselle paces a little more. "That is where they took her," she says in a measured tone. "You were right, and that's probably all this guy knew. Once the others found out we had him, they must have changed their plans."

"There's nothing else we can do," Christophe says.

"There's got to be!" I say. I look at them desperately. "We can't just stand around here doing nothing! Didn't any of you get a license-plate number? Can't we call the police? Rayne's been kidnapped, for God's sake!"

Giselle stops pacing. "We did get a license number, but it was a fake. Trust me, that was the first avenue we tried. The police are no good to us in this situation, and the attention will only make it worse."

Christophe takes a sip of his water. "Janine and the other Sekhem are going to come back and we'll regroup, see if there is something else we can try. Once you calm down, maybe you can try to read him again—see if you can identify any of the people he was with."

"It's not your fault," Giselle says. "You did what you needed to do." She looks at the guy, whose eyes are still wide on us. "You told us what he knew. It's just too bad it wasn't enough." Giselle heads for the door. "I'm going to see what's happening upstairs. Make sure our guests are doing okay." I know that she's as frustrated as I am. I'm sure she just wants to get out of here.

"I'll come with you," I say. Part of me doesn't want to see Drew and Peter right now. I don't know if I'll be able to explain to them what's happening. That I failed. But I'm not sure I can stay in this room any longer.

"Stay here with Christophe," she says. "We have a rule to never leave a prisoner alone with just one person. When I come back, you can go." The door shuts behind her with a tight seal.

Christophe finishes a text and looks up at me. "Why don't you just relax? You can't function if you're agitated. Calm down and you can try again."

I shake my hands out. "I'm okay. I want to see if I can get

anything else from him before everyone gets back. We don't have a lot of time to waste."

"I don't think that's a good idea," Christophe says. "You said yourself that you needed time to recover." He smiles at me, but I can tell it's not sincere. Something passes over his features, and I can see that he doesn't want me to read the guy again. But why? It can't all be out of concern for me.

"I feel fine," I say, walking over to the chair. Christophe reaches out to stop me by grabbing my left hand. He's stronger than he looks. "Ow!" I cry, yanking my arm away.

"I'm sorry," Christophe says. "I didn't mean to hurt you." He looks down at the scar that runs the length of my forearm. "What happened?"

I rub the spot where he twisted my wrist. "Veronique," I say. "And a broken window. That's what happened." I'm suddenly wary of him.

He tilts his head as if he's interested in the story. "Veronique caused that? Looks like a nasty scar."

"It is," I admit, watching him carefully. "Ended my cello career." I flex my left hand. "There was some nerve damage that will probably never heal."

Christophe nods slowly. "That must have really pissed you off," he says. He raises his eyes to mine. "Enough to make you want to get back at her."

The tone in his voice is vaguely accusatory, and now I'm on total alert. "What do you mean by that?"

"Nothing," he says, holding up both hands. "All I meant was that permanent physical damage would be enough motive to want someone gone from this lifetime."

I take a step toward him. I don't like where this is going. "Are you saying that you think I had something to do with Veronique's death? Are you crazy? Rayne's my best friend. I'd never do anything to put her in danger."

Christophe's eyes widen. "You have to admit, that would be a good cover. Having your best friend kidnapped. It would totally throw the scent off of you." He sniffs the air as if to demonstrate.

"Do you honestly think I could kill someone?" I ask.

I can almost feel his eyes on me as he scans my dress. "I don't think you'd get your hands dirty, no. But there are other means to the same end, aren't there?"

I can feel my hands clenching into fists. "I had nothing to do with any of this. I'm just here to try to help, that's all."

"Fine," he says, but I can tell he doesn't believe me. "Janine may trust you, but in situations like this, nobody is above suspicion." He gives a little nod. "You understand."

"Right." I slump into one of the empty chairs and stare into space, my mind whirling with possibilities. My eyes are half-closed when some movement in the room makes me suddenly alert. I keep perfectly still, but watch both Christophe and the guy in the chair until I see it again. There's nothing I can pinpoint directly, just something in the way they make eye contact, but I'm as sure of it as if they'd been speaking out loud. Christophe and this guy know each other, and not just from tonight.

I get a cold chill down my spine as I watch them through half-closed lids. I've never really paid that much attention to Christophe before—he's just a guy who came from Switzerland to work with Griffon on the lab, but he's always been there in the background. He's had access to all of the information about

Veronique, about the formula and about Rayne, and I'm sure Griffon didn't hesitate to tell him anything he didn't already know. They're friends, and he's a trusted member of the Sekhem. But like he said, in situations like these, no one is above suspicion.

Stretching in my chair, I pretend to stifle a yawn.

"Tired?" Christophe asks, apparently under the impression that we've got a truce.

"A little bit," I lie. I get up and walk over to him. If he is what I think he is, I'm going to have to make physical contact to find out. And Christophe isn't under a nerve block, so I have to do it so that he doesn't suspect anything. "Connecting as an empath does take a lot out of me." He's leaning against the wall, one hand hanging down, the other in his pocket. I lean against the wall next to him, as close as possible.

"I'm sorry about getting angry with you," I say, looking up at him through my eyelashes. Good thing I've watched Kat do this a million times. "This whole situation is just so stressful. I know you're only doing your job." Just getting the words out requires effort, when what I want to do is spit in his face.

I can see him relax. Amazing what a few words can do that fists can't. "I'm glad you understand. We have to rule out all of the possibilities."

"I do," I say. "I just hope you know that I'm not one of them."

Christophe grunts in reply and bends over a text again.

"So, what do you think they're going to do with him?" I ask, nodding to the guy in the chair, who has his eyes trained on us. He may not know what we're saying, but he knows he's being discussed.

"They won't kill him," Christophe says, looking up briefly. "So in a way, he's safer here than he is out there."

"The Sekhem don't kill prisoners?" I inch my arm along the wall to get closer to his, but he must sense it, because he moves just a tiny bit to the left.

"No. Not anymore." Christophe grins. "Not like in the old days, when we could pretty much do whatever we wanted."

We're only about two inches apart now. I think about pulling the falling trick like I did on the bridge, but I have a feeling that would only make him suspicious. Christophe's got one leg bent against the wall, so I casually bend mine the same way, tilting my body just the slightest bit so that I can make contact with his leg, hoping that I don't fall off these heels at the same time.

Making contact and conversation at the same time is tricky, so I focus on the last words that he said in an effort to keep him talking. "What was it like back then?" I ask.

"Easier," Christophe says. I can still see his lips moving, but all my concentration has gone to the point where our bodies connect. I feel a surge of overwhelming confidence rush through me, almost a euphoria that something he's been working on is going really, really well. I also feel a split; loyalties are divided, and there's a hesitation to cross over a line completely. I close my eyes, still aware that Christophe is talking, and try to let my mind go, to allow any images that are in his consciousness flow over to me. I get flashes of airplanes and the long empty space of a runway.

My eyes fly open as I hear a crash. The kidnapper has fallen over—he's still tied to the chair, but he's moving now and shouting something in a language I can't understand. Christophe rushes toward him, breaking the connection between us, speaking quickly in the same language. I may not understand their words, but I get what he's saying by the way he's staring at me. The nerve block has worn off, and the kidnapper knows I've been reading Christophe.

I run for the door, but I'm exhausted from the effort of reading him, and in seconds, Christophe's on me, grabbing me around the neck and smashing my head into the wall. My vision fades for a moment and pain rushes through my brain. I can feel a warm wetness trickle down my neck, and my arms flail as my hands grab for anything I can find to get him off me.

Christophe's face is just inches from my own, and I can see flecks of spit fly as he speaks. "You think you can use your empath skills to read *me*?" he asks, his voice a harsh whisper. "I'm not going to let someone like you destroy all of the work we've put into this." He tightens his grip around my throat and I can hear myself choking, even as shadows creep in around the edges of my vision. With the last bit of energy I have left, I bring one knee up into his groin as hard as I can. His hands loosen enough for me to pull away as he shouts in agony, and I stumble for the door, gasping for air. I push on it hard before I remember that it opens inward, but only manage to give it a small tug before Christophe jumps up behind me and slams it shut again, twisting an oversized lock that will keep anyone out.

I look around frantically for anything to defend myself with. The kidnapper is moving on the ground, but he's still secured to the chair, so I focus on Christophe. He's coming at me, slowly this time, like he's going to make sure he enjoys every second of whatever's going to happen next.

"Even if they hear you," he says in a ragged voice, glancing upstairs with a grin, "it doesn't matter."

I push myself against the wall, as far from him as I can get in the small room. "But they'll know you did it," I say, trying to buy some time. "They'll know you're not one of us."

He looks at me like I'm stupid. "I may not be Sekhem, but I'm still Akhet." He glances down at the guy on the floor. "Good thing he's here to take the blame."

I can feel cold sweat running down my back as I frantically look for a way out. Christophe's reflexes are lightning fast, and he has my left hand bent painfully behind my back before I can even move. I close my eyes and reach for one end of the tall metal shelving against the wall and pull with everything I've got, bringing them crashing down onto the floor. Canned food and bottles of water spill out all over the room and the heavy shelf catches Christophe's leg, knocking him to the ground as I twist out of his grip.

I race for the door, clawing at the lock until I can finally turn the knob and wrench it open enough to slip through it. I manage to scream for Giselle just as Christophe bursts through the door and throws me to the floor. Christophe's knees are on my legs, pinning me down on the ground as he looms over me, and I know that this time he'll finish me. His hands go around my throat again, tighter this time, his face red and distorted from the effort. I'm trying to grab at his arms, but he's so much bigger than I am that I'm just clawing at the air. I'm starting to lose consciousness when I suddenly feel the weight lifted off of me, and I roll onto my side with gasping, coughing breaths.

Someone pulls at my shoulder and I'm on my back, looking up at Giselle. Her face is a mask of concern as she shakes me gently.

"He's one of them," I gasp, stopped by a fit of coughing. "I saw airplanes. A runway." I can't manage any more words. Her face is swimming in front of me and my ears are rushing with static. Christophe knows where they've taken Rayne; she's got to get it out of him.

"It's okay," Giselle says, her breathing hard and quick. She gently checks the lump on my head before pulling herself up off the floor. I can barely hear her last words as the room fades around me. "It's all in Christophe's phone."

I hear voices, but it's so nice and comfortable where I am, I don't want to open my eyes.

"She's coming around," I hear someone say, and I force myself into consciousness, everything that's happened in the past few hours rushing back to me in a flood of images and emotions.

"Where's Rayne?" I sit up quickly as my vision fragments into stars and my head pounds.

I feel hands on my shoulders pushing me back against soft cushions. "She's fine," Drew says softly. "You need to take it easy. You've been out for almost an hour."

I squint in the light coming from the lamp on the table next to me and look around. I'm not in the safe room anymore, but in what looks like a library straight out of a Sherlock Holmes novel, with wood-paneled walls and shelves full of books. There's a blanket over me, and my heels are neatly positioned next to the couch. "Where is she?" I repeat, putting a hand to the lump on the back of my head. I can feel dried blood back there too, but my fingers come away clean.

"They're on the way back here," he says. "They found Rayne and the others at the executive airport, about to get on a plane." He leans down and kisses me gently on the forehead. I can see the concern in his eyes. "God, I was so worried about you."

I look around. Peter's in a chair by a curtained window staring at the two of us, but there's nobody else in the room.

"Where's Giselle?" I ask, remembering her face downstairs. She must have pulled Christophe off of me. My heart pounds at the memory of his hands around my neck.

"In the safe room still, watching over the prisoner."

I try to sit up again more slowly. "What about Christophe?"

Drew shakes his head. "Gone."

"But he was part of the plot the whole time," I say, struggling to sit up again. "He knew about everything, he was in on it with the kidnapper—"

"'Gone' as in 'dead,' Cole," Drew interrupts. "Giselle snapped his neck. She had to, to get him off you." He glances back at Peter. "He'd been texting the kidnappers right out in the open, telling them everything we found out. Figured nobody would suspect him, I guess. Until you did." He gets up and crosses the room, bringing back a glass of water. "Drink this; you'll feel better."

The glass trembles in my hand, but the water is cool on my throat. "I saw the way they looked at each other," I say. "And I knew right then he was one of them."

"So you can read minds?" Peter says from across the room. They're the first words he's spoken since I woke up.

I glance at him. He looks a little disheveled and confused. He's slouched in the chair with his arms crossed in front of his chest, and I don't blame him. I'm not sure how much he knows, but it must be a lot to deal with. "Not exactly," I say. I look at Drew.

"I didn't know how much to tell him," Drew says.

"I can't read minds," I say. "But I can read emotions and sometimes interpret images in other people. I'm good at visual cues that other people miss. Does that make sense?"

"Not really," he admits. He looks from me to Drew. "What are you people, anyway? Nobody wants to tell me, but I know something's going on."

I decide he deserves to know the truth. "Akhet," I say. "People who remember their past lives. Rayne became one of us when Veronique gave her the ergotoxin she created. Which is what the guys who took her are after." I can see him struggling to accept what I'm saying. "You should really ask Griffon. He's better at explaining all this."

We hear the front door slam and footsteps echo in the entry-way. Drew pulls the door open and sticks his head out into the hallway. "We're in here."

I stand up at the sound of feet pounding down the hallway, just as Rayne bursts through the door. For the first time since this all started, my eyes well up at the sight of her, as she jumps up to hug Peter, who looks like he's never going to let her go. "Oh my God, I've never been so freaked out in my whole life!" she says, breathless, when he finally puts her down. "I was so scared, but I knew you would come and get me." She comes over to give me a hug, but pulls back and puts one finger on my neck. "What happened?" She looks into my face, confused.

I put one hand up and feel the welts where Christophe was choking me. "I got into a little fight. But I'm fine." I grab her and give her a hug. "The important thing is that *you're* fine."

"You should have seen it," she says, her eyes shining. "I was trying to figure out how to get out of there, you know? I could see that we were going to the airport, and there was no way I was getting on a plane with these guys, guns or no guns. We parked the car on the blacktop next to this little plane, and the next thing I know bullets are flying all over the place and Griffon is pulling me into a car." She shakes her head, and I can tell she's overwhelmed by everything that's happened tonight. "It was so crazy."

I look past her to Janine and Sue standing in the doorway. I can hear deeper voices talking out by the front door. "Is everyone okay?"

"On our side, yes," Janine says, walking into the room. "But we had to eliminate the kidnappers." She nods to Sue. "Luckily, this one still knows how to handle a gun."

Sue smiles at her. "We were able to recover some of the files from Veronique's office and what appears to be all of the formula that she'd already made. Everything was wrapped up in a suitcase, but we're still trying to figure out where they were going."

"And who they were meeting," Janine says. I can see her eyes on the bruise on my neck.

"Did Giselle tell you what happened?" I ask.

"She did," Sue says. "So hard to believe Christophe turned. If you hadn't been there, he'd have gotten away with it. They all would have."

Drew walks over and pulls me to him. "I can't believe I was only two floors away when that bastard was trying to kill you." I can hear a hitch in his voice as he speaks. "I'm never letting you out of my sight again." He bends down to kiss me and I lean into him, grateful to be able to relax at last.

"Um, I'm going to help Giselle and the guys deal with the safe room," Griffon says from the doorway. He glances quickly at the two of us and then focuses on Janine. "Do you need me for anything?"

"No," says Janine. "That's a good idea. We'll have a briefing in the morning."

"Right," he says, not looking back at me before he turns to go downstairs.

A tall grandfather clock in the corner starts to chime, and I realize it's already midnight. "Why don't you come stay over at my house tonight?" I ask Rayne. Even though it looks like the kidnappers have all been killed, I'm uncomfortable leaving her alone. "My parents will be less pissed that I'm late if you're with me." It's almost funny that I'm worried about my parents after what went on here tonight.

Rayne looks down at my dress. "How are you going to explain the fanciness?"

"Your other clothes are in my car," Drew says. "You can change here and I'll drive you home." He kisses me quickly again. "Unless I can persuade you to come stay at my place?"

I can feel Janine's eyes on me. Even though I know she's not my mom and wouldn't say a word about it, I still feel funny talking about this in front of her. "Not tonight. It'll be okay. I'll see you tomorrow."

"And the tomorrow after that?" he asks, a bright smile bursting through the concern on his face.

"Yes," I say. "I promise."

Thirty

I curl up on my side and stare out the window of Drew's apartment, unable to shake the inexplicable feelings of helplessness and dread that have been following me for days. The afternoon fog is rolling in, tucking itself around the skyscrapers, and the damp gray light outside matches my mood much better than the summer sunlight we've been having. I know I shouldn't be depressed—Rayne is safe, the formula was recovered, and all Drew wants is to make me happy. But still I feel a heaviness in my chest that I just can't loosen. I play with the knot on the scarf I've been wearing to cover up the bruises on my neck. In a few days they'll be gone completely. I wish the memories of that night could go with them.

Drew's next to me on the couch, talking on the phone. "How much?" he asks the person on the other end. "Twenty million? I was thinking more like fifteen. That should be enough to get them started." Another pause. "Screw that. Tell them it's take it or leave it. If they can't come to some sort of an agreement, there are plenty of start-ups who can." Drew scrolls through pages and pages of numbers on his tablet faster than I can see them. He stops abruptly and peers at one page. "What about ADM?" He listens to whoever is on the other end. "Good. Put fifty percent of that back in the company. Hold the other fifty." Drew's fingers play with mine absentmindedly as he wraps up his conversation. "Is that it? I'll talk to you in the morning." Drew pulls the headset off and tosses it on the table.

I put my book down and lean back against him. "Two truths and a lie."

Drew keeps tapping on the screen. "What?"

"Two truths and a lie," I say, poking him in the side. "It's a game."

He sighs, not taking his eyes off the tablet. "I'm no good at games."

I slide over to the end of the couch as I feel hot tears at the back of my eyes for no reason at all. So what if Drew hates games? He's busy, and it's stupid. So why am I crying?

"What's wrong?" he asks, looking surprised.

"Nothing," I sniffle. "It's just been a rough few weeks."

Drew puts the tablet down and reaches for me. "Thank God all of this Sekhem business is over and we can get on with our lives."

I lift my head up to look at him. "What do you mean, over? I'm still going to work with Janine. They need me. They need what I can do."

He looks confused. "But it's dangerous, you saw that. And you're not obligated to help them anymore."

I can tell this conversation isn't going my way. "Well, I'm still going to see Janine."

"Fine," he says, but I can tell he doesn't really agree. "But I don't want you doing any more dangerous assignments." He kisses me. "I need you here, in one piece." Drew sits back on the couch and I lean against his arm. "I told Sandoval I'm buying the boat," he says. "So I think we should run away to an island somewhere until you turn eighteen. You won't have to do anything except lie in the sun and swim in the water, surrounded by tropical fish."

I snort. "Sure. That would be great, but what about school? I'm going to be a senior this year. I have to finish."

"Quit!" Drew's eyes light up. "Just bail on all of it! Why do you need to finish?" He looks like he really doesn't understand the concept. "Don't you get it? From now on, you don't have to do anything you don't want to do. I have more money than we can spend in a lifetime. A high-school diploma isn't going to give you anything I can't." I can tell he's getting excited about the possibilities. "Anywhere you want to go. Europe, the South Pacific . . . maybe Thailand. I'll do a little bit of work here and there, but the rest of the time we can just hang out together playing duets and watching the sun set."

"But what about my family? The studio?"

"Once they see that you're fine, they'll forgive us. Parents always do." Drew lifts my left hand and kisses the scar that runs down the length of my forearm. "I'll buy you your own studio," he says. "I'll stock it with the finest instruments in the world. You can teach, you can perform, you can even tour if you want. You won't have to work for a thing."

I look at Drew's face and see the excitement in his eyes, the smile on his perfect face. His life is full of possibilities, of people who never say no to him. He quit school at sixteen and never looked back. He's sitting here, offering me the world, saying things that any girl would kill to hear. So why do they just make me uncomfortable?

"What's the point?" I sit up on the edge of the couch, pulling my sweater tighter around me. I feel myself walking to the edge of something, dipping my toe off the cliff to see if there's anything there that will support me. "What's the point of being alive if you're not working toward something?"

"But you will be," he says quietly. "We'll both be working toward creating a family. The family that was cut short the last time."

"I thought you said you didn't want to have kids right away."

"Not *right away*," he laughs. "But I don't want to wait too long. All you talked about last time was how you wanted to have babies. Our babies."

I look at Drew and see that he's already got it all planned out. Just like last time. "I'm not that girl anymore," I say quietly but firmly. "I'm Cole."

Drew's mouth sets in a hard line, but his eyes soften as he looks at me. "I didn't mean it like that."

"But you did! You've said it over and over. You want me to go right back to that lifetime." I take a deep breath, forcing myself not to cry. "But I'm not Allison anymore. I can't be that for you, wearing beautiful dresses that you buy for me and staying home having babies." The last words come out in a whisper. "That's not what I want this time."

"This is crazy," Drew says, sitting up next to me, one hand on my knee. "I don't know what kind of bullshit Janine's been feeding you, but—"

"It's not Janine," I say to Drew. "It's me. I have my own dreams, things I want to do. And I can make my own decisions." As I say it, I realize it's time that I do. We both want all of me, and only one of us can win. I reach up behind my neck and unclasp the ankh. I fold it into my hand one last time, feeling its warmth, keenly aware of the connection between its past and my present. In one motion I pull the earrings off as well and place them all in Drew's palm, closing his fingers around them. With that one gesture, I make a statement that propels me forward. I take a single breath, drawing air deeper into my lungs than I've been able to in days.

"Don't do this," he says, shaking his head. "Don't do this to me. To us." He lifts his hand and I flinch, but his fingers barely brush my cheek. "This is our destiny. We were meant for each other. We always have been. You can't do this."

"I have to," I say. Drew's beautiful blue eyes look suddenly panicked, and I realize that what's right is usually what's most difficult. "Maybe we were meant for each other once, but you deserve better than I can give you. There's someone else out there who can give you what you need."

Drew looks down momentarily and then lifts his eyes to mine. "As long as your essence is walking this earth, there is nobody else for me."

The weight of his words hits me full force, but as hard as this is, I can't make my decisions for him. I have to make them for me. "I'm so sorry. I can't be the person you need me to be."

He looks like he's about to cry, and I see the muscles in his jaw working. "This isn't over," he says. "As long as I'm still breathing, this isn't over." He reaches for me again, but I'm already gathering my shoes and my bag. I can't look at him, so I keep my eyes on the floor until I hear his footsteps in the hallway and his bedroom door slam.

I'm waiting for the elevator when the full weight of what I've just done washes over me. I had everything at the tips of my fingers—a gorgeous guy, more money than I could ever spend, a lifestyle most people can only dream about—and I just threw it all away. For what?

Thirty-One

The last notes echo through the music hall as I look over and give all of my students a big smile. I lean over and whisper, "Now everyone stand up and take a bow."

They all bend awkwardly at the sound of the applause, Zander bowing deepest with a toss of his head that irritates me. The lights go up and everyone begins to pack up their instruments as their parents gather at the front of the stage.

Olivia Miller walks over holding a small pink box wrapped in a ribbon. She hands it to me. "My mom made this for you," she says. "To say thanks."

I open it to see a tiny cake with a cello piped in frosting on the top. I put one finger in and take a taste. Lemon, my favorite. I give Olivia a hug. "Tell your mom thanks for me. And no practicing until Monday. That's an order."

"Yes, ma'am," she says with a grin as she runs off.

I turn back to my music stand as Herr Steinberg walks up. "That was wonderful," he says, looking stiff and formal in the suit he always wears to recitals. This place isn't as big or as fancy as the concert hall at the Conservatory, but I love him for always taking every recital seriously.

I stand up, lifting my case upright. "They were," I say. "I'm really proud of how well everyone did."

"Your students were great," he agrees. "But I was talking about you. You had total command over the instrument today. It's almost impossible to believe that only a few months ago, we thought you might never play again."

"It was okay," I concede. "But not like before."

"Not like before *yet*," Herr Steinberg adds. "I'm serious. If you keep moving forward like you've been doing, your future as a cellist is wide open. I'm not going to say it will be easy, but with a lot of hard work and a little luck, you will be able to do whatever you dream of." He watches me intently. "Do you know what it is you're dreaming of?"

I look down and fiddle with the latch on the cello case. Being a cellist is all I ever thought about doing, but now things are different. My Akhet skills and knowledge are growing every day, and things that I never thought about doing before suddenly seem like they could be within reach. "I'm not sure anymore."

"Well, I hope you'll keep working with me at the studio," he says. "I know you'll have to cut back on your hours when school starts next week, but you have a job here as long as you want it."

"Thanks. I'm not planning on going anywhere."

"Excellent news." Steinberg puts his arm around my shoulders and gives me a hug.

Dad pops his head around the curtain. "Need help carrying anything?"

"You can grab my bag if you want," I say, hauling the strap for the cello over my shoulder.

"Got it." He bends over and kisses me on the forehead. "That was wonderful, honey. Don't tell your mom I said so, but she went through more than one tissue during your performance."

"Thanks. I'm glad you guys came."

"You couldn't have kept us away." He holds up his phone. "Kat asked me to record it for her. She's sorry she's not here."

I stare at him. This is the first mention I've heard of Kat since she left. "Thanks."

We walk out into the main hall, where Rayne and her mom are waiting for me. Even though her memories are still brief and scattered, I've had her meet with Janine a few times to help her adjust to her new Akhet life. For as much as Veronique succeeded in opening up her memories, she got one thing wrong—Rayne was never Alessandra. The two of us have tried and failed to make that connection. "This is for you," Rayne says, shoving a bamboo plant into my hands with a grin.

"Thanks," I say. "Just what I needed. Way too many people bring flowers to these things."

"You and your students were wonderful, Cole," her mom says.

"Thanks."

Rayne leans in toward me. "Don't know if you saw him, but Drew was sitting way in the back of the room near the door. The second you were done playing he practically raced out of here."

Drew. Hearing his name makes me feel unsettled. He's tried to get me to see him in the past couple of weeks, but despite the guilt I feel about how things ended, I always refuse. Drew is gorgeous and kind, and I know his only flaw is that he loved someone too much. Unfortunately, that someone was just a ghost from the past, and I can never be the person he wants me to be. One thing I do know is that he isn't the type to stay just friends. Better for everyone if we stay far apart. So what was he doing here?

Mom comes up and gives me a hug. "I loved your performance, honey. And it looks like that little blond girl is going to give you a run for your money."

"I'm not competing with anyone, Mom. Olivia's just my student, that's all."

"I know, I'm just joking," she says, bending down so that her lips are close to my ear. "Besides, you were much more accomplished when you were her age."

"Seriously, Mom. Stop it."

"Okay, okay. How about we all go out for ice cream to celebrate?"

"Maybe in a minute. I need to put some things in the practice room." I turn to see Griffon standing behind me, red tulips in his hand, just like the last time he was at one of my concerts. It's been a month since the night we rescued Rayne, but I still feel the rush I always get when I see him, and I hope my face doesn't give me away.

"Am I too late to celebrate?" he asks.

I'm so unnerved by the sight of him that I say the first thing that pops into my head. "As usual."

"I deserved that," he says, keeping his eyes steady on me. "But I couldn't miss your big comeback."

"And that was so nice of you," Rayne says for me. She cuts me a look. "Wasn't it, Cole?"

I nod, temporarily out of words. This isn't the same Griffon who barely spoke to me the night we rescued Rayne.

"You know," Rayne says, looking directly at Mom, "I'm really tired, so I think I'm going to skip ice cream for now. Plus, Peter's coming over later this afternoon."

Mom picks up the thread. "And I just remembered an appointment I have in less than half an hour."

Dad just looks confused. "What appointment? It's Saturd—" Mom doesn't give him a chance to finish before she elbows him in the ribs.

"An appointment I didn't tell you about," she says to him through clenched teeth.

I'm mortified because none of them will ever win awards for acting, but Griffon just smiles. "If you don't mind, I'll make sure you get home."

"That would be great," Mom says with uncharacteristic enthusiasm. "Let Dad have the box and the bamboo plant." She takes the pink cake box from me and stares at the flowers in Griffon's hand.

"Oh—these are for you," he says, handing the bunch to me.

"Thanks," I say, slightly mystified at the flowers and the smiles. I'm not sure how to feel at this point.

"We'll take those too. I'll make sure they get in some water," Mom says. "Keep your phone on, and don't stay out too late."

"I won't," I say, giving her a hug. Apparently all it took was one career-ending arm surgery and seeing someone way too old for me to get her to lighten up.

A whirlwind of hugs and good-byes, and Griffon and I are alone. I point vaguely to the back of the theater. "I have to go put this music away," I say, holding up the folders in my hand.

"I'll come. If that's okay."

I nod, but can't think of a single thing to say.

We walk toward the back room in silence, dodging the students and their parents as they put their things away and head toward the door. "I hope you don't mind that I showed up like this," he says.

"Free country," I say, knowing it sounds bitchy, but I can't help it.

"Janine told me you were playing again." He glances at me. "I couldn't miss your triumphant return."

I allow myself a small smile. "Just a student recital," I say. "Hardly triumphant." I point to an open door. "In here."

We walk into the practice room just as Zander is putting his music stand away. "Hey, it's the Etch A Sketch boyfriend!" he says with a slight sneer. "Are you getting any yet?"

Griffon looks surprised and slightly amused, but I've finally had it with this kid. I can deal with a lot, but Zander is working my last nerve. "Knock it off," I say.

Zander shrugs, and as he moves, I catch a glimpse of something under his polo shirt. I reach for the chain around his neck and pull out an ankh—a silver one with a black stone and hieroglyphic writing around the edges.

"Where did you get this?" I demand. It's the same ankh that Veronique gave Rayne, I'm sure of it.

He brings his eyes up slowly to meet mine. "I found it," he says, a challenge in his voice. Zander turns to go, but I grab him by the arm to stop him, and that's when it all comes crashing over me in waves of emotion and powerful Akhet vibrations. An essence so dark and evil that I have to look away from its center. I get images of death and the taste of blood and a craving for power so complete it blocks out almost every other emotion. I drop my hand as though I'd been burned as a sly smile creeps over Zander's lips.

"He's Akhet," I say to Griffon, who takes a step toward us, not totally sure what's going on.

"Akhet?" Zander repeats innocently. "I don't know what you're talking about. I'm just a kid." He grins, his features momentarily looking much older than his eight years. "A little boy you can say anything in front of, whispering your secrets into your phone because he's not paying attention." He waves his hand in a strangely adult gesture. "And even if he was, he wouldn't have a clue." He stares at me in defiance. "Isn't that right?"

I think back to that time during his lesson when I'd talked to Janine on the phone. I'd told her all about Veronique and the formula while Zander was right there. Listening to every word. "You did all this?" I say in disbelief.

Zander takes a step so that he's inches from me, his light brown hair flopping into his eyes. "You can never take back what Veronique started. Once the genie is out of the bottle, it stays out."

I grab his arms with both hands, rage practically blinding me as I pull him off his feet. "You almost got Rayne killed!" I shout at him, digging my fingers into his arms so that he can't wriggle free. "We need to take him to the Sekhem," I say to Griffon, my words coming in a rush. "They have to know—"

"Mama!" Zander screams, in a high-pitched little-boy voice so different from the one he was just using. He kicks his feet and wriggles in my grasp.

Griffon's hands are on mine. "Let him go," he says, calmly but firmly. "You have to put him down."

I hesitate and Zander wrenches himself from my grasp just as his mother appears in the doorway, her face full of concern. "What's the matter?"

Zander takes one glance back at me and then rearranges his features into the picture of innocence before he turns back to his mother. "Nothing. I'm ready to go. Can we get ice cream on the way home?" Hearing him sound like a normal little boy makes me want to scream.

"Of course," his mom says, taking him by the hand and leading him out of the room. She looks over her shoulder at me. "See you Monday."

"No!" I reach for the door again, not willing to let him get away, when Griffon grabs me around the waist and holds me back.

"He's gone," Griffon says, gripping me tight. I hear anger in his voice, but more than that, I hear resignation. "In his current state, Zander is untouchable."

I try to twist out of his grip. "But he can't be! That's crazy! You can't just let him walk out the door like that." I slide down the wall to the floor and put my hands over my face, my whole body shaking. "We need to lock him up. Make sure he doesn't have access to anyone again."

Griffon sits down next to me and puts one hand lightly on

my shoulder. "There's nothing we can do to him. At the moment, he's an eight-year-old boy."

"But you saw him! He's *not* just an eight-year-old boy. That thing is pure evil."

"And thank God we now know who and where he is," Griffon says. "Just because we can't do anything to him doesn't mean we won't be watching him carefully. He made a huge mistake by revealing himself to you just now. The greatest danger of an essence like that is when you don't know where they are."

"Can't you just get rid of him? Make it look like an accident or something?"

"For what?" Griffon says. "So that he can come back ten years from now in another body that we don't know about, stronger and angrier than ever?"

I can feel my breathing slow down just a little bit. "It's just so wrong!"

"I agree," he says. "But sometimes you have to accept wrong now in order to make it right later." Griffon stands up and holds out his hand. "Let's walk. You need to get outside, and I was told something about ice cream."

I shake my head and brush his hand away. "I don't want to walk. And I definitely don't want any ice cream."

"Fine. Just come with me while I get some. There's a great place with weird flavors just a few blocks from here."

"Caramelized bacon," I say quietly. "That's their best one."

Griffon wiggles his fingers and I take his hand and let him pull me up, keeping my fingers wrapped around his for just a second longer than necessary. There are so many things I want to say, but everything is so messed up that I don't know where to start.

"Finish putting your things away," he says. "I'm going to call Janine and tell her about Zander, so I'll meet you out front."

I shove my things into the closet. The rage and fury that took up so much space in my body has vanished, leaving me feeling empty and spent. I duck out into the hall once I make sure that it's empty. I can't face anyone else right now.

Griffon is just hanging up when I walk out the front door. "Janine thinks you're a genius, in case you were wondering," he says. "She was calling a Sekhem meeting before we even got off the phone." He matches his step to mine as we walk down the street. "I think she's going to want you to be a part of this."

I nod. "I wouldn't have it any other way."

Griffon walks in silence for a few steps, but I can tell there's something more he wants to say. "I . . . I never did apologize."

My heart races at the words I've been wanting to hear.

"For leaving you alone with Christophe," he continues, and I look away to hide my disappointment. Out of the corner of my eye, I see him glance at my neck. The bruises are gone, but I know he can still see them in his memory. "I never would have, if I had any idea what he was." There's pain in his eyes, and I see him swallow hard. "I trusted him. I trusted him enough to leave you with him."

"You didn't know," I say. "Nobody did. Christophe was good at hiding who he was."

Griffon shakes his head. "But I should have known. At the break-in at the Swiss lab, one of the best Iawi Sekhem was killed. We all thought it was outsiders. But putting the pieces together now . . . I'm sure it was Christophe."

"It's always easy to see things after the fact. It's not your fault." It seems like it's just moments before we're in front of the ice cream store. Neither of us says much, lost in our own thoughts as we order and walk back out onto the sidewalk with our cones.

"You didn't get the bacon," Griffon says as we walk slowly down the street. He feels like a stranger to me, like we're miles apart. "I'm a little disappointed."

"Peanut-butter curry was calling me today." I take a lick from the bottom, feeling slightly better with the sharp sweetness flooding my mouth. "Want a bite?"

"Sure." He leans down and takes a small bite out of the side of my ice cream. I take a bite right after him in the same spot. This is as close to kissing him as I've been in a long time.

"I thought you hated peanut butter," I say.

"I'm trying to be more flexible," he says. "Want some strawberry jalapeño?"

I shake my head. "Too spicy. And a little weird."

We walk in silence, one of those times where you're not really walking to get anywhere, just walking to be somewhere. I stop and look into the window of a jewelry store. Hanging on a velvet board are a bunch of necklaces, the one in the middle a silver ankh with a purple stone. I reach up reflexively before I remember that I'm not wearing one anymore.

"Yours is gone," Griffon says, and I'm not sure if it's a statement or a question.

I nod slowly, still staring into the window. "I gave it back."

Something seems to shift in Griffon as we stand there looking at the display. "Let me get that one for you." He glances over
at me. "For your birthday next week."

I feel myself blushing. "You remembered."

"August twenty-seventh," he says, glancing at me.

"Of course you wouldn't forget," I say. I look back at the necklace. "Thanks, but no. I'm going to get another one, but I want to
wait until I find one I love. And then I'm going to buy it myself."

He nods as though he understands and turns away from the
window. "Two truths and a lie," he says.

I can't help but smile. "Okay."

"I broke my leg so badly the first time I went snowboarding,
they had to get a sled to carry me down the mountain. Totally
embarrassing. And painful."

"Aw!"

He shakes his head. "Shh. Not done."

"Sorry."

"When I was five, I shaved my legs because I thought they
were too hairy."

A laugh slips out as I picture that, and he gives me a look.

"And my newest Akhet skill is the ability to rewind time."
His face is serious as he looks at me. I hold his gaze a beat longer
than I need to before I turn away, my heart pounding.

"Too easy," I say. "Nobody can rewind time."

"Doesn't stop me from wishing I could," he says.

"And the beauty—and the curse—of being Akhet is that we
can never forget. Any of it." There's a silence as the words settle
between us.

"Right," Griffon says, squinting into the distance. "It's such a nice day. Do you want to go down to the beach? We could ride along the Great Highway for a little while before I take you home."

I think about how it feels to ride behind him, the sun shining on the water beside us. "I'd like that," I say as we walk back toward the recital hall. "But I need to make a stop first."

Griffon looks at the shiny blue convertible with the white interior and the big silver bass clef hanging from the rearview mirror. "This is yours?"

"Yep," I say. "A convertible VW Rabbit." I see Griffon's grin. "Don't tell me you had a car just like this when they first came out."

"Nope," he says. "I wasn't really a Rabbit kind of guy. I did always want a convertible, though. When did you get your license?"

"A few weeks ago," I say. "I had all that money from giving cello lessons, and one of Dad's friends sold it to me." I shrug and look at the car that I've come to love in such a short time. "I got tired of always being the passenger. Of not being in control of where I was going." I lean against the car and hold my breath, feeling the moment change. "Or who I was going with."

Griffon hesitates, then plants both hands on the hood behind me. Shivers run down my spine as he presses me against the car and whispers in my ear, "You are totally amazing." As my lips meet his I feel a rush of emotion as everything that's happened in the past several months collides.

"I'm so sorry," he murmurs, his lips still on mine. "God, I'm so sorry I was such an ass." He pulls back slightly and buries his face in my neck, and I reach up to run my fingers through his short hair, feeling the soft fuzz instead of the curls I'm used to, not wanting this moment to end. For a second I feel dizzy and I'm afraid that I might be drifting into a memory, but then everything comes back into sharp focus. With Griffon, there is no past to fall back on, no memories of another relationship, no expectations to meet. With him it's all about what's now and what's next.

"It wasn't all your fault," I say, my voice wavering and uncertain as I speak.

"It was," he says, reaching down to brush a strand of hair away from my face. "I almost let Drew ruin the best thing that's ever happened to me. All because of something that took place hundreds of years ago that had nothing to do with you. It was stupid. I knew you weren't seeing him. But I needed it to be your decision. I couldn't live the rest of my life with what might have been hanging over us."

"Why couldn't you just be honest with me? Just tell me what happened in the past that was so bad."

Griffon hesitates. "I should have. It was a long time ago in Italy. I fell for someone who was dealing with a relationship in the past. It . . . it didn't work out so well for me, and I was afraid to go through that kind of pain again."

My memory flashes back to the woman at Drew's party. Chiara. That's what she'd said her name was when she knew Griffon. She'd also said he wasn't the forgiving type. I put my fingers in his belt loops and pull him to me, wanting nothing but to feel him close again. We kiss and touch for a long time, our hands exploring familiar territory that at the same time is completely new. Without a doubt, I can do this forever. A passing car honks at us and I pull away, the happiness that's building up inside barely contained. "How about that ride to the beach?"

Griffon smiles at me. "I'm cool staying here for the next couple of days."

I push him gently. "Me too. Although I can think of a few more comfortable spots." I picture his big, wide bed, shining with a square of afternoon sunlight, and have no doubt my face is red. "Come on, let's go."

I unlock the doors and put the top down, praying and then cheering when she starts the first time I turn the key.

Griffon buckles himself into the passenger side and grins at me. "I like it."

Looking for a break in the traffic, I ease the car onto the road, smoothly switching gears like Dad taught me.

In a few short miles, we turn onto the Great Highway as the late afternoon sun sparkles on the waves below. I push down on the accelerator and the car gains speed, racing down the hill toward the beach. I've been on this road a million times, but it's like I'm seeing it for the first time, not balancing on the rear seat peeking around Griffon's back or watching out the window from the passenger side, but staring straight ahead, controlling every motion.

Griffon turns toward me, grabs my right hand, and gives it a gentle squeeze. I grin back at him with my hair blowing behind me, the asphalt speeding beneath me, and the horizon stretching in front of me, knowing that without a doubt, this moment, right now, is the best one of all.

Acknowledgments

A sequel is like a middle child—people make an extra effort to let it know that it's loved. This manuscript was loved by many people who helped make it a reality:

My agent, Erin Murphy, who always answers e-mails in a day, anguished ones in minutes.

My editor, Mary Kate Castellani, who knows what I want to say and then helps me say it.

My publisher, Emily Easton, and the team at Walker for supporting all of us from the very start.

My amazing friend Daisy Whitney, who is the guru of my writing life and always makes me rethink my footwear choices.

My writer friends Malinda Lo, Gabrielle Charbonnet, Cheryl Herbsman, and Robin Mellom, who always "get it."

My friends Karen Ryan, Jessica Romero, Barbara Stewart,

and Jill Raimondi, who know nothing about writing but everything about friendship.

My neighbors Denise, Ed, Juliet, and Lukas for loaning me Griffon's memory and their unflagging support.

My family—Mom, Joe, Dad, Suzanne, and Jessica, for their constant interest and cheerleading. And my sister Wendy for naming her sons Connor and Griffin.

My boys, Jaron and Taemon, for being the most understanding kids a writer can have and not minding my constant muttering.

My husband, Bayo, for holding down our lives when I'm mentally elsewhere. I couldn't do it without you.

My readers—your e-mails and tweets about the sequel kept me going in the middle of the night.

9/13, 11/14, 9/15, 4/17, 12/17